The Richn

Stephen Driscoll

North Staffordshire Press

Newcastle-under-Lyme

Staffordshire

The Richness

ISBN 978-1-9160152-1-0

Published in 2019

North Staffordshire Press

10 Queen Street

Newcastle-under-Lyme

ST5 1ED

Dedication

To the 97

This story is being told from a historical perspective, recounted as a tale that should be remembered for the tremendous amount of human upheaval involved. At times, the narrative is interrupted from a modern perspective, indicated by occasional notes from the narrator.

A note on language:

For convenience, this novel is written in English. Most of the words and expressions used are relevant to the period of time that the narrative covers. However, other languages would have been spoken and heard including: the European tongues of French, Spanish, Portuguese, Dutch and Italian; African languages of Berber, Tuareg, Fula and Wolof; Algerian Arabic; and Irish and Scottish Gaelic. A number of words from those dialects have been used and a glossary at the end of the book explains their meanings. A new pidgin language eventually developed in Algiers and surrounding areas for trading purposes; it was called Sabir and took words from French, Spanish, Portuguese, Italian, Berber, Turkish, Greek and Arabic.

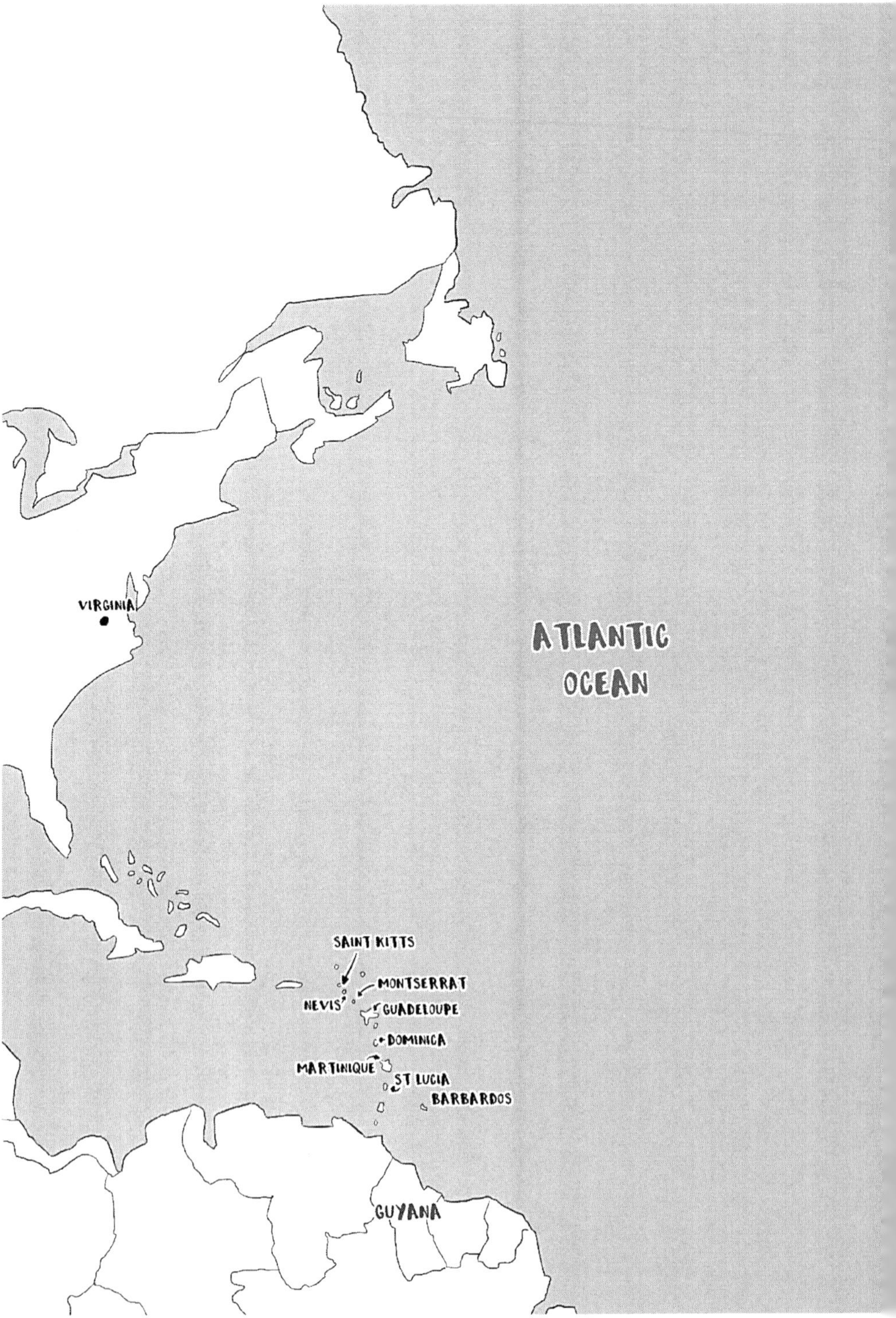
VIRGINIA
ATLANTIC
OCEAN
SAINT KITTS
MONTSERRAT
NEVIS
GUADELOUPE
DOMINICA
MARTINIQUE
ST LUCIA
BARBARDOS
GUYANA

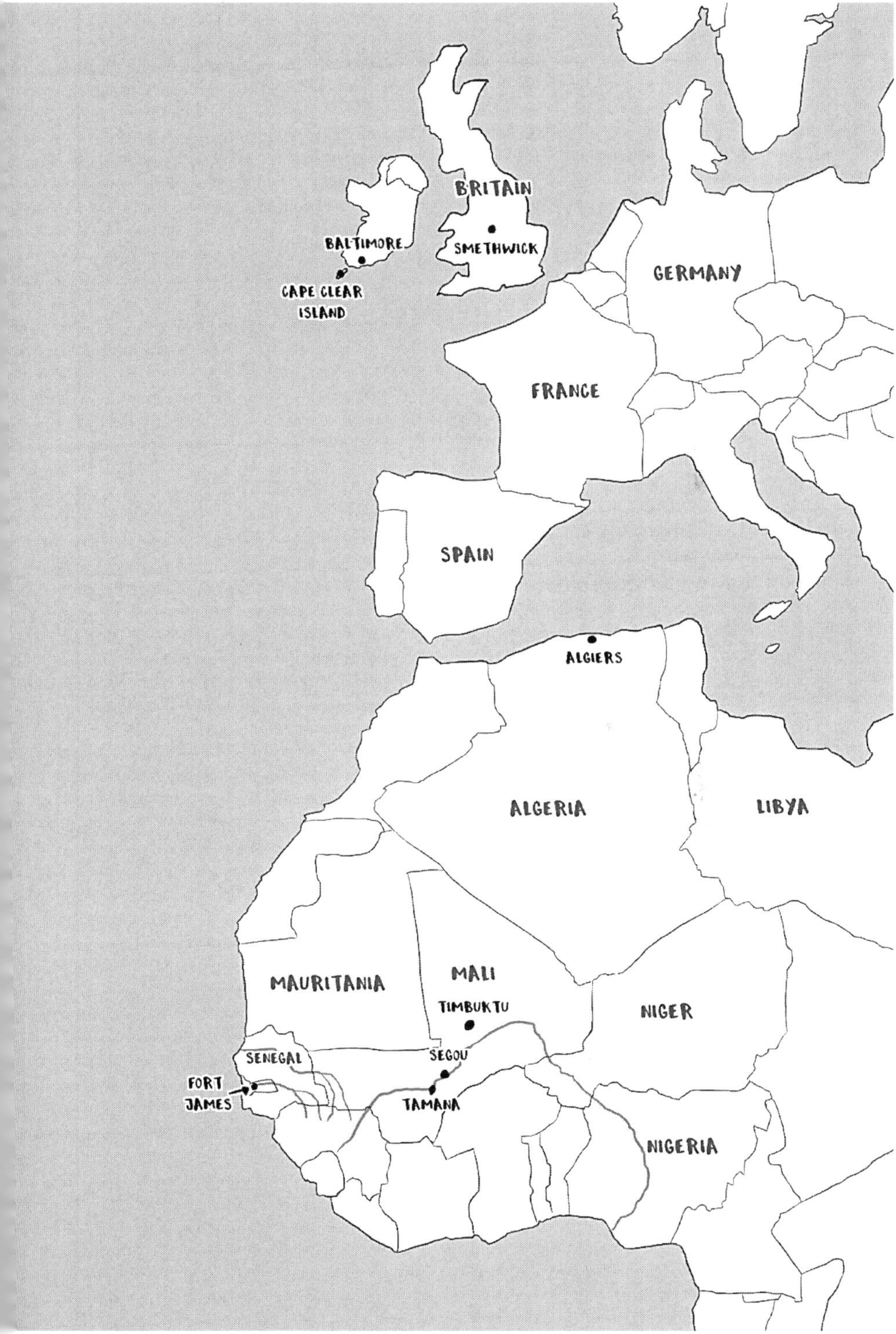
BRITAIN
BALTIMORE
SMETHWICK
CAPE CLEAR ISLAND
GERMANY
FRANCE
SPAIN
ALGIERS
ALGERIA
LIBYA
MAURITANIA
MALI
TIMBUKTU
NIGER
SENEGAL
SEGOU
FORT JAMES
TAMANA
NIGERIA

Words to a song.

Never pretend that you're always right,
When you're at least fifty percent wrong.
Otherwise the human race will have difficulty getting along.
Something needs to change.
If you are ignorant of your history,
You will never fully understand why the world is as it is,
And that fear and war go hand in hand.
We believe in so many lies.
Examine your prejudice, ask 'where did it come from?'
Was it the media, your parents or your friends?
Then meet the victim of your hatred with an open mind,
And your life will start to climb.
But you've got to be meek, ever so meek, meek and mild.
Forget your self-importance, because you're not.
If you listen, think, reflect and think again,
Your fear will wither away.
So, never pretend that you're always right,
When you're at least fifty percent wrong.

Contents

PART ONE

Chapter 1 – Kinsale, Ireland

April 1626

It was cool, windy and rainy; some might say a typical day of weather in Hibernia, the land of winter, the name the Romans called the island of Ireland. A pair of physically fit, six-feet-tall, fresh-faced, 18-year-old young men stood sheltering under the extended roof part of a warehouse on the wharf of Kinsale Harbour on the south coast. Both being of medium build, they were often assumed to be brothers.

"I still think you're mad to do this, but you always did like an adventure," said Eoghan O'hEidirsceoil (from now on, John O'Driscoll, the Anglicised version) to his best friend and first cousin, Padraig O'Mathghamhna (from now on, Patrick O'Mahoney).

"It's going to be an adventure, that's for certain," responded Patrick. "I wish you were coming with me."

They were watching two sailing ships, *Faith* and *Hope*, being loaded in preparation for a journey across the Atlantic Ocean. Sailors carried tools, equipment and food, and rolled barrels of water onto the vessels. Live pigs, goats, chickens, ducks, cows and horses were driven aboard. As the final animal was penned in, a squall rattled the ropes on the masts, causing the fibres to hum in a deep throaty bass.

John shivered and wrapped his long hooded cloak tightly around himself. "If you think I'm going to get on a boat with a load of strangers and sail off thousands of miles into the unknown, you're madder than I thought," he uttered. "I couldn't leave my family, friends and horses."

"Stop it," grumbled Patrick. "You're supposed to be encouraging me and wishing me good luck, not trying to put me off. This is a great opportunity to do something different."

xxx

Three weeks previously, Patrick had been in Cork looking for work. His experience and knowledge of working with horses had secured him a position at a coaching inn on the outskirts of the city. He had celebrated by having a beer when, by chance, he had struck up a conversation with an English gentleman called Mr Wallett. Mr Wallett, feeling generous, had bought Patrick a couple of pints; eventually, chat steered away from horses to tales of adventure. It transpired that Mr Wallett was looking for volunteers to travel to the West Indies, and specifically, to the island of Saint Christopher. Although he hadn't been there himself, he seemed to know everything about the island – beautifully green and fertile, plenty of fresh water, fish, fruit and a healthy climate. It sounded idyllic. Patrick's mind began to picture the place and a thrill of excitement rippled through him, warmed by the effects of malted hops.

"So, there's a deal in this for you, if you're interested," said Mr

Wallett, carefully lighting his pipe from the flame of a beeswax candle that illuminated the roughly hewn table they were sitting at. "My employer, Mr Hilton, an Englishman of some note, plans to start a tobacco plantation, and he seeks healthy young men like yourself to travel to Saint Christopher. There's good money in this stuff," he continued, tapping his pipe. "You would be expected to work for four years. The great news is that your transport to the island would be paid for and you will be provided with shelter, food, drink and clothing. In addition, at the end of the four years, you will be entitled to the freedom dues of Saint Christopher, so that you can start to make your own way."

"And freedom dues are?" enquired Patrick.

"Ten pounds in cash," Mr Wallett elucidated.

"What sort of work would I be expected to do?" asked a shiny-eyed Patrick, excited by the sound of ten pounds; an amount he had never possessed in one go.

"Anything really," Mr Wallett replied, "clearing land, planting crops and probably looking after horses, especially with your undoubted skills and interest in them. Several horses will be shipped across. They will need to be cared for."

Patrick was exhilarated. Here was a perfect opportunity – travel, adventure, money, and horses, all paid for.

"I'm interested," he said, dismissing thoughts about what his family might think. He had no specific commitments and, anyway, once he told people about this they may accede that it was a good idea. "What's the next step?"

Mr Wallett smiled, reached inside his jacket pocket and pulled out a folded page of paper. "This," he said, unfolding the blank sheet, "will become what is called an indenture contract. Have you ever heard of one?"

"No, and how can it be a contract?" challenged Patrick. "There are no words on it. Don't take me for a fool, I can read you know!"

"Calm down, it's alright," placated Mr Wallett, "as you have correctly pointed out, this is an empty sheet of paper. You will understand more after we, or rather I, have filled it out. If you agree to what has been written, we both sign and date it. Don't worry, it's not a legal document until there are signatures on it. Now, how about getting us another beer, while I fill my pen and get on with the writing?" he said, handing Patrick an English sixpence.

Patrick went to purchase two ales. On his return, he found Mr Wallett had an ink bottle and a brown goose quill placed on the table next to the paper. Positioning the pewter tankards carefully on the uneven wooden surface, so as not to spill any liquid, Patrick sat down, as Mr Wallett picked up the feather, dipped it and wrote the following:

"This indenture, made on the Twenty-first day of March in the year of our Lord, One Thousand Six Hundred and Twenty-Six, between Patrick O'Mahoney and Mark Titus Wallett, honorary agent for Anthony Hilton, does promise that the said Patrick O'Mahoney, from his arrival at Saint Christopher, will serve in the employment of the said Anthony Hilton, for a term of four years and that said Anthony Hilton will pay for said Patrick O'Mahoney's travelling expenses, providing him with lodging, food, drink and clothing during that time. At the end of the said term, Patrick O'Mahoney will be paid ten pounds, according to the custom of the country."

This was written on the top half of one side of the paper. Mr Wallett copied the exact wording underneath. When he had finished writing, he put the pen down and took a long pull on his beer. Wiping his lips, Mr Wallett explained that once Patrick had agreed to the contract and signed both halves, the paper would be torn into two pieces, in a jagged fashion, with Patrick keeping one half and the other being delivered to Mr Hilton.

"The reason is," clarified Mr Wallett, "if there were ever to be a dispute about this document, you can produce your copy and Mr Hilton can show his. The two halves will match along the notches like a jaw coming together. That will prove that it's genuine."

"What if I don't sign it?"

“Then you will have missed out on this opportunity. I tell you what. Mr Hilton’s ship is due to sail from Kinsale in three weeks, so you have some time to think about your decision. If you sign this and turn up, then off you go. If you don’t, you don’t. I’ll destroy Mr Hilton’s portion. Simple, yes? I will always find someone to take your place.”

“What’s the name of the ship?” asked Patrick as he signed, tore the sheet and pocketed his half carefully.

“Faith,” replied Mr Wallett, finishing his drink. “And congratulations, you are now an indentured servant.” He shook Patrick’s hand. “I'm off now,” he continued. “I hope to see you in three weeks. And you can keep the change from the sixpence,” he added as he walked away, smiling.

“Sorry,” apologised Patrick, jangling the two pennies in his pocket. “I forgot all about it.” And he had. His mind was all over the place. He calmed himself down by having a slow drink, to consider what had just occurred. The next day, Patrick expressed regret to the innkeeper, explaining that a new chance of a lifetime had come his way, and galloped his horse back to his home village of Baltimore.

Reactions to his other worldly venture were varied from Patrick’s family and friends. Overall, though, there had been an understanding for his desire to leave. Ever since the last Irish chief of the area, Fineen O’Driscoll the Rover, had, contrary to Brehon Law, handed over most of the land rights of the O'Driscoll clan fifty years ago to Queen Elizabeth I of England, Baltimore had changed. The English had settled, land and employment for the original inhabitants had become scarce, the Gaeilge language and Catholicism were banned and the Irish punished for recusancy. This was as good a time to leave as any.

XXX

"You're right, Pat. I wish you luck, fortune and good health," said John. "Who knows when we will meet again? Write if you can and tell me what it's like. Maybe I'll join you if it's as good as you make it sound."

"That would be just great John," Patrick replied as they heard the final call for passengers to board the ships.

They looked at each other. A smile, a hug and a grip of hands said the rest. Patrick hoisted his kit bag over his shoulder and, in the drizzle, walked over to the gangplank to board his barque, joining a group of gabbling, excited men. Mr Wallett was at the bottom of the brow checking paperwork. He nodded to Patrick and allowed him through. John turned away with mixed feelings, mounted his horse and made his way home in the rain to Baltimore.

Chapter 2 – Baltimore, Ireland

Saturday 18th June 1631

It had been an unusually dry, hot summer so far. Baltimore roasted in glorious Atlantic high pressure air masses, full of warm westerly breezes. Temperatures had hovered around the late twenties and early thirties on the Centigrade scale. Thin, blowy skirts and kilts were the order of the day.

John perspired. Not only was it muggy again but he had been toiling with the horses owned by his boss, Corent Croffine. John, like his cousin Patrick, was a natural with horses. Mutual love flowed between man and beast. He calmed them with a special whistle, made them whinny with a few quiet words, and always greeted them by name. They were his escape from the fact that he worked long hours, six days a week, for an Englishman.

John's older, reckless brother Conor was mocking, acerbic even, jibing and jeering at him every time they met, about him working for the English. Conor's whole purpose in life it seemed, like their father's, was to fight against the intruders, who had been trying to conquer Ireland, on and off, for the best part of five hundred years. Conor and John had grown up hearing, witnessing and feeling the injustices imposed on the

Irish by the English. For Conor, this had developed into an almost pathological hatred towards anything Anglo-Saxon. Consequently, from a young age, he had joined a band of kernes and taken part in guerrilla warfare tactics around Munster, against the imperialists. He was a wanted man by the English authorities but he was a cunning kerne. John, however, although angry at the treatment dished out by the colonisers, hadn't let it consume him. Mr Croffine treated him kindly enough and the horses were more important anyway.

Sweaty and dusty, John stopped spreading hay and propped up the pitchfork he'd been using. He surveyed the stables with a satisfied smile - all neat and clean, with the horses contentedly chewing fresh feed. That was it for the day and the week. Tomorrow: a day off. He had been anticipating this exact moment all day when he could relax. Not only was it payday but in his pocket, was a letter he had received yesterday. He knew it was from Patrick, who he had not heard from personally since they parted company in Kinsale, five years previously. Patrick's parents had received an annual report from him which they shared with John. All Patrick ever said was that he was alive and well and the weather was superb.

Initially, John had frequently thought about Patrick, but over time, this became less and less. It was a pleasant shock to receive his letter in the post. He had opened it immediately, to find two pages of close writing. Instead of reading it straight away, he skipped to the end, affirmed that it was from Patrick, then decided to wait a day to study it whilst relaxing on a Saturday evening at the local alehouse.

Stripping to his waist, John washed in the horse trough before climbing the ladder to his room above the stables. He slipped on a clean leine, combed his shoulder length jet-black hair and dropped a few coins in his pocket. Just to put him exactly in a befitting mood, John spent fifteen minutes softly practising scales on his clairseach, a triangular Irish harp, made from seasoned hornbeam wood with brass strings. This had been a gift from Fineen, his paternal grandfather, who had also been quite a proficient harpist. Performing loudly or in public was too risky these days. The English could not understand how the uncivilised Irish managed to produce such civilised enchanting music. Consequently, to put an end to that unnatural coupling and to stop musicians strumming patriotic tunes, a Proclamation was issued to pluck the fingernails of people caught playing. On leaving the stables, out of habit John patted the collar of his brat, hanging by the stable door.

"Check," he said to himself.

John breathed in the temperate air as he walked towards the alehouse, eagerly anticipating drinking a couple of coirms and taking his time to read the letter slowly. The atmosphere, cooling slightly as evening fell, was scented with aromas of sea, fish and baked earth. He scanned his surroundings in the extended light of mid-summer, his deep green eyes taking in a few men fishing from their currachs on Roaring Water Bay, amongst its many islands. Two of the islets, Sherkin and Cape Clear, had skylines of ruined O'Driscoll castles, Dun na Long, Fort of Ships, and Dun an Oir, Fort of Gold, respectively, both destroyed following a dispute with the men from Waterford in the previous century, over some allegedly stolen Portuguese wine. He smiled as he listened and watched house martins and swallows twittering, dipping and diving across the fields catching insects. The martin's sharp white rump and throat contrasted acutely with its brown-black wings and glossy blue-black back and cap, the colours shimmering in flashes from the sunlight.

Chapter 3 – The Letter

Written September 1630:

"My dear esteemed cousin, friend and brother I never had.

Finally, I have some time and space to bring you up-to-date with what has happened to me since I left you in Kinsale, over four years ago. Your last words to me have been constantly in my mind; without luck, fortune and health, I would be dead by now!

It took exactly 40 days to get to Saint Christopher; we call the island Saint Kitts for short. Many of my fellow travellers suffered badly from sea sickness, but I was lucky. We were welcomed by the Governor, Thomas Warner, who had already settled there on the leeward side, a place called Old Road. It was decided that our group would form a settlement on the windward side. That was really hard work. In blazing heat, we had to clear the land from scratch; felling trees, removing stumps, digging up and clearing jungle underbrush, so that we could plant tobacco, indigo and vegetables. However, whilst working we were attacked by the local natives, the Caribs. They were out to murder us and they did. Some of us escaped and fled to Warner's place for protection.

There are French settlers here as well and they joined us to fight the Caribs. It was an unfair contest. We had muskets. When I say we, I was actually in the second line of attack, armed with a machete but I didn't have to use it. The guns did the job. The Caribs had bows and arrows tipped with poison from the local manchineel tree. One of the first things you learn about this place is not to eat the fruit of that tree. They're like small apples but the toxins send you mad with pain and can kill you. The battle was a massacre. We killed hundreds. But it was either us or them.

After that incident, things settled down for a while and we actually grew some great tobacco and vegetables. Very fertile land, only two types of weather, mainly sun and short, outbursts of torrential rain. Occasionally we get vicious storms called hurricanes, named after the Carib's god of wind, then more sunshine. Some days it's that hot you can't do anything, it's stifling. No mizzle, ice or snow though!

A few of the servants I came with have died here. Not only from fighting the locals but also profound exhaustion or disease; ghastly fevers and dysentery from infected water. You've got to be careful but like I say, I've been lucky.

Out of the blue, a group of fear and mna gorma arrived. I've never seen people with such dark skins. We call them Negroes... Spanish for black if you didn't know! They'd been brought from Africa to help us on the plantation. I must say, they were an emaciated bunch. Apparently, their journey was hell on earth but they were soon fattened up on our diet of fish, veg and rats. Aye, huge rats! Much bigger than ours at home. Tasty though! As you know, ni mor riachtanais when the devil drives.

After about a year, the man I was working for, Hilton, decided to move to another island nearby called Nevis. Apparently, there had been a plot to murder him! He took me with him, mainly because he trusts me with his horses, and we started a new settlement. It was going well, 'til some Spanish ships appeared and wrecked the place, taking us all prisoners. Talk about an adventure; but, as you can tell by my letter, I survived. I was put on a ship that was supposed to take us to England but after we set off we noticed that the Spanish were leaving, so once they were out of sight, we returned to settle again. Bizarre, right?

So, now I'm back here on Nevis and flourishing. Oddly, the name Nevis comes from the Spanish word for snow! Apparently, Columbus mistook the clouds at the top of the mountain for the white stuff, when he sailed round these parts. It's a beautiful place. Nature's greens, reds, browns and yellows are everywhere in the trees and flowers, and the sea is warm and vividly blue. In June, I completed my indenture service and was given ten pounds. I've rented a few acres off Hilton, bought a horse and started cultivating tobacco and veg for myself. Everything sprouts quickly here; there's more than one growing season. I'm earning a living but have hopes of making much more with the tobacco. Have you started smoking yet? I make extra cash by tending to Hilton's horses as well.

More Africans are arriving all the time. They're forced to be slaves, bound and shackled, bought and sold like horses, and I've heard that some are treated terribly badly. It's not surprising they're extremely angry about it. Hilton's purchased a few but he manages them with respect and he lets me use them when it's necessary. If I profit enough, I think I might buy a beautiful slave woman and treat her very well!"

That's the only way he'll get a woman, thought John, *he's hopeless with them*. He read on.

"... Hilton's been pretty good to work for, but I've had to keep quiet about my religion. I've heard him talking to other Englishmen about us Catholics and it's not complimentary. There's talk of persecution. I'm keeping my head down. Still, he's been firm but fair and kept to his word. Made me work hard though. I've got muscles where I've never had them before.

Anyway, my friend, of course I miss you and the fun we had, but I'm glad I came here. It's been awful for some but overall, I've got no complaints. Let me know what's happening at your end when you get a chance. Fancy joining me?

I've written to my parents each year to tell them I'm alive. If they replied, I never received anything, probably due to the upheavals I've described. Don't tell them what I've told you, they'll just worry. Tell them I'm just fine, which is what I am.

Anyway, that's all for now, I'm off to catch my dinner! What shall I eat tonight, fresh fish, lobster or turtle? The choice is huge! It's not pilchards every day! And, 'til next time, I wish you luck, fortune and good health.

Your loving cousin, Patrick.

Sent from: Nevis,
Leeward Islands,
West Indies."

John had been reading whilst sitting on a bench outside the front of the alehouse. He quaffed his beer, went inside and asked for another. His head buzzed from what he had read.

What a story he thought as he sat down outside again to re-read the letter. Engrossed as he was, his concentration was barely disturbed by a presence who sat down nearby. But when the surrounding air changed unsubtly from sweet summer scents to a sour stench, John looked up and stared at the dishevelled state of his bench fellow. Slowly, recognition dawned.

"Conor!" John exclaimed, quietly. "What are you doing? You shouldn't be seen round here. You stink."

"Thanks brother, I love you too," responded Conor, grinning and revealing yellow-stained teeth. He was the epitome of grime. "Don't worry, nobody's seen me. I came hidden in a jaunting car under a pile of hay driven by a friend. I've got some business to attend to, then I'm off. Chance brought me your way."

"I haven't seen you for months, where've you been?" asked John, holding his nose.

"Oh, here and there, there and here. You don't need to know."

"What have you been doing? Or shouldn't I ask?"

"The latter," smirked Conor. "How are you? Still being a fecking egit and working for that English bodach?"

"Yes. I'm fine, good mostly."

John looked at his brother two years his senior, lean and wiry and always with that appealing glint in his soft hazel eyes. Conor was seen as a hero in the area, a legendary freedom fighter, for his commitment to campaign against the English. Infamy had its rewards – younger men looked up to him, women of all ages lay with him, old folk fed him.

"I've had a letter from Cousin Patrick in the West Indies," John said.

"That's interesting," said Conor. "What's he saying?"

"He's had a tough time, reading between the lines, but it hasn't broken his spirit. He's doing quite well now, by the sounds of it."

"Where did he go again?" asked Connor.

"He started off in Saint Christopher, or Saint Kitts as he calls it, but now he's living on an island called Nevis."

"Neeevis," said Conor, extending the 'e', "Saint Kitts and Nevis in the West Indies, eh! That rolls off the tongue nicely; sounds quite exotic. Maybe I'll go and visit him when we've got rid of the English. Is the seal safe?"

"Of course," replied John.

"Good. Guard it with your life. It's the link to our past and hopefully future. Well, it's been great bumping into you but I've got to go. You haven't seen me. I'll be in touch."

As quietly as he had arrived, Conor left and the whiff dispersed. John shook his head thinking, *what I don't know, I can't lie about*. He started to re-read the letter.

I'll visit Patrick's folks tomorrow, he decided, suddenly remembering with a sigh that he'd have to go after attending church. *I don't need a fine*, he thought, shaking his head.

For the important part of their lives, John and Conor had been brought up by Patrick's parents, their aunt and uncle, Bridget and Sean O'Mahoney, who were Catholic tenant farmers struggling to make ends meet from a few acres of potatoes and a small herd of Dexter cows. Bridget was their mother's sister, who had died giving birth to John. Their father, Conor senior, was a fugitive, either fighting or on the run from the English, sometimes running as far as Spain. John was tired of hearing about his father's antics and had mentally blocked them out. His brother had done the complete opposite and adored and emulated their absent parent.

Chapter 4 – Baltimore

Sunday 19th June 1631

John prayed the sermon would be short. He took his place at the back of Tullagh Parish Church, where cramped seating was reserved for the Irish, behind the comfortably spaced English. He saw his aunt and uncle sat at the far end of a pew, squeezed up against the wall. They nodded and smiled.

I wonder if my grandfather turns in his grave at how things have turned out, thought John, *it wouldn't have been like this in his heyday*. But the irony was that it had been Fineen O'Driscoll who had unlocked the door to the English settlers. *Fancy selling out to the English for a knighthood*, accused John.

Fineen, an ex-fearless freebooter, double-crossing knight of the realm and finally, a penniless, ruined man, had been the last chief of the O'Driscoll clan. Hoping for some power rather than none-at-all, Fineen, in breach of early Irish Law, had signed over the majority of the clan's lands to the English, selecting to side with them when he saw that Ireland was falling to their influence and strength. In return, he had been knighted by Queen Elizabeth I, allowed to remain at his family home An Cloghan, Stony Place, on Lough Hyne, and have a renewable yearly lease on Dun na Sead, Fort of Jewels, the last remaining O'Driscoll fortress still functioning in the area. *It's better than being kicked off your land completely and transplanted to Connaught*, Fineen had reasoned, secretly pleased that he could insist on people calling him 'Sir'.

The English had established themselves and taken over the lucrative pilchard fishing industry. This was all before John and Conor had been born. Some, like Fineen's son, Conor Snr and John's brother, Conor Jnr had castigated Fineen for betraying the clan and acting unlawfully and had strong feelings about it all. They truly believed that, at some point in the future, the O'Driscolls would reclaim their ancestral lands.

My father and brother are daft, thought John, not listening to the rituals of Protestantism but standing, kneeling and sitting when others around him did.

xxx

Flashback to 1629:

When Fineen had died a couple of years ago, his measly remaining amounts of property were divided up within the family. It had been a rare occasion when John's father had been present. The odd building and plot of land and other items of value, like the symbol of authority the White Rod, old Celtic jewellery and several good vintage bottles of

Spanish and Portuguese wine, had been taken by the bailiffs to pay off debts. But there was one thing of worth in the O'Driscoll's minds that they didn't get: the seal.

The story was that Fineen, on becoming a Sassenach knight, had been granted Armorial Bearings. The symbols were a ship to denote a notable sea expedition, of which he had had many, especially pirating, and a cormorant, because, in his opinion, it was the king of fishing birds. The colours were argent and sable with a motto that read *Spes Mea in Deo*: 'My Hope in God'. In his vanity, Sir Fineen had registered the manufacture of a seal to be made from local oak with the Coat of Arms carved into it. It was skilfully crafted, as round as a two-penny cartwheel copper coin and the thickness of a sardine. To grip it, two grooves had been chiselled out on the reverse. However, by the time the seal had been completed, Fineen's financial circumstances had taken a plummet and he never found himself in a position again to use it. He couldn't afford the wax anyway. Consequently, it had not been used once, not even for fun.

It was just the three of them in the dusty unkempt living room of An Cloghan where Fineen had died: Conor Senior, Conor Junior and John.

"This," said Conor Snr, holding up the seal, "is the crucial piece of evidence we have from the past to the future. We must keep it safe if we are ever going to be able to claim legal ownership of our lands from the English. It proves who we are and our direct ancestry to the chief of the O'Driscolls. Someone must look after it. I would usually give it to you, Conor, because you are the eldest. But you are too much like me and you will lose it because you're not settled nor the settling type."

Conor Jnr listened attentively, his eyes fixed in awe of his father. He frowned as he tried to work out whether he had been paid a compliment or not. John squirmed in his chair, wondering what was coming next.

"So," continued their father, "I have decided to place it in your care, John. You are calm, quiet and stable. Can we trust you to safeguard it?" John looked at his father who had never been present in his life when it mattered. *What do I make of him?* he thought. He had no specific feelings for his father or, at best, confused ones. "Honour your parents," he had been taught, but had always questioned. Not having known his mother, John had always assumed that she would have been like his aunt, Bridget; a wonderful, kind-hearted woman; easy to honour.

"Of course, Dad," said John, unemotionally but dutifully.

"Good. That's resolved then," concluded Conor Snr placing the well-waxed seal into a green velvet pouch and handing it to John.

xxx

John's reflections were jolted by the movement around him. It was the end of the service and people were leaving, English first. He bided his time, left the building and waited for the O'Mahoneys.

"Can I come around in about an hour?" asked John. "I've had a letter from Patrick."

"Oh! Have you John? That's great. Of course, you know you are welcome anytime," replied Bridget fondly.

"I need a walk first, to get that service out of my head. I'll take the long way round and see you there."

John walked and contemplated. *I never want to leave this place*, he mused, thinking of Patrick's experiences and taking in the slightly browning but usually verdant, productive, undulating countryside and the ever changing, ever fluctuating seascape. *I belong here. I don't care who owns the land, so long as I can stay. Whether the seal is important or not, I'll look after it, because I said I would.* John had sewn the seal into one of the fringe corners of his mantle, which he kept on a hook just inside the stable. At first, he felt a heavy sense of responsibility about it all but after applying the final stitch and examining his handiwork, peace descended. *Not a sign*, he had thought, pleased. Now he enjoyed the habit of just checking. There was a reward for his commitment. Each time he touched the hidden seal, a warm feeling enveloped him like a thin veil.

John entered the O'Mahoney family cottage, bowing his head to avoid the stone lintel above the front door, just as he had done hundreds of times before. The next few hours were spent chattering and filling his belly. Sean always took an interest in John's life, and Bridget was a feeder. Huge portions, plenty more, choice of puddings, something to go home with. She was an incredible provider, wouldn't listen to you and treated you like royalty. Patrick was the main topic of conversation. John exaggerated the positive news in the letter and left out the negative and controversial. It was a warm, friendly time. Finally, John bid farewell and walked home, carrying enough food for two days. A gentle horse ride took up the rest of the day before he retired to bed.

Chapter 5 – The Cove, Baltimore

Monday 20 June 1631

It was the dark hours before daybreak. John was in a deep sleep, but something was awry. A shout, a scream, a whinny, banging, more banging, getting louder, more neighing. He awoke with a jerk. The smell of smoke; the horses moving about in the stable, snorting. The cries of women and children; male voices shouting. In his loft, John waited for his eyes to acclimatise to the darkness. *What the feck?* he thought. The screams were unfeigned, piercing and shrill. He heard the distinctive crackle of fire on thatch. With vision adapted and a rush of panic and fear, he jumped out of bed, hastily put on his clothes and shoes and climbed down the ladder. The horses were agitated, jostling each other by the stable door. He spoke gently to them and they calmed a little, but still bolted into the yard as soon as the door was opened.

John looked out. The scene bewildered him. There, within spitting distance of the stables, was the Croffine's cottage with its roof ablaze. He automatically grabbed his cape and turned to run to the front of the cottage, where all the noise was coming from. As he rounded the corner of the stone building, he ran straight into a huge dark-skinned man holding a flambeau in one hand and a yatagan in the other. John observed an overriding perception of red as he tried to bounce off and away. But the man, dressed in a vermillion kaftan and crimson turban, was quicker. He dropped the torch and grabbed John with the strength of someone who you know you have no power to resist. John wasn't a fighter in any sense and succumbed.

"Don't fight or..." the man said, deeply and roughly, as he brandished his sword.

John just nodded in shock, guts churning, mind a blur. He was half-dragged, half-walked to the street and placed alongside the Croffine family, Corent, his wife, daughter and Corent's two other servants, Liam and Niall, who shared a minute room in the cottage. They used to, anyway. John looked up and around. The roof was completely burnt, as were just about all the others on the twenty-six cottages of the small coastal neighbourhood of Baltimore that made up the Cove. The parched sedge, tinder dry from the heat wave, was no match for the fire torches.

John wasn't focussed. He was numb. Blankly, he looked around, trying to make some meaning of all this. He was suddenly man-handled and pushed, along with the Croffines. He saw the Roberts and Gunter families, and then what seemed to be the entire population of the Cove being shoved and harried down the road, by as many, if not more, red-turbaned men. Some had skins the colour of a raven. *I've never seen a fear gorm before*, thought John, dazed at the sight. *So, that's what Patrick's on about. What are they doing here? What is all this shite?*

Some of the women and children cried, most were in their nightgowns and John felt cock-a-hoop, strange given the circumstances, that he was fully dressed. Others were looking morose with thousand yard stares, obviously traumatised. A bellow of "Allahu Akbar" jounced his hearing and John looked at one of the captors. He grinned when he noticed the baggy dimije and gaudy cariks. The man noticed John staring and smirking at his trousers and shoes, and flashed his scimitar. John recognised blood on the blade, a deeper red than the clothing and quickly averted his eyes. *Someone's been hurt*, he realised, as he carried on stumbling down the road towards the beach, an unfamiliar situation in familiar surroundings.

He came up against a wall of people. It was a queue, moving slowly as the captives were placed into rowing boats and taken to two awaiting ships, anchored in Baltimore harbour. Faint signs of dawn were appearing on the horizon as John took his place, unquestioning, nestled between Liam and Niall. He wrapped his coat tightly round himself, caressing the concealed seal; a touch of reassurance. Lodged firmly between the only two other Irishmen in the group, he shut his eyes and tried to settle his feelings.

Chapter 6 – Baltimore to Algiers

20 June 1631 to 28 July 1631

John woke muzzily from a short, disturbed sleep. Something was crawling over his face. He slapped his cheek. A small black bug was smeared on his hand. His eyes adjusted to the pale light, seeping through cracks in the planked ceiling of a sail locker, where he was imprisoned along with the other men. Closely packed and chained by the legs to each other, there was little room to move and his bum was numb. He lifted a buttock to help the blood flow. His intestines stirred. He needed to defecate. John looked around. By a ladder, leading to a trap door, sat two of the captors, keeping an eye on their hostages.

"Oi!" John shouted, attracting their attention. "Privy," he said, hoping they would understand. They did, one unchained him and led him up on deck. John breathed in the fresh air, deeply, and took in the fact that he was now at sea, on a three-masted sailing vessel that lurched comfortably over the swell. The only land in sight was an indistinguishable speck on the horizon, which he assumed was Baltimore. The sun had just risen on his first day of captivity.

John was directed to the heads, a wooden slatted area at the front of the ship, leading up to the bow. Keeping his balance, he squatted, eased his bowels into the sea below and wiped himself with white oakum. The bodily function lightened his mood a little and he made his way back to the deck. The soldier who had been policing him beckoned.

"Come with me, the captain wants to see you," he ordered.

John surveyed his surroundings as he was led by the arm and taken to a cabin at the stern of the craft. The different body hues and varied visages of the crew revealed a global navy. Men from a variety of regions, including China, India, Scandinavia, Arabia and East Africa, made up the workforce. Some were busy tying or loosening ropes, others were climbing around the yardarms or performing chores on deck. He noticed another smaller ship sailing behind the one he was on. He felt the boat surge forward as the sails filled with wind. The guard knocked the door.

"Enter!" Came a shout from within.

Inside, John was told to stand in front of a desk where a middle-aged, heavily moustachioed, Caucasian man sat staring at paper charts. After a long pause, Mr Whiskers looked up.

"Good morning, Christian," he said. "How are you?"

John knitted his brows, surprised at the question. *How am I? And that's not my name*, he pondered but replied, "I've been better."

Mr Whiskers laughed inwardly but didn't say anything.

John went on, gaining confidence. "I don't really know how I am. I'm alive, hungry and very vexed. That's how I'd sum it up. Who are you, what are you doing with us and why am I here?" he ended, feeling relieved to offload the chaotic queries that had been bickering around his brain.

"Good questions, very good questions," Mr Whiskers replied calmly. "And I will answer them shortly, but first, let me introduce myself. I am Captain Morat, from Algiers. What's your name?"

John smiled when he realised his mistake in thinking he'd been called Christian. *He must have called me by my religion*, he thought, *how strange*. John answered and Morat made a note on a clean sheet of paper with an inked swan's plume.

"I have picked you out, John, because you are the only one who is actually fully dressed. By my reckoning, to be able to manage to dress yourself in the chaos of a raid, makes you a lot more capable than most of the others. Unless you sleep in your clothes, of course." Morat smiled in a cordial manner. "I am going to charge you with the importance of remembering what I say, so that you can tell your fellow captives about the situation you are in. Can you do that?"

"I suppose so," said John, still bewildered. *Is this real or a bad dream?* he thought.

"Good, well listen up then," said Morat, twiddling his

moustache. "You've all been taken prisoner. I'm in charge of the two ships and the crews. We're on our way to Algiers, where your community will be sold as slaves." Morat paused to let the information sink in. John felt a thud in his chest; he had heard of this type of thing. Pirates seizing ships and crews, taken into slavery, never to be seen again. But not near Baltimore nor attacks on land.

"We will treat you well," continued Morat, "so long as you don't cause any disruption or try to escape. The men you see in red are Janissaries, the most highly trained division of the Ottoman army. They know their stuff, so don't even think about playing up or being troublesome. The other sailors all have a vested interest in you. They will share in the money I can get for you at the slave market."

John didn't know what to say. Trying to imagine the future seemed pointless somehow. He was powerless. His stomach rumbled.

"You are hungry," remarked Morat. "You will be fed. It won't be what you're used to but it will keep you alive."

"Am I supposed to be grateful?" retorted John, astonished at being so abrupt.

"Now, now. I can understand your anger, but you'll have to deal with that quickly or it will only get worse for you."

Worse, thought John, *I wonder how*. He nodded in response.

"Good," said Morat. "I imagined you would see sense. Now, do you have any questions?" *Probably hundreds,* thought John, *but I can't get my head straight.*

"Where are the women and children?" he finally asked.

"We separated them from you men. Some are in a different hold to you, on this ship, and the rest are on the other one. They're also being informed about what will happen. Don't worry, they'll come to no harm; our religion respects women. They are under the protection of Allah and the Janissaries. The other sailors dare not mistreat them."

"What religion are you?" asked John, unexpectedly interested. Church had always befuddled him. Having been brought up secularly Catholic, within the O'Mahoney household, he had secretly always questioned the doctrine. Trying to remember which saint did what was impossible. The idea that everybody was a miserable sinner and should feel guilty about Adam's fall from grace didn't make sense, nor did the notion that all pleasure was sinful. *I want to feel contented,* he had challenged, *not blameworthy the whole time. I certainly don't want to be like those moaners who mither and pretend to be in a position to cast the first stone, and then judge everyone else as if they are perfect. And I don't want to eat the body of Christ or drink his blood either, how disgusting! As for turning the other cheek? It's just not realistic.*

The English had brought their new religion, Protestantism, with them. What the real difference was, John couldn't tell, apart from a few rituals. The message seemed similar, the *do unto others* type of thing. But the Protestants had no time for the Pope or the Irish friars, and the English had been very forceful about imposing their beliefs; banning Catholicism, although he had never understood why. *Both the Anglicans and the Catholics are Christians who believe in Jesus, so shouldn't they all be friends, accept their differences and have a mutual understanding?* he had reasoned. For all the scriptural instruction he had received, none of it had satisfied him. There was always doubt.

"I'm a Muslim," Morat replied, "and so are the Janissaries. I can't vouch for the others on board. They come from all over the place, so we've probably got worshippers of Mazda, Shiva, Buddha and Confucius on board. In fact, I know of one blond out there who can't stop talking about Odin and Thor. The point is that these ships are under the protection of Allah."

"Who is Allah?" inquired John, racking his brain for a vague memory of that name.

"The one God; the Creator," replied Morat, matter-of-factly.

John wondered. His religion had a God, or was it three Gods? Was Allah one of them? And this business of taking slaves, was that what Allah wanted? "Well, I believe in God," said John, hoping this would make a difference. Perhaps they were on the same side after all.

"You don't believe in one God," returned Morat. "You have at least three – God as the Father, God as the Son and God as the Holy Spirit. Then you worship Jesus and almost as many saints as the Hindus have Gods. Christians are idolaters. In comparison, Muslims pray directly to God, as only Allah should be glorified." *Interesting*, thought John. *A new perspective.*

"So," said John slowly, trying to construct the question in his head, "does the Muslim religion say you can go and take people at knifepoint out of their beds in the middle of the night and ship them off as slaves?"

Morat shrugged. "I'm not saying I'm a perfect Muslim. I do my best, that's all. Taking slaves is what I do." He shifted in his chair and grew serious. "Ghazi," he called to the Janissary who had brought John to the cabin. He had been quietly standing by the door during the conversation. "Check with Pedro to see if there are any ships following. I'll be all right here."

"Yes sir." Ghazi left.

Morat looked at John. "I can tell that you're a thoughtful man," he said with respect. "We might get time to discuss this in more depth over the next month. That's how long this journey takes, by the way. But, the answer to your question is a mixture of yes and no. Firstly, it is not the Muslim religion. My religion is called Islam and followers of Islam are Muslims. Islam says that I can take slaves if I am fighting in the name of Allah, but only so long as I'm not the aggressor and I'm fighting to defend Islam, or when Islam is being prevented from spreading."

John listened intently, forgetting his current predicament. "If I've heard you correctly, you have gone against Islam then," he said. "We weren't attacking you, nor were we preventing Islam from spreading."

"True," smiled Morat, putting his hands up as if he had been caught out. "There's the rub." He paused. "Ah, business and religion, profit or piety. In strict terms, Allah may not approve of my actions; however, on the other hand, he may see it as a good thing, as we now have the opportunity to convert some infidels into Muslims. You may think it's hypocritical but with the profits I make from you lot, I can give something to the poor and contribute more to the mosque. That's our equivalent to your house of prayer." John shook his head. *He's the same as some of those serious church goers*, he thought. *Blaspheming, lying, cheating and fornicating for most of the week, then turning up on Sundays, asking for forgiveness!* "And don't forget it was one of your Popes who sanctified slavery, in order to Christianise Africans. No-one is innocent," Morat continued. The door opened and Ghazi returned.

"Not a sail in sight sir," he reported. John's belly grumbled again.

"Take him back and give them breakfast," commanded Morat. "I'm sure we'll talk again, John. Now go, tell the others what you've heard."

Gripping John's arm firmly, Ghazi walked him back to the hold. He smelled something cooking; a completely new, but unappetising, smell. John felt encumbered by the task set by Morat, all because of a set of clothes; to inform a group of distraught captives that slavery beckoned. He caressed the heaviness of his other obligation, hidden in the corner of his cape. *I've got to get through this though*, he thought, *even if it's just for my ancestors. I must survive and keep that hope alive, and find my way home*. Feeling burdened, his appetite weakened. *Stay strong*, he said to himself, *stay bloody strong*.

"You don't have to hold me so tightly," John said to Ghazi. "I won't jump overboard or anything."

"You promise in the name of Allah?" asked Ghazi.

"If that's what it takes, I promise in the name of Allah."

Ghazi released his grip and grinned. His smile was disarmingly friendly. John shook and rubbed his arm.

"Thank you," he said.

"He likes you," said Ghazi. "Morat, I mean, he likes you. If you keep in his favour he may be able to help you in Algiers." Ghazi opened the trap door and secured John back in his place. It stank in the hold.

"Can you grant us some fresh air, please?" John asked.

"I will ask," responded Ghazi, climbing the ladder and shutting the door.

John's eyes accustomed themselves and he looked around. Some of the men had been sleeping but they came to following the disturbance. On waking, their reality hit them like the heaviness of a blunt blow; initially stunning them, followed by a sudden charge of adrenaline.

"Did you have a good cac?" asked Liam.

"I certainly did," chuckled John.

"You were a long time," stated his other neighbour, Niall.

"The captain wanted to see me. We had a chat. I'll tell you all about it soon. Meanwhile, I think we're going to get some breakfast and hopefully, fresh air."

At that, Ghazi appeared at the trap door. "To start with, half of you can come up and have breakfast on deck," he said. "Then the rest of you afterwards." John stayed back to be part of the second half. He'd already taken some air.

Breakfast consisted of some sort of fish-based gruel. Something in it smelled rotten, but out of sheer desperation, they ate it anyway, forcing it down with the help of a tasteless ship biscuit. After Ghazi had shackled everyone back in the hold again, John informed the group of Morat's plans for them. Many asked questions, but John had few answers.

"I have told you all I know. If I find out more, I will update you," he promised. There was silence, followed by quiet murmurings, as the prisoners discussed their new knowledge. Ghazi kept a close eye, ready for any negative reaction from his charges.

Corent Croffine, John's now ex-employer, spoke up. "Does anyone else think that we would be better off with an Englishman talking to the captain?" There was an undertone of assent.

"Please yourself," John said flatly, not bothered in the slightest. It wasn't as if he had offered his services to Morat anyway.

"Any volunteers?" asked Corent. Not a peep.

"All right then," Corent continued. "I will. Excuse me," he said to an alert Ghazi, who, having been looking at John, turned his head slowly and looked at Corent. "I demand to see the captain."

"Why?" asked Ghazi.

Corent paused, taken aback at being questioned. "I want to offer myself as the person representing this group. In place of John there," Corent said, pointing.

"What's wrong with John?" queried Ghazi, seemingly amused.

"Well, seeing that he's Irish and I'm English, I have more authority," postured Corent.

Ghazi laughed, his teeth gleaming in the gloom, eyeballing Corent as he responded. "The skipper asked for John so that's that. If he wanted you, he'd have asked for you. But he doesn't and didn't. You have as much authority here as one of our ship's rats. Do not demand anything again."

Corent flushed and looked away, his ego deflated. John smiled and nodded at Ghazi, who had returned his gaze to John. There was no more dissent. The boat creaked and rocked its way south, travelling past France, Spain and Portugal, entering the Mediterranean Sea through a thin gut flanked by the peaks of Jabal al Tariq to port and Jebel Musa to starboard.

xxx

Narrator's note:
The name Jabal al Tariq was anglicised to Gibraltar, when the British took over the area in 1704.

xxx

During the voyage, John was summoned back to Morat's cabin on several occasions. Their conversations ranged from the plight of the imprisoned to slavery and religion. John grew into the role of mediator, helping the captain compile a list of names of all the detainees. With John's pledge to be held accountable for the captive's behaviour, Morat allowed his cargo to be placed on deck when the weather permitted. Two days out from their destination, John was called in for the last time.

"Soon, we arrive in Algiers," Morat told him. "Today, you will all have a sea water wash and be provided with some clean clothing. Make the best of it. I want you all looking as healthy as possible for the sale."

Finally, thought John. *The journey is coming to an end*. Creeping sensations of apprehension attacked his stomach, completely extinguishing a growing feeling of boredom with the ship's routine.

"Have you no questions?" asked Morat. "This is your last chance; we will not see each other again in this manner." He leaned over, conspiratorially, even though there was no-one else in the cabin. "I like you John. Is there something you think I can help you with? You would be a terrible waste in the galleys."

John shuddered. He had learnt about the slaves forced to row in the galley ships from Ghazi, who had endured such experiences in a previous life. The punishing physical work killed many.

"Do they have horses there?" John blurted out.

Morat laughed. "Horses! Hundreds of them, why?"

"I miss my horses back home and I'd like to work with them again," said John, simply.

"I'll see what I can do," said Morat. "Don't mention this, I can't promise anything for you or any of the others. Business is business, and if Allah has preordained it, most of them will end up rowing their lives away."

Chapter 7 – Algiers

28 July 1631

John felt slightly uplifted when he noticed swifts, swallows and house martins flitting in and around the rooftops of the sun-bright, white-washed buildings of Algiers. Having been herded off the ships, the Baltimore captives were marched through the narrow streets, squinting at the glare, to the Pasha's palace. Along the way, the locals subjected them to cheers, jeers and insults. The Pasha's dwelling, a grand detached mansion, was set inside a fortified Casbah, protected by high, windowless stone-walls, pierced only by a gateway, the top of which had been delicately masoned into an arch. Passing by the bowaab, the sentry manning the entrance, the stolen goods traipsed into the compound. John could only admire the gardens, full of mature date palms and cedar trees; vividly variegated ivy bushes and jasmine hedgerows, with numerous blooming flowers of which the striking purple iris took some beating.

Now, as they stood waiting in the huge main hall, John tried to alleviate his anxiety, distracting himself by focussing on the view from the nearest window, whilst stroking the seal. Everything was about to change again. Although the ship's routine had become tedious, there had been a strange kind of comfort in its familiarity and confinement. At this precise moment he had no idea what was in store for him, apart from the cruel fact that he was going to become someone's slave. Morat had explained that, before they were all taken to the bedistan to be sold, the Pasha had first choice of the thralls.

Pasha Hassan Khodja, descended from aristocratic Arabian ancestry, entered the hall, followed by several other dignitaries. He approached Morat, who bowed obsequiously. John watched the pair as they greeted each other; entranced by the Pasha's shimmering jewelled sash, the sheathed scimitar hanging from his side, and his white turban, bedecked with gleaming gems and ostrich feathers.

Morat suddenly pointed straight at John and the Pasha's head turned in his direction. John stopped breathing. He caught the Pasha's eyes briefly, looked away, then back again. The Pasha and Morat were engaged in discussion with each other once more.

What was that about? John thought, exhaling. The Pasha and Morat walked around the human merchandise, all of whom were now dressed in uniform roomy trousers and loose tops. John had his cape over his shoulder. It was getting threadbare and some holes in the fabric needed fixing. The corners were still strong though, even the one that he continued to caress nervously. The Pasha and Morat had stopped a few feet away from him, reviewing a couple of the females. Eventually, they came to John.

"Your Excellency," said Morat, addressing the Pasha. "This is the man I mentioned earlier. He assures me that he is good with horses, but I have no evidence apart from his word."

The Pasha scrutinised John. "Well, let's see if his word is true. In fact, this could be serendipitous. You see, my daughter is driving me mad; she has acquired the unruliest horse I have ever come across. It refuses to calm down, but she insists on taming it. The ostlers have tried to no avail. If the horse can't be broken I'll have to order for her throat to be cut. And then, of course, if I do that, my daughter will never let me hear the end of it."

The Pasha addressed John directly. "If you can perform miracles and break this beast, then I will consider putting you to work in the stables. If you can't, you are a prime specimen for the galleys." The Pasha clicked his fingers. A particularly large, brawny black man, part of the entourage came forward; yellow robes whishing and his tasbih swaying across his broad chest. A curved sword swung loosely. "Mahmood, take this slave to the stables and arrange for him to have a one-to-one with my daughter's nightmare. Give him one chance."

Mahmood smiled and bowed. He looked at John, beckoned him and turned towards one of the many doors leading out of the hall. John followed; his mind spinning, mixing a concoction of hope and fear. As he left, he glanced back at the rest of the Baltimore victims. He didn't realise then that that would be the last time he saw any of them. They walked through several corridors, passing numerous rooms to the left and right. None of the doors were open, nor could John hear any noises coming from behind them. Cooking odours, pungent, savoury and spicy, tickled John's nose. These were new smells to him, rich and mouth-watering. He felt a sudden pang of hunger. Mahmood took him to a set of steps which led outside and down into a courtyard. As John stood on the top step, he noticed a balcony to his left that overlooked the enclosure. A fresh, sweet scent emanated from around the gallery, reminding him of a mixture of honey and fruit. He paused, breathing deeply. It was an overwhelming fusion of aromas. Mahmood noticed and looked at John.

"You like the perfume?" he asked.

John nodded. "What is it?"

"You're experiencing the aura of the harem," Mahmood replied. "Behind that balustrade live the odalisques and women of the household. You are not allowed anywhere near it without express permission from me. Otherwise..." He stopped talking, looked sternly at John, whilst taking out his blade and pretending to cut his throat with it.

"I get the message," said John, "but the smell is wonderful."

Satisfied that he had made his point, Mahmood re-sheathed his weapon, and smiled. “That is the scent of frankincense, mixed with other essences. However, that is of no concern to you. Your job is to subdue a horse. If you don’t, your life will be miserable and most likely, very short.”

They descended and walked across the dry, dusty ground towards a small group of men. The yard was flanked on two sides by stalls; half open at the top, with grey, black and brown horses’ heads protruding out from the frames. Just one stall was left closed; outside of which, the men were talking. They went silent as Mahmood and John approached them.

“Where is the princess’ horse?” enquired Mahmood.

“In there,” replied one of the men, gesturing to the fully closed door, with a bandaged hand.

“Get her out,” ordered Mahmood. “This slave is going to try and tame her.” The men laughed.

“Don’t dally,” demanded Mahmood. “It’s an express instruction from the Pasha.” John could hear shuffling behind the stable door.

“Stand clear,” said another man, as he slid the bolt that released both halves of the door. He didn’t have to open it. The horse barged it out of the way and raced into the courtyard, jumping and braying. John watched, transfixed as the beautiful chestnut mare stamped and trotted around its confines.

Magnificent, John thought, as he admired the quality pedigree of this fifteen hands high, high-tailed Arabian equine. The reality of his situation receded as he averted his concentration solely onto the beast in front of him; registering every flick of the head, tail swish and stomping of hooves. Then he noticed it. The horse seemed reluctant to put much pressure on its rear left foot; dangling it just above the ground when standing still. Instinctively, John knew what to do. This animal wasn't wild in temperament, it was in pain.

"Has anyone inspected this horse properly?" he asked of the men. They shook their heads. The man with the strapping spoke up.

"We've had this horse for two days. No one's managed to get near to her. It was hard enough to get her in the stables; six of us ended up having to use ropes. When I got too close, she bit my hand. We don't know what to do with her."

John looked back at the horse. It was waiting, breathing heavily, lolling its head from side to side and taking in its surroundings. *Now or never,* thought John as he began to advance, slowly. He exhaled. His breathing calmed, resonating between a murmur and a low whistle, undulating in tone. The horse pricked up one ear, and then the other. Its head stopped moving, transfixed on John. *So far, so good,* he thought, drawing nearer, beginning to feel a mutual wavelength between him and the nag. He continued his low humming until he was within touching distance of the creature. Suddenly, the horse rushed away, kicking out and shaking. John heard laughter behind him, but didn't bother to look round.

Staying still, he continued his susurration. The horse stopped and looked towards John again. *That's good*, thought John, *maybe this time*. Mustering his most gentle intonation he started muttering cajoling words. "Pretty girl, very pretty girl, keep calm, I can help." The horse snuffled shallowly. John moved closer and closer; close enough now to touch the mare's face. He had no fears or other cares. In that moment, there was nothing else in the world except him and the horse. Still murmuring sweet phrases, John slowly raised his hand, allowing the filly to see it, and petted the fur above the nostrils. The horse made a sound like a sigh. John's other hand moved to the animal's left ear and scratched it. He raised his head to whisper in the ear. The horse seemed to relax.

Gradually and methodically, John moved down the left-hand-side of the steed, wittering away and smoothing his hands along the neck, withers, barrel and flank, keeping constant contact. As he reached the hock it twitched involuntarily. John's undertones grew slightly louder and deeper. Gingerly stroking the leg, he raised the fetlock and inspected the foot. Feeling a warmth of achievement, John spotted the problem. He saw the tell-tale sign of a small stone, wedged in between the bone of the hoof and the skin of the leg. The flesh around it was swollen, a polyp, almost covering the stone. *If I can get that out, I can hopefully secure a position here*, he thought.

Turning slowly to face the men who were watching silently open-mouthed, he indicated with a curved finger that he needed something sharp to dig with. A hoof pick was thrown his way. Cautiously, John pressed his fingers against the angry skin, pulled it back and revealed the stone, smeared in blood. *This must be extremely painful*, he considered; reassuring the horse continuously with his low-tone and hushed words. The mare was still. John felt the trust. He placed the pick at the edge of the hoof, gained a small purchase on the pebble and eased upwards. A slight but distinct sucking sound was heard and the stone came free. The horse reacted with a trembled shivering, starting at the end of its mane and travelling down its back. John released the foot, picked up the offending piece of rock, patted the pony's rump and walked back to the gawping men.

"The wound needs to be bathed. Have you water and liniment?" he asked. "This was the problem," he said, holding up the bit of grit.

From behind him, John heard someone clapping. He looked around and up at the balcony, to where the applause was coming from. His throat gulped, and with a sharp intake of breath, his vision widened at the beautiful high cheek-boned face of a young woman looking down at him. She was dressed in thin, brightly-coloured red and yellow robes topped by a mauve hijab that covered her hair.

"Stunning", he said to himself, forgetting where he was again as he soaked up the texture of her smooth, pampered dark skin, and even darker, shining eyes.

"Well done, half-cloak," the woman called down at John, who felt as if his face was being pierced by her falcon-like focus.

"Anais, go back inside immediately," barked Mahmood.

"I will not, Mahmood," countered Anais. "I am the Pasha's daughter, that is my horse, and I will do as I please."

It's her horse, John realised, still drinking in the aura of Anais.

"Please return to your quarters Anais or I will have to inform your father," said Mahmood, tiredly.

"You do what you need to do," responded Anais, haughtily. "I, meanwhile, am going to take a look at my horse." She slipped through a side door and came down the steps.

All the men except Mahmood and John averted their gaze. Even just a sneaky peek at any woman of the harem could be punished severely. Mahmood saw John ogling, hypnotised by her eyes; the sclera as clear as pearl, the irises and pupils merging as deep dusky circles with a lustrous sheen.

"Don't look anymore, slave," said Mahmood, sternly. "You need to learn to know your place quickly or you will lose your life. Anais, I will have to report your disobedience." John looked away. But Anais, ignoring Mahmood, came up to him.

"How did you calm her?" she demanded. John didn't respond, but looked at Mahmood, questioningly.

"Answer her, but don't look," was the advice.

"Come on. Tell me," Anais said, impatiently.

"I talked to your horse," replied John.

"You talked to her!" exclaimed Anais, laughing. "So, you speak horse, do you?"

John stayed quiet. A man stood near with a wooden bucket of water and some other liquid in an earthenware bowl.

"I will watch while you treat my horse," said Anais.

John did as he was told. The horse was placid now and he had no difficulty bathing the laceration and applying some soothing lotion. He had a heightened awareness of Anais' close presence. From her clothing, faint wafts of frankincense flavoured the air. *In your dreams*, he thought, trying not to reveal any sign of uneasiness.

"You've done well, half-cloak," Anais said softly. "What's your name?"

John didn't know whether to answer. He looked to Mahmood for guidance but it seemed that he had given up trying to control Anais and was busy talking to the men.

Without looking at her, he answered. "John."

"Well, John. I only called you half-cloak, because of this thing," she said as she flipped a corner of his cape. "What is it? I've never seen one before."

"It's called a brat. For the cold," he said, automatically pulling the garment together, protectively.

"Well, it's hardly cold, now, is it?" she said in an obvious tone.

"I know, but I've only just got here. I haven't found a coat-hook yet."

She laughed. "Thank you for helping my horse. I shall speak to my father about you. In return for curing her, perhaps I can find a new coat for you?"

John was shocked. It was like she was talking to him as if they were friends. "Thanks, but I don't need a new one," he replied, "just some repairing."

"In that case, I will mend it. I am very good at sewing. Take it off and let me have it."

"Can I trust you with it? It's very important to me," John said.

"Are you questioning my integrity?" snapped Anais. "If I wanted to, I could have you stripped and whipped for that. And I could destroy your precious brat!"

“I’m sorry,” apologised John, suddenly losing the feeling of friendship and remembering his situation.

He handed over the clothing. John’s success with the horse resulted in him becoming a stable slave. Considering the alternative, he was jubilant. After eating a tangy and fiery mutton stew in the servant’s kitchen, he was shown to where he would lodge, in the loft above the horses. Climbing the ladder to his bedding, he stripped and lay down, exhausted. *A home away from home*, he reflected. *Life can be so strange sometimes*.

Chapter 8 – Slavery in Algiers

August/September 1631

John had to wait many days before he saw his cape again. *Just don't lose the seal*, was a recurring thought. He quickly settled into his new role; tending to the horses. His new acquaintances, the other grooms, treated him with respect having witnessed his talents first-hand. As a slave he was confined to the stable area most of the time, where he became enamoured with the different species of horses the Pasha owned. The greys were low-tailed Algerian Barbs, and the piebalds, bays and one black stallion, used for stud duties, had been imported from the Iberian Peninsula. Comparing the characteristics of these breeds, in contrast to his experience with Irish Hobby horses, captivated him. As he worked in and out of the courtyard, he couldn't help but look up at the harem sometimes, hoping for a glimpse of Anais. He never saw her but other women enriched the balcony occasionally, some wearing full burka veils.

One afternoon, whilst daydreaming and calmly brushing Anais's horse, John noticed a change of fragrance in the stable air. A breath of frankincense mingled with the aroma of horse, hay and sweat. He was working topless, methodically stroking the beast's rear quarters. As he turned around, he was startled to see Anais, leaning against the door, watching him.

He detected her eyes moving over the shape of his chest and arms. *Is that a faint smile?* he asked himself, automatically standing more upright. He quickly deflected his gaze but not before noticing that she was carrying his brat.

"Hello, Christian slave," Anais said mockingly, walking towards him. "Your cold weather gear is mended. Here, what do you think?"

John held out an arm and she placed the coat over it.

"You can look at me, you know," said Anais. "We're alone for the moment. But if somebody comes, then you must look away. Did you think you wouldn't see your brat again?"

It had crossed his mind. "I would never question your integrity again," John replied instead. He examined the garment, checking the fringe first. With a sigh of relief, he felt the shape of the seal. There was new stitching and brightly coloured patches of cloth covering the worn parts of the fabric.

"Good as new." John smiled, looking up at Anais. "Did you do this yourself?"

"Of course. I'm glad you like it. But, I do know what's inside it," she said with raised eyebrows.

John didn't know what to say; unnerved by her beauty, the

alluring scents, and the heightened awareness that he was half-naked, he felt vulnerable. Although it was hot, he wrapped the cape around him, glancing up to catch Anais' knowing, amused smile. She strode past him to her horse.

"When I felt it, I unpicked the original thread to see what it was. Then I sewed it up again. It's a seal, isn't it?" She scratched the horse's chin.

"Yes," said John, simply.

"And why would you carry a seal in your clothing?" she asked.

It was one of those moments when his defences were down and he wanted to tell her everything about himself. Just as he went to answer her, the sound of approaching footsteps stopped him. He quickly faced away and reverted to the posture of a slave; bowed and subservient. He began brushing the horse again. Mahmood appeared, with his tall bulky frame blocking out the sunlight.

"There you are, Anais. I've been looking for you everywhere," he said despairingly. "Your father wants you."

Anais breathed deeply and stamped her foot in displeasure. "Another time, inshallah," she whispered to John and tramped out purposefully, not even looking at Mahmood.

Mahmood shrugged his shoulders as she went by then looked at John and with inquiring brows asked, "Are you cold? How come you're wearing that?"

"No. Anais repaired it for me and I tried it on, that's all. I can take it off now."

"You're doing well, Christian. You seem to have resigned yourself to your place in life. I can't say that for all of your group," Mahmood said, enigmatically. John had, at times, speculated about what had befallen the other Baltimore captives.

"What do you mean?" he asked.

Mahmood explained that all the others had been auctioned at the slave market. Many families had been split up and sold separately. A few unlucky women became the objects of some men's sexual fantasies, while other females had been bought to spend their lives as seamstresses, cooks and domestic servants. Children were acquired by childless couples, or tradesmen wanting free labour. All the able-bodied men had been scooped up by corsairs to be used as oarsmen in the galley ships. One older man had been purchased by a wealthy mature widow to keep her company. He didn't argue when she revealed that she was a dominatrix.

"One man in the galleys has died already," Mahmood said straightforwardly. "I heard he wasn't rowing hard enough and had to be whipped. It sounds as if he expired from the punishment. Another one tried to escape by jumping overboard, but he was soon caught. He now sits in a dungeon. So, you can count yourself lucky."

John shook his head in dismay.

"I think you ought to know that there's an English consul trying to negotiate a ransom for your crowd," mentioned Mahmood. "But don't get your hopes up, it seldom happens."

And certainly not for an Irishman, thought John.

John deliberated this news. He did want to go home, but, newly ascertained, a sense of discovery had revealed itself, completely unlike Patrick who, since early childhood, had always dreamed of doing something adventurous. He smiled at a recent memory, when he'd thought that he never wanted to leave Baltimore. But now that he had, albeit unwillingly, John's mind was opening. Recognising that he was much luckier than the other villagers, he endeavoured to embrace his new experiences; whether it was an opportunity to discourse with someone from another culture, observe the differences in architecture, the food, a religious debate or just fresh ways of thinking. With everything that had happened since he'd arrived, he hadn't even started considering the practicalities of returning to Ireland.

"Can I ask you a question, Mahmood?" John enquired.

"I'm all ears."

"Is there any way I can leave here and go home?"

Mahmood pouted his lips. "Well, there are ways," he replied

slowly. "You could try to escape, but no one has ever done that from this household. If you had money, you could pay for your freedom, but you don't. Or, by doing something which raised the Pasha's opinion of you he could, through a merciful act of manumission, release you from your bonds. Converting to Islam may strengthen your cause. In fact, it would be beneficial even if you remain in bondage."

John weighed up his options. Escaping would be difficult, perhaps something to consider in the future if he was desperate to go home. There wasn't any obvious way of raising a monetary sum for his release. However, discussions about Islam with Morat had stimulated his interest. Recent events had reignited that enthusiasm. In wonder, he listened intently the first time he heard the mesmerising nasal incantations of the muezzin's call to prayer from beyond the boundaries of the Pasha's home. Since then, he had learnt that the adhan came from a place of worship, the Ketchaoua Masjid, where people attended to perform their prayers five times a day. Inside the Casbah, Muslims stopped work, washed, gathered together, placed cloths or small rugs on the ground and prayed; all facing in the same direction for about fifteen minutes. This all piqued his curiosity, being so different to the tedious boredom of both his Catholic and Anglican religious participation.

"How do I become a Muslim?" he asked.

“I can teach you if I get permission and the time, inshallah,” replied Mahmood.

“What does inshallah mean?” John enquired, remembering Anais’ whisper.

“If God wills it,” answered Mahmood. “Why would you want to become a Muslim, Christian?”

“Well, for one thing, it might stop people calling me Christian. My name is John. I'm not a true believer anyway. To start with, I disagree that you have to believe in Jesus to enjoy a decent life after death.”

“But you are more Christian than anything else, are you not?” inquired Mahmood, investing himself into the conversation.

“That's true, but only because I’ve never had access to any other religions. The idea of God has always interested me, but I’m plagued by doubts about some of the scriptures I've read. I'd just like to learn more, so I can make up my own mind,” John replied. He couldn’t help but think that Anais might be pleasantly surprised if he converted.

“That’s a good answer,” approved Mahmood. “Keep an open mind. I have not always been a Muslim. I used to worship my ancestors, but now I know the truth about God.”

“Can I ask you another question?” said John.

“My ears are not full yet.”

“Where are you from?” came the query.

"Ah," Mahmood sighed, "the south. South of the Great Desert; very far from here."

"How did you get here?" John asked, inquisitively.

"How? I was stolen and enslaved, just like you," was the reply.

"But you're not a slave now, are you? You carry a weapon and have some sort of authority and privileges."

"I'm still a slave. It's a long story." Mahmood pulled up a stool and sat before he continued. "When I was six, war came to my village. The victors found me and my five-year-old sister, Dalanda, hiding. Our parents had been killed. We were sold to slave traders and brought here to Algiers. The Pasha's family took us in as playthings for the harem. That was thirty-two years ago. Dalanda is no longer with us. May she rest in peace," he paused and shuddered.

From his pocket, Mahmood produced a sebsi pipe and pouch. John watched as he filled the clay bowl with a green vegetable material. He put the pipe in his mouth and, from another pocket, brought out a flint and piece of wool, which he put on the ground. Unsheathing his scimitar, Mahmood struck the flint three times before a hot spark landed on the wool and smouldered. He quickly re-sheathed the weapon, picked up the wool and blew until it flared. Placing the flame to his pipe, he sucked. The dudeen smoked. On the fourth pull, he inhaled deeply. John was intrigued. He had never smoked, nor really come across it either. A fleeting thought caused him to wonder how Patrick's tobacco crop was growing. John waited, expectantly, for Mahmood to take a breath. Finally, he exhaled the smoke, and with a great gasp, and to John's relief, gulped some fresh air.

"That is definitely not frankincense you're smoking," said John, sniffing and wrinkling his nose at his first smell of cannabis.

"This is kif," Mahmood explained, putting down his pipe. "It's good for the mind."

John, riveted by Mahmood's story and behaviour, had stopped grooming the horse until it nudged him, as if to remind him; he complied, combing its mane. He wanted to hear more details of Mahmood's past and hoped he was in the mood to continue talking.

"So, you've been enslaved here for thirty-two years?" he prompted.

"Yes," responded Mahmood, "that's better. I needed the kif to talk about the aftermath. When I was about eleven, they cut off my genitals."

"What?" exclaimed John.

"Yes, and I remember it clearly."

John crossed his legs involuntarily. "Why?"

"They do that to some of the younger male slaves, so we lose our desires; to tame us," Mahmood replied, mournfully, repeating the lighting ritual, dragging in a lungful of smoke.

"How do you go for a piss?" asked John cheekily.

"Like a woman. Anyway, moving on, I had become a favourite amongst the women and when I was old enough, I became the eunuch to the harem. I am a trusted slave, with a little power."

John felt sympathy for the man. After a short silence he asked softly, "what happened to your sister?"

"I tried to protect her," Mahmood replied, his speech beginning to slow, "but she grew into a beautiful young woman. She was the Pasha's gozde, his favourite. He wanted a son, but his wife was barren, so he chose Dalanda as a concubine hoping that she would bear him a boy. She did, and he is called Mohammed. The Pasha made her his second wife and soon Anais was born. Dalanda fell ill when Anais was only seven-years-old; she eventually died from the plague." Mahmood had been struggling to express himself and now fell silent.

John managed to keep up with the information. "So, your niece, Anais, obviously lives here. But then where is your nephew, Mohammed?"

Mahmood stared at the floor with tired, droopy eyes. "Mohammed is away studying. Now, that is enough for today. You have listened well," sighed Mahmood, getting to his feet. "We will talk again soon, inshallah."

"I hope so, inshallah," mimicked John as Mahmood pocketed the pipe. He felt a sudden deep yearning to be at home amongst familiar surroundings. "Do you ever want to go back home?" he said before Mahmood left.

Mahmood nodded, looking directly at John through bloodshot eyes. "Before I die," he said, "to my village of Tamana. I want to make sure my parents were buried according to custom. If they weren't, their souls will be trapped and won't reach the ancestors. If that's the case, I must perform a ceremony to release them. Now, no more questions today, my ears are full." He walked out into the sunshine. *Has he been crying?* wondered John.

Chapter 9 – Slavery in Algiers continued

October 1631 – September 1641

It was the constant raised sound of chirping that caused John to notice a richness of house martins gathering along the rooftops of the residence. A few red-rumped and barn swallows shared the space. He had seen this behaviour, during autumn, many times before in Baltimore. *It looks like they're getting ready to leave*, he thought. *I wonder where they go to*. He watched them, jumping and fluttering, anxious to move. Suddenly, without any apparent warning, the birds launched themselves upwards as one and flew off inland. For the next month, he observed a steady stream of swallows, house martins and swifts, flying by, all heading south. A few flew around the stables for a short time, ducking and diving, stocking up on insects before moving on. They were notable by their absence.

Months went by and there was no news from the Consul. John had been thinking about Anais. He saw her on the days when she took her horse out, but she was always surrounded by other women. They all wore niqab veils, but he could tell who she was as they approached the stables. Her sharp eyes, the easy, confident gait and slight hint of her shape through her flowing garments, tucked into her calf-high leather riding boots, gave her away. To his disappointment, she always acted as if he wasn't there, not even acknowledging him when, having prepared her horse, he held the bridle out for her. Without moving her head, she took the reins, jumped into the stirrups and rode away.

Spots of light rain were falling on a spring morning, when a couple of things changed. First, John noticed the return of some house martins. Then, Anais had come for the horse, veiled, with her friends as usual. But, just as she walked past John to take the halter, she bent her head towards him, whispered "tomorrow," quickly mounted the horse and trotted off. *What just happened?* he thought, his heart flipping at the sound of her voice. *I can't let myself fall for her. Nothing could happen anyway... not between a princess and a slave.*

The next day, John was resting; sitting on a bale of hay with his back against the wall, wondering when, or even if, Anais would materialise. Not long after the Zuhr prayer, he heard soft footsteps just outside the stable and Anais appeared in the doorway.

"I can't believe I managed to slip away unnoticed," Anais said, as she checked behind her and entered. John stood up, his chest heaving as he waited. "Hello John, are you well?" she asked pleasantly. He nodded, stupefied by her beautiful, unveiled face.

"Come on then, tell me about this seal," she said excitedly. *So, that's all she's interested in,* he thought, deflated, his shoulders dropping slightly.

He paused then said, “Anais. I’m confused. Sometimes you seem to treat me like a friend and other times like a piece of horse dung.”

Anais had seen the change in John’s posture and stepped closer. “I want to get to know you better, John, but it can’t be anything more than what it is, at present. It would be dangerous for both of us, if we were seen behaving outside our positions in life.”

John nodded his understanding relieved that his growing feelings for Anais weren’t being rejected outright. “That’ll do as a compromise,” he grinned.

“I’m glad we’ve been more honest with each other,” she said, genuinely. “Now please, while I’ve got some time, tell me about the seal.” So, John did.

“That means that you’re the grandson of the King of Ireland, then” stated Anais, admiringly. “I knew there was something distinguishing about you.”

“No, not the King,” laughed John, “a chief, one of many.”

“Chief, King, same thing, but you shouldn’t be left a slave!” she protested. “You are of noble blood, equal to my own family.” She stopped talking, thinking.

John said nothing, knowing his place, but was nonetheless burning to know more about Anais. There was a comfortable stillness, broken only by the swishing of the horse's tail. When he felt that he had given her enough time, he threw caution to the wind, desperate to ask her something about herself. "What do you want out of life, Anais?" he asked.

Anais tilted her head slightly and looked him in the eyes. "I want to find the right man to marry," she said in a serious tone.

Trying not to reveal that his heart was in his mouth, he sputtered, "I hope you find him soon."

"Oh," said Anais, nonchalantly but with tenderness in her eyes, "I think I might have already done that," and left without saying goodbye.

xxx

Whilst working one day, John heard the soft notes of a stringed instrument. He discontinued mucking out, walked into the yard, and looked up at the balcony where the music seemed to be coming from, but he couldn't see who was playing. Mahmood came down the steps and John took the opportunity to ask him.

"What's that music?"

"The enchanting tones of the oud," replied Mahmood.

"It's gentle on the ears," agreed John. "I don't suppose I could see one, could I?"

"Not unless you become a trusted slave. Now, I've come to

escort you to the Pasha."

"Why? What's going on?" asked John, anxiously.

"I don't know," shrugged Mahmood.

"Have I done something wrong?"

"I don't know. All I know is you have been summoned to see him."

Mahmood led John to a massive study. The walls were decorated with maps and the corners housed shelves of books. A sublimely carved wooden desk was in the centre of the room behind which the Pasha sat in a grand chair.

"Sit down, Christian." The Pasha spoke in a deep, velvety voice. "I'll get to the point, I'm a busy man. My daughter has been giving me ear-ache about you. What have you been telling her? I mean, I know you sorted out her horse but now she's full of some idea that you are the son of a King. Is this true?" John sighed and explained his history.

"... So, it is true. You are blue-blooded," said the Pasha, surprised. "Perhaps I should ransom you back to your family. They would be rich, yes?"

"Unfortunately, no," said John. "The English have taken over the land and my family has ended up penniless. My father believes that we can get our rightful territory back so long as we have the seal, and eventually get rid of the English."

"You would like to remove the English?" the Pasha enquired.

"Oh yes, very much," John replied. *Some more than others*, he thought, thinking of his brother, Conor.

"Maybe Algiers can help you fight the English, but what could we get in return?" The Pasha didn't seem to direct this at John, more to himself. John just shook his head.

"Getting back to the matter in hand - my daughter. She's put in a word for you to get promoted. To please her, you are now in charge of all the stables; a higher position for which you will receive a small remittance. You have worked well. In addition, I also hear that you are interested in learning about Islam. That is good; I give Mahmood permission to instruct you. Anais has also requested that you be allowed to become a trustee so that you can leave the premises to run our errands. I have denied her that request. After all, I could never trust a Christian completely." The meeting closed with a dismissive rising of his hand and a turning of his head.

xxx

Obviously, there were times when John's mind tuned in to thoughts of Baltimore. In those moments, he simply wished to meet a familiar face, eat a plain, traditional Irish meal or gaze across a well-known landscape. He wondered if the horses had survived the fires and how his aunt and uncle had fared. As for Conor, John knew that he would be fretting about the seal. But there was no time to pine for home. John was satisfied taking each day separately; surviving and keeping the seal safe were his main priorities. Newfound interests were keeping thoughts of returning to Ireland at the back of his mind, although he knew he would have to begin thinking about it seriously, at some point. Whenever their duties allowed them, Mahmood and John spent time together.

"I'll start with the history of Islam," said Mahmood.

During these junctures, John learned about the Prophet Mohammed; a moderate man who married legitimately in the spirit of the time. The learning curve was steep and long. He found out that the Qur'an, Islam's Holy Scripture, was the word of God, religiously recorded word for word. In essence, it conveyed the message that one should: 'believe in the one and only God, and that Mohammed was the final messenger; stop idolising Jesus and trust that Mary was his mother and a virgin; treat Christians and Jews with respect as they believe the Gospels. Furthermore, one must: forgive others; dress modestly; not be greedy; accept that everything is preordained; treat women equally and give them their rights; not kill your daughters; not go to war unless you have to defend yourself; spread the word of the Qur'an; be just and fair; love one another as brother and sister; give two and a half percent of your savings to charity; fast during Ramadan; and do the Hajj at least once, if you can. Finally, there is no coercion in religion and you are allowed a maximum of four wives, although only having one is best... Oh, and drinking alcohol or eating pork is discouraged.'

John was eventually able to slip in a question. "So, when you pray, do you do it in the name of Mohammed?"

"No," replied Mahmood. "We pray directly to Allah; not through an intermediary."

"Did you know that Christians believe that every prayer has to be said in Jesus' name and that without complete faith in him as a saviour, you are doomed in the afterlife?" queried John.

"I didn't," responded Mahmood. "Muslims accept that he was a prophet, but not divine, just a man who..."

"Who was crucified for our sins," John interrupted.

"I was actually going to say that, rather than being crucified, he was taken up by Allah," Mahmood said. "Worshipping Jesus is idolatrous according to my doctrine. There are obvious differences in our religions and it is probably impossible to know all the beliefs of every faith. Our own scholars find it difficult enough to understand all the laws of Islam, let alone other creeds. And even then, there are arguments about different ideas and interpretations. If you want to know everything about Islam, you will have to study the Qur'an yourself. I could lend you a copy of the scriptures, but it's written in Arabic and there are no English translations. And then there are all the hadiths too."

"Can you read Arabic?" asked John.

"Of course."

"Then how about reading it and translating it?"

"That's a huge ask," sighed Mahmood.

"It would be interesting to see one though," said John, fascinated by this religion which seemed simpler, easier to comprehend and just more believable than his Christian background. *Islam even loves Mary and Jesus*, thought John. *It all seems very straight forward. It's just an updated edition of Christianity. If there is a God, why wouldn't you believe this version of him?*

"That won't be difficult," declared Mahmood. "I will bring one next time. Do you feel that you're beginning to understand Islam now?"

"Yes, I do. It's absorbing, but a couple of things bother me."

"And what are they?" asked Mahmood kindly.

"Firstly, is it a requirement for Muslim women to wear full face veils?"

"In Islam, no," responded Mahmood. "It's a matter of choice. I don't know all the reasons why women wear them because I haven't asked every Muslim woman who does. But I do know that for some it's an expression of their devotion and piety; that they are going the extra mile to dress modestly. I believe that other women wear it because they're fed up with men leering at them."

John nodded, remembering another aspect he had had some trouble understanding. "But what about slavery? I spoke to Morat about it on the ship. He told me he was a Muslim, but he still nabbed and imprisoned us. How can he be a Muslim and participate in the slave trade?"

"Slavery's been around forever John; before Islam, before Christianity. It's traditional. I admit that it's a tradition that must stop, but it is what it is. Never mistake cultural or human behaviour for religious actions. However, yes, your assessment is correct. There are some people who say they are Muslims but do not follow the true word of Islam. Morat was not acting in accordance with the Islamic rules on slavery. That is his choice, his free will, his business with God, and not mine or yours. Islam allows slaves only as prisoners of a war where Muslims have been defending themselves against aggression. In that case, they must be kafirs, not other Muslims, and they must always be treated with respect. Do you feel you have been respected?"

"Mostly, I suppose," said John. "I bet you don't."

"No, but then, I am better off than those who are forced into the galleys."

"I guess so," said John, thinking how lucky he had been. "It doesn't make sense though. If everyone is Muslim here, and deals in slaves, aren't they all acting hypocritically?"

“Not everyone deals in slaves,” responded Mahmood. “But before you make that judgement don’t forget that first and foremost we are all human beings, full of the frailties that humanity brings. We all have desires and cravings. We all feel anger. Our fathomless minds, the peak of creation in my opinion, can cause us to think irrationally, but that’s just our nature. Although people are physically different, we’re all born with similar traits, varying strengths, and plenty of weaknesses. None of us are perfect, although some seem to think they are. There are far more upright Muslims than false ones, those that practise what they preach, and don't support slavery or other sinful practises. They are wonderful people. It’s those who use the name of Islam as an excuse for their selfish behaviour that gives our faith a bad name. I think you'll find that in most religions. Are you telling me that every Christian is a good Christian?”

“No way!” exclaimed John. “Some of them hit high on the hypocrisy scale. I know of a so-called Christian priest who does disgusting things to young boys. He always seems to pick on the poorest and the meekest. And then there are those who turn up to worship in their Sunday best, pray fervently, put money in the collection tray, but once they get home, maltreat their wives and commit all manner of sins. That’s not Christianity. But, of course, there are good Christians too,” John conceded, thinking of his aunt and uncle. Lowering his voice, he said, “but the Pasha must be complicit in all that’s going on.”

“The Pasha is basically a good man, but there are difficult politics in this city and he does what he has to do,” explained Mahmood. “Much of the power is in the hands of the pirates, who are very well connected. I take little interest. I have decided on the simple life and keep Allah in my head as much as possible.”

John had plenty of time to consider the teachings of Islam between their meetings. Mahmood could only find time every few days, often short-lived, to meet with John in the stables. *How do you make sense of that?* thought John when he first saw the immense, neatly written Arabic manuscript of the Qur’an. Reading from right to left, starting at the back, Mahmood did his best to translate, but some words were just impossible. What he did manage to do, was to transfer some of the feelings and concepts, so a message of sorts was inferred. John was impressed and hungered to understand more. He decided to learn Arabic, and become a Muslim. After studying hard, he eventually declared the Shahada in Irish-lilted-Arabic, in front of a beaming Anais and proud Mahmood.

“You are now my brother in faith,” said Anais.

I want it to be something else, ruminated John, but simply smiled and said, “Who’d have thought?”

Shortly after that, and because of his new set of beliefs and hard work, John became a trusted slave. One of the first things he did with his new privileges was ask to see and try to play an oud. It didn't go well. He found it uncomfortable holding the instrument in his arms and couldn't fathom the tuning. It was the one and only time he missed his old harp. Thoughts of home and Baltimore were diminishing; it wasn't where his heart was anymore. Now able to leave the confines of the household and deliver messages or run errands, John enjoyed walking through the crowded, tall-walled, shady alleyways; watching street vendors plying their trades in spices, gems, and boldly coloured textiles. Beggars, some with severe physical defects, all half-dressed in filthy rags, pleaded to passers-by. When empathy clutched at him, John donated a coin or two, not with the intention of eradicating poverty but simply to help the pauper feel more comfortable that day. On more than one occasion, his tasks occurred at the same time as a call to prayer.

He took these opportunities to visit the mosque, admiring the marble columns and octagonal minarets. Although he received a few enquiring looks, he was accepted by the other supplicants and enjoyed the feeling of camaraderie during these times when everyone was equal in their devotions. There were no reserved spaces for so-called important people. The little money he earned, he saved until the cheapest range of jewellery in the souks came within his budget.

Through the seasons and passing of shifting moons, John and

Anais' relationship developed from occasional flirtation to deeper emotions. The attraction that had been there from the start germinated, grew and blossomed into love. It was complicated. Most of the time they had to act as princess and slave, which amused them as equally as it frustrated them. The courtship consisted of short celebrated moments; sometimes only a few minutes long. With care and patience, both revealed their feelings and commitment to each other. Having established reciprocal adoration, they knew it was only a matter of time before they could be more overt about their involvement; ten years after John's capture, to be exact. During this time, there were other suitors who sought Anais' hand in marriage; some very rich, others very handsome and all appearing highly suitable to the Pasha, who could not understand why his daughter deflected their marital attempts.

"I will choose who I marry," Anais told her father. "Please do not encourage or make any arrangements on my behalf, for further potential bridegrooms. I will let you know when I have made my decision." The rejected bachelors slunk away, each smarting from their encounter with Anais.

As soon as he could afford a ring, one made from silver alloy with a yellow stone, to represent sunshine, hope and happiness, John bought it. At his first opportunity, he presented it to Anais.

"I don't have wealth to offer you, but you have my heart. Will you marry me?" he asked.

"Riches aren't important. You are. I'm confident that you can provide enough for me in our life together, and that's all I need. Yes, I will," she replied without hesitation, extending the fourth finger of her left hand, allowing John to position the ring. It was too big, but slipped comfortably onto her middle finger.

"I'm sorry," apologised John, "I had to guess your ring size."

"It doesn't matter," she whispered and they stole their first kiss with only her horse as witness.

"How are we going to do this?" John asked, heart pounding, a little breathless. "I'm a slave; how is your father ever going to allow you to marry me?"

"He will," Anais said confidently. "And when he does, what happens then?"

"Well, at some point, I want to go home," he said.

"As do I, and so does Mahmood."

"Home?" queried John. "Surely this is your home?"

"It is for now," she said, "but for all of my life, I've wanted to visit my mother's village. She told me about it as a child. Although I was only seven-years-old when she died, her descriptions made a lasting impression. I want to see what it's like. It's called Tamana, across the Great Desert." There was a break in the conversation, as both tried to think of some way to make their wishes come true.

"I've got it," Anais said brightly. "We get married as soon as possible; I tell my father I want to visit Tamana, and that I want Mahmood to escort us through the desert. This is the best time of year to travel, temperature-wise. Your marriage to me automatically releases you from slavery and I'm sure I can get my father to emancipate Mahmood. He's going grey now and there are plenty of other eunuchs who can take his place."

"That gets us to Tamana, but how do we get to Ireland from there?"

"As soon as I have seen my ancestral village, we'll work out how to get to Ireland. I'd like to see where you're from, and meet your family. Then we can decide where to settle."

I think I know the answer to that one, thought John, stimulated by the notion of returning home and remembering the cold, wet winters. Their marriage wasn't common; in fact, it had been totally unheard of before. The wedding of a princess, with a joint black African slave and Arab Pasha heritage, to the grandson of a white Irish chief turned slave, became quite a talking point in the city. Contrary to all the gossip, the ceremony was a quiet affair, with certain nuptial celebrations carrying on late into the night. The Pasha acquiesced on every detail of Anais' plan, down to, and including, the donation of three camels to take the party south. Frankly, he was relieved that Anais was happy, no longer his responsibility, and out of his hair!

As for Anais, the one drawback to her plan was that her horse had to be left behind. Horses don't fare well in desert conditions and it wasn't practical to carry extra food and water just for one. Besides which, it is questionable as to whether the mare would survive the distance. She was now middle-aged and beyond her prime. Anais assured herself that the beast would continue to be well cared for. John was sad to be leaving all the charges he had grown attached to, especially Anais' horse, which had played such a vital role in the outcome of his situation. The newlyweds cheered up when Mahmood informed them that his village had their own small but hardy horses; John looked forward to working with yet another equestrian breed.

Mahmood couldn't remember a time when he was ever this excited. He thanked Allah for his blessings, over and over. *I'm going home*, he thought, *I can't believe it*. He was up early on the day of their departure. In his mind, he relived some of the tumultuous journey he had made as a six-year-old, across the Great Desert. His name was Yaya then. He remembered the heat of the days and the cool nights, the light of the stars, the tiredness, but also the beauty, the feeling of smallness. The unbroken vision of pure sand, and the slow, methodical marching combined to create an almost trance-like state. The focus of keeping himself and Dalanda alive, eating and drinking enough, distracted him from the trauma of having witnessed his parents' murder. Now he was returning at nearly fifty-years-old to the home of his ancestors. With so many thoughts racing through his mind, he lit his pipe. The kif calmed him, enabling him to concentrate on the task in hand – to look after these two lovebirds. He was pleased for them. With spirits lifted, Mahmood wandered off to organise the camels.

Chapter 10 – Algiers to Tamana

October 1641 – February 1642

John tried to ride a camel, but fell off twice, much to the good-humoured amusement and banter of the group of blue-turbaned men that he was about to embark on a journey with across the Sahara Desert.

"Come on," he said to himself, "if I can ride a horse, surely I can ride a camel."

The first time, he failed to realise, and deliberately nobody had informed him, that he had to lean back as the animal raised its rump. On the second occasion, he didn't lean forward as the beast mobilised its front legs. Having mastered those lessons, he grasped the rest and was soon swaying his hips in equal rhythm to the oscillations of the dromedary. The Pasha had negotiated for the team of three to join a trans-Saharan trade caravan, an azalai over one thousand camels strong. This provided safety in numbers as they passed through areas where Berber and Tuareg gangs of bandits robbed defenceless travellers. Most of the animals only carried empty, intricately woven saddle bags, while some were burdened with wood for fires, and food and water to nourish their minders in between oases.

Anais was the only woman. Being married and from high society, she was afforded a great level of respect. She, John and Mahmood travelled together, towards the back of the convoy. The leader of the group, Aderfi, a large Berber man with hands like shovels, sometimes joined them. He knew the desert intimately, as did his men.

"When we get to the desert in a few days' time, we will start travelling by night," Aderfi explained at the start of the journey, "that way, we avoid the heat and it's more comfortable. By day we will shelter from the sun in the shade of wadis, and sand dunes. Try to sleep when you can. You need to maintain your energy, and remember to drink enough water. We don't want you to dehydrate. Our first stopping place will be Adrar, in the Tuwat region, but we will only stay for a maximum of two days while we replenish supplies. Then we'll travel to Taoudenni where you can get some proper rest."

"What's there?" enquired John.

"Salt. That's the whole purpose of our trip. We will load our empty camels with salt and take it to Timbuktu. There, we trade the salt for gold, ivory and slaves." Mahmood's ears had pricked on hearing the word Timbuktu and even more so when slaves were mentioned.

"I remember Timbuktu," he said. "You don't forget a name like that. The last time I was there, I was six-years-old and my sister was alive. How long have you been employed in this trade, Aderfi?"

"On and off for twenty years. My father did it before me and his father before that. It's in the blood, so to speak."

"It could have been a member of your family who took me as a slave to Algiers then," said Mahmood, calmly.

"I suppose that could be true," agreed Aderfi. "But the past is the past and you never knew that it had been written for you to return as a free man, did you?"

"Allah is merciful," nodded Mahmood.

Before arriving at the desert, the company had to traverse the passes and valleys of the high Atlas mountains. These were exciting times for Anais and John, something like a camping trip. After a meal and prayers at night they took themselves off a distance, away from the caravan, to a private place. Huddled together in blankets, they made love and gazed at the dark, jagged peaks reaching up towards the millions of stars, each glittering as sharp as the spark of a flint strike splayed against the pitch of the sky. Even when moonless, there was enough illumination to create starlight shadows.

The routine changed when they came to the start of the Grand Erg Occidental, an area of seemingly endless sand dunes that rose and dipped in waves and ripples. They travelled through the night, resting by day. Prayers were only said in the morning and evening. Sometimes they passed small groups of people, bivouacking around the bases of stoic acacia trees; sleeping, eating or warming themselves by fires.

These were Tuareg nomads, making a living from their herds of camels and goats.

"Where do you think they feed them?" John asked Anais, taking a swig from his gerba, a goatskin water bottle.

"They know the place thoroughly," she replied. "It could be just around the corner for all I know."

John shook his head. "It looks like a tough life."

"They're born to it; it's normal for them. It would be hard for you and it certainly wouldn't be my first choice."

"It would be impossible for me. I'm glad you don't want that lifestyle, I don't think we'd survive," John joked. Two weeks into the journey and the excitement had worn off. Anais was saddle sore. She allowed John to rub a mixture of beeswax and olive oil into her thighs and buttocks.

"That's nice," she sighed. "I don't know how I'm going to withstand another few weeks of this."

"We must be getting near Adrar soon," said John, enjoying the intimate moment. "Then we can rest for a couple of days. If you need more time to recover, perhaps we can stay there for longer. We're in no rush."

"Mahmood is," she highlighted. "He can't wait to get home. And I don't want to delay him. I will ride with some more soft blankets under me and you can rub my thighs every day. What do you say?"

John smiled, "I'm not going to argue with that."

Relief arrived three days later, when they entered the oasis of Adrar. Date palms grew everywhere. The fruit: fat, shiny and as brown and long as an adult cockroach, melted in the mouth, oozing flavours of honey and toffee. John gorged on them until he realised they were a very effective laxative. Two days turned into three, much to Aderfi and Mahmood's frustration. Water was the delay and couldn't be rushed. The level of the aquifer that the oasis relied upon was low and the trickle from the foggaras slow. On the plus side, it meant that Anais had more time to improve the friction burns, with the help of healing lotion and loving hands.

"At least we know what to expect now," Anais said to her companions as they started the next leg of their odyssey.

"For the moment," said Mahmood, ambiguously.

"What do you mean?" asked John.

"Well, after Timbuktu, we must travel by boat to the town of Segou. Then find more transport to the village itself. If I remember correctly, that's at least another day further along the river. We don't know what Tamana will be like or how the villagers will receive us." Mahmood paused. Receiving no response from either Anais or John he continued. "There are some things you need to know, John. Anais and I are from the Fula tribe. Our people are simple animal herders, mostly. My parents kept cows. I think that's what the war was about: cattle-rustling. I've probably seen more of the world than everyone in the village put together. Most of them won't have seen a white man before. They might think you're a god, or worse, a devil spirit! They're superstitious, and don't know much about the wider world, so try not to attract any more attention to yourself than necessary. I'll have to explain ourselves to the village headman before we can do anything."

"Is that what you want to do when you get back, keep cattle?" asked John.

"I don't suppose there will be many vacancies for a harem eunuch," chuckled Mahmood. "It's an idea though. First, I want to see if any of my relatives survived the war."

"Do you know if there are any Muslims in the village?" queried Anais.

"Oh yes, Islam was around, but my parents preferred the old religion of ancestor worship. I've never really talked to you about that, Anais. I will leave it until we get there and see what the situation is."

John was struck by the knowledge of the camel drivers. To him, every dune, wadi and rocky outcrop looked the same. *I'd get lost within hours,* he thought. Apart from other humans and their domesticated animals, he had seen evidence of other life in the desert; notably scorpions, lizards and mice, and once three wide-winged vultures, circling. Some days, if he was awake, he saw birds, flying so high that he couldn't identify them. They were small black specks, fleeting across the true-blue sky, travelling in the same direction as the caravan. *I wonder*, he thought, thinking of the house martins.

The trio continued their trek, gratefully reaching the salt mining town of Taoudenni three weeks later. They were all exhausted and made full use of the period of rest that came.

xxx

Narrator's note:
They had crossed a stretch of sand that, over two hundred years later, would become a national border between Algeria and Mali during the European Scramble for Africa.

xxx

John was fascinated by the place. He wandered around the slabs of salt, hewn from the bed of a parched salt-pan lake. His presence caused the men who were cutting and handling the wedges to pause in their work and stare. Their intense look radiated honest, natural curiosity, not animosity. Not having been exposed to previous reports about white people, let alone seeing any in the flesh, there was no malice or prejudice attached to their enquiring eyes.

xxx

Narrator's note:

One is not born with preconceived ideas, they are learnt, and can therefore be re-examined, usually found to be false and, finally, unlearnt, if one wants to change of course.

xxx

Nearby, a man on a camel cracked a whip, and the scrutinisers returned to cramming the sodium chloride into the saddle bags, four pieces per animal. All the labour was being performed by a group of men whilst being supervised by half a dozen camel riders. Aderfi's crew sat about, waiting. John had a hunch.

"Do you think they've been taken captive, like we were once?" he asked Mahmood.

"Who are you talking about?"

"The men working and loading the camels."

"Indeed they have but in a different way to your ordeal," said Mahmood. "Most of them will be prisoners taken in local skirmishes between warring tribes. All menial tasks around here are consigned to slaves. You could have ended up here."

John didn't know whether to take Mahmood seriously and said nothing. It hadn't been that long ago since he had been a slave. Now he didn't really know what he was. *I'm free, yes, but what am I doing with my freedom?* he thought. At that moment, he wasn't sure where he was in the world, mentally or physically. The fact that he had recently raised his societal position at the same time as being totally in love and newly married, and was standing in the middle of terrain which was so contrary to anything he had experienced before, was as daunting as it was exhilarating.

The loading of the camel train took the best part of a week and Aderfi was pleased when the final oont was laden. Everyone felt refreshed and eager to move onwards. The convoy set off again. After two more weeks they paused for one night and a day at the oasis of Araouane, replenishing water and food. Aderfi boosted the spirits of his passengers by informing them that they had completed the most challenging part of the journey and should reach their destination within six nights.

As dawn appeared over the horizon after the sixth night, the city of Timbuktu, with its wattled and thatched huts, and Djinguereber Mosque, composed of mud bricks and wooden buttresses, came into sight. A cry of joy went up all along the caravan from man to man to woman. Aderfi came up to his three fares.

"We shall part company when we arrive in Timbuktu. You have been easy companions and I wish you well on your onward journey," he said sincerely.

"You have looked after us magnificently," responded Mahmood warmly, "and your desert skills are second to none. We won't need these camels after this. I'd like to reward you for attending to our needs, by giving them to you."

"That's very generous," said Aderfi.

"But there's a condition attached to this generosity which I hope you will agree upon," added Mahmood.

"And what is that?" Aderfi asked.

"I'd like you to promise that if you come across very young boys and girls in your business transactions, you won't enslave them but help them to either return home or be cared for safely. Can you do that?"

Aderfi looked at Mahmood for a few moments before replying, "I can. In future I will only buy adults."

"Do you swear unto Allah?" pressed Mahmood.

"Wallahi," was the response.

"Thank you," smiled Mahmood, shaking Aderfi's hand. "I only have one more thing to ask. Would you direct us to where we can catch a boat to Segou?"

"Of course. If the waters are high enough, you can get all the way."

"I hope so," said Mahmood. "I hadn't thought of that."

The closer they came to civilisation, the more they witnessed the evidence of desertification in the area. A combination of drought and overgrazing had caused the topsoil to blow away and be replaced with encroaching sand. Former healthy gardens were now the furthest beaches from the sea. John scratched his leg and flinched. He had noticed the insect bite a few days ago. The irritating itch had turned sore; a flared redness had grown larger and started to swell. He didn't complain. *It'll go,* he thought as the group enjoyed a few days recuperating from their long haul across the Sahara, in the once resplendent ancient city of Timbuktu. It had been, until recently, renowned as a seat of Islamic scholarship.

John forgot about his leg when he noticed house martins sweeping around the buildings and trees on the first day. They were there again the following day and throughout their stay in town. *So, this must be where they end up,* he thought in wonder, relishing the idea that some of these birds could have flown here all the way from Ireland. *Maybe I'll see some of you in the spring, next year in Baltimore, if I can find a way back.*

Mahmood was right to be uneasy about the height of the river. The dry season had begun and water levels were slowly reducing after the spate of rainy months. John was overawed when he saw the River Niger for the first time, he could barely see the opposite bank. *Look at the size of it. The Ilen is a rivulet compared to this,* he thought, trying to visualise the waterway that purled through his home area, entering the sea near Baltimore. The trout fishing fun he had had with Patrick seemed like a lifetime ago. Mahmood found a friendly boatman, Karim, who assured him there was enough water to travel to Segou for now. The navigation season was coming to an end though, and if they had arrived two weeks later, it would have been impossible. He agreed to take the three travellers as paying customers on his long wooden pinasse. They would have to share the space with the crew, as well as the cargo of salt. Having agreed a price for the six-day journey, John, Anais and Mahmood created an area for themselves under the boat's canopy and tried to settle comfortably. Mahmood and Anais found it straightforward and soon fell asleep in the drowsy heat, to the rhythmic motion of the boat's paddlers.

John, however, was perspiring heavily; more than the usual amount of sweat caused by the arid climate. His head had been aching for the last couple of days, but he hadn't felt it necessary to mention it. Thinking it was just dehydration, he drank more water, but the pain refused to ease. Within two days on the river, the situation took a turn for the worse. He could no longer hide his physical discomfort, and started to vomit. Anais was immediately perturbed and comforted him. It was only now that John revealed the mark on his leg which had swollen into a large boil.

"Why didn't you tell me you had been bitten?" admonished Anais, examining the inflammation.

"It was just a bite, nothing serious," he replied, sheepishly.

"Well, it's serious enough now," she said. "You've had a nasty reaction to something. You should have told me; we're meant to be together in everything, aren't we? Good and bad?"

John nodded weakly, suddenly heaving as he experienced a severe stomach spasm. Karim noticed John spew over the side and approached.

"You have motion sickness?" he asked.

"I don't think so," replied John. "I've never had it before."

Anais showed Karim the furuncle on John's leg and his eyes widened. He noticed John's beads of sweat and his pallid skin.

"Does your head throb?" he asked John.

"Yes, it feels like a megrim."

"I've seen these feverish symptoms before," grimaced Karim. "They can be very severe, even fatal. We should be able to get some help in Segou, but we won't be there for another three or four days, minimum. Try and keep him cool and hydrated," he said to Anais.

Anais took her role as wife and carer seriously. She stayed by John's side, bathing the wound, gently mopping his brow when his temperature soared, holding him when he shivered and rubbing his back when he retched. She poured water into his mouth and tried to feed him flakes of boiled fish. He vomited it up before it provided any nourishment. John's symptoms grew worse. When the fever took over, he lost awareness of his surroundings.

In one of his lucid moments, Anais had told him, "John, you are seriously ill. I will try and get Karim to stop at a village for medicine."

"I'm sorry," groaned John. "I don't want to delay everyone."

"Don't be silly. We have to make you well," she paused, "and I've got something to tell you."

"What?" he prompted.

"I think I'm pregnant. I've missed my last period and I just know we have a baby." John felt a tingling surge of happiness at the news.

"That's wonderful," he voiced, his mood lifting briefly before another wave of sweating and nausea hit him. He groaned. "Damn this illness, I must get better."

But he didn't.

xxx

Narrator's note:

John was infected with what became known as Plasmodium falciparum, the most virulent of malarial parasites.

XXX

Karim agreed to stop at two riverside villages. He managed to acquire some dried roots of the nibima plant. This was boiled into a beverage and fed to John, but it was too little, too late. John became weaker and weaker whilst Anais prayed.

"I don't know if I'm going to survive this," he confided to Anais during a moment of respite from the ague.

"Of course you will," she replied brightly, hiding the fact that she had also considered this.

"If it is written, and I do, then fine. But if I don't, I need you to do something for me," he said.

"Anything, my love."

"First, never forget that my love for you is deep and true," John declared.

"I can certainly do that," she said, "and you know it is completely mutual."

"I do. You have made me very happy. But there is something else; I need you to try and keep the seal safe and somehow return it to my brother, Conor, in Ireland."

Anais had no idea how, but she would try and find some way. "I will, my darling, I will. Now don't worry, just rest," she urged, full of worry.

The next day, just one day out from Segou and proper medical care, John died. His body was dropped overboard according to the region's custom, to be devoured by crocodiles. He who died on the water was handed over to the River Spirit. Nonetheless, his soul was at rest; he had been true to Anais and Allah right up until his last breath. Anais cried all night, inconsolable at this cruel turn of events. Mahmood stayed awake and tried to comfort her. By the morning, Anais, drained from her emotions, had decided that God was testing her. She drew some strength from this thought and was determined to stand firm during this examination of her faith.

xxx

Narrator's note:

A line from the 1976 song 'Have Mercy', written by the Jamaican reggae band *The Mighty Diamonds*, sums this up perfectly: 'Man was made to suffer, yeah, and women was [sic] made to feel the pain.'

xxx

John's death had been quick and unexpected. Anais reflected that although their marriage was only four months old, they had been devoted to each other for much longer.

"We've been luckier than some," she sighed, "but Allah knows best."

Anais distributed John's clothes amongst the crew, all except for the old, frequently repaired cape. That stayed with her. She rubbed the collar, feeling the lump of the seal, smiling when she remembered calling John "half-cloak". During the next few days, Anais was grateful for Mahmood's support. Preoccupied, she focussed on keeping herself and her unborn child healthy. At Segou, Mahmood took control, quickly organising another boat to Tamana before the river became unnavigable. He was both excited and sad. A guilty relief swept over him, now that he did not have to explain the presence of a white man to the village headman.

Chapter 11 – Ireland

Summer 1631 – Winter 1642

The English continued to oppress the Irish. Their insistence to take over the land and subjugate the people caused more and more locals to try and undermine their efforts. Feelings simmered and seethed, culminating with an Irish revolt. Bands of filthy, slimy-haired, unkempt men, in half-organised, semi-affiliated groups, toured the countryside, literally frightening the life out of the English and Scottish settlers. Armed with knives, pikes and pitchforks, they killed many indiscriminately and chased the rest away to the well-defended area of The Pale. The Irish stayed beyond it.

Conor O'Driscoll Jnr was in the thick of these actions. 'God has given me this cause', he truly believed. 'Get rid of the English', was his motto. 'Bullies, thieves and liars', was his opinion of the invaders. Conor had been living rough for years, it was a way of life. He and his gang were sheltering in woodland, weighing up how to attack the village of Clonakilty.

"It should be simple," he told his troupe. "As always, we'll creep down just before dark, surprise them, kill some, set fire to a few houses and then run back. After this, we'll have cleared the area. The rest won't stay; they'll be too scared. They can hide and whimper in Dublin while we can go underground for a while. Job well done." The men cheered. A straight forward guerrilla attack; maximum surprise, maximum shock, maximum fear, minimum time, minimum effort. It worked. Fourteen corpses later and a bonfire of thatched roofs, the brigade returned to the woods and regrouped, unidentified, unidentifiable. The surviving villagers deserted the small town. The kernes shook hands and went their separate ways. Initially, Conor hid on a relative's farm in a remote part of the Munster countryside for a while to see what consequences there might be. Of course, there were repercussions for the uprising.

"We must burn these rebel tories and flush them out with fire," insisted Murrough O'Brian, the pyromaniacal, Irish turncoat in charge of the English retribution army, for the province of Munster. It was an effective tactic and many Irish outlaws were caught and hung. There were informers, a lousy lot. When the heat became too close, Conor moved away from the farm, dodging the flames by moving from place to place until he felt it was safe to settle undercover again. This time, at the O'Mahoney's.

Conor, in his late thirties, was a veteran of many battles against the English and hailed as both a feinne and a liberator by many of the Irish in Baltimore, none more so than the O'Mahoneys. Now in their early sixties, and set in their ways, they had decided to stay in the half-destroyed village after the pirate raid that had happened ten years earlier. Many of the survivors had moved away from the coast and set up the community of Skibbereen.

XXX

Flashback to September 1631:

After leaving John all those years ago, it had been three months before Conor had heard about the sacking of Baltimore. He had managed to get back home to establish the true news.

"It was crazy," Bridget said, piling up a plateful of mutton stew and potatoes in front of Conor. "We heard a commotion, and then warnings from our neighbours. We ran for it but the Turks never got as far as the cottage in the end."

"What about John?" Conor asked.

"He must have been taken with all the others," she replied, her voice dropping. "We only found two bodies: Tim Curlew and Johnny Davys."

"No damage there then, they're English," Conor said, contemptuously, trying to hide the deep worry he had for John's whereabouts. "What about John's place, his possessions?" he asked, thinking of the seal.

"Nothing," said Sean. "It's all gone. Completely razed by fire."

There was a silence before Conor asked, “Is there any chance he could have been burnt?”

Sean coughed. “We have considered that,” he wheezed, “but we don’t think so. The horses survived. We believe John escaped the blaze, but was taken away. There’s no evidence of any bones, and although the flames were high, I don’t think it would have been hot enough to burn a full body.”

Conor loured. “But we can’t be sure,” he said, quietly.

“I suppose,” said Sean, equally as hesitant.

“Do we know what happened to them?” asked Conor.

“Word has it that they were taken to the North of Africa.”

Conor visited the stable where John had lived. It was as if it had never existed. The stone walls of the cottage were there, blackened with soot, but without a roof or any repairs. The place was desolate, along with other similarly derelict buildings. Conor kicked at a pile of dirty ash where the stable had stood, revealing a mangled mass of charred wires. *Harp strings*, he thought. *At least it wasn’t hot enough to melt them*. There was nothing else to find. He looked out over Roaring Water Bay, seeing it and not, in and out of focus. Eventually, his eyes rested on the ruins of Dun an Oir, the old O’Driscoll fort on Cape Clear Island.

“Well John,” he said aloud, “if you’re out there, you had better find your way back with the seal, or I'll come and find you. Once I'm done with the English."

Chapter 12 – Munster

March 1643

Somewhere in the depths of the Munster countryside a baby boy was born, wailing and flailing.

Chapter 13 – Ireland

Spring 1643 – Winter 1651

Conor was a wanted man by the English, and had been for a long time. He had built a reputation for himself, with his seemingly magical ability to attack, fight, withdraw and just disappear. Although he knew many people in Baltimore, he still had to be careful and only visited those he fully trusted. The British garrison in Baltimore, currently housed in the fort previously owned by his family, Dun na Sead, would be more than interested to learn that he had returned to his home area. But the soldiers were disadvantaged; none of them knew what he looked like, only his name.

"You're better off here," said Bridget, making colcannon; mashing up potatoes and cabbage, mixing in the cream. "We'll keep you safe. Part of me is glad that Patrick left this sad country when he did, although I miss him terribly. It's good to have you around again, Conor." Conor smiled, feeling relaxed in comfortable surroundings with his aunt; her unaffected warmth uplifting him.

"Have you heard from Patrick at all?" he asked.

"Not for a couple of years," answered Sean. "He's writing less often or his letters just aren't getting here. The last we heard he was growing sugar."

"We have written back to him," added Bridget, "but we don't know if he receives our news because he never answers our questions. We pray he's safe and well."

"What's the name of the island he's on?" queried Conor. "John did tell me but I've forgotten it. I'm sure it began with an N."

"Nevis," said his aunt and uncle in unison.

"Nevis," Conor repeated, with a nod. However, it wasn't long before Conor became restless; when he heard that a Catholic Confederate army had been mustered in Kilkenny, within the province of Leinster, he decided to join up. Through his contacts, he enlisted and persisted with his raison d'etre, solely to expel the English.

xxx

"They've done what?" exclaimed Conor, incredulously.

"They've chopped his head off," was the reply.

King Charles I of England didn't need a tam o'shanter anymore. The news shocked all combatants, causing the mood in Ireland to change and a lull in the conflict, as if everyone had downed weapons to work out what to do next. Conor took the opportunity to return to Baltimore, to reconsider his position. He was confounded when he heard that another army from England was being prepared to combat the English forces already in Ireland. *How can this be?* ruminated Conor, confused. *Fucking politics!* For the first time, he was hearing expressions of 'Roundheads' and 'Cavaliers'.

XXX

Then, the storm hit. It was true. The English were fighting their own. The name 'Cromwell' filled Royalist and Irish heads alike with fear and trepidation. Oliver Cromwell wanted to convince the King's supporters that they were wrong, and had decided that the Irish needed to be punished further for the Revolution of 1641. It was time to cleanse the productive lands of Ireland, once and for all, from the troublesome followers of the Anti-Christ, the Pope. Cromwell irrationally believed that it was the laws of nature and God that made it his duty to kill and instil terror. His reputation for barbarity and religious puritanical extremism spread like a net around the country. Panic reduced the resistance. Towns and cities, bands of kernes and innocent victims became entangled, wriggling helplessly in the trawling of the New Model Army.

Conor's anger and hatred for the English only deepened, but his appetite for war was weakening. Now in his forties, most of which had been spent living wild and fighting, Conor was starting to slow down. Although his resentment towards the English was unrelenting, his body was telling him to rest. Injuries, aches and pains took longer to recover. *How many more battles can I endure? When will it end? Is it worth it?*

What have I got to show for it all? he started questioning himself. *What do I want now?* He smiled at the memory of one of his Uncle Sean's favourite sayings that: "if you don't know what you want, you won't know when you've got it." In his heart, Conor yearned for a more peaceful life. Doubt had crept in. A few years ago, it felt like the Irish were winning. Yet, now it sounded like a tsunami of trouble was headed his way. Rumours that Cromwell encouraged the massacres in Drogheda and Wexford with no quarter given to soldiers and civilians alike, especially priests, monks and nuns, increased the weight of dread.

"We've heard that Cromwell is on his way here," Sean said to Conor one evening as they tucked into a supper of thick soda bread sandwiches, flavoured with cheese and pilchards. Conor stopped chewing and sighed.

"You know, I don't think we're ever going to get rid of the English. They're too strong, too determined and there are far too many; worse than a plague. I'm losing the will to fight. I don't understand it anymore. It was simple in the old days; it was us against the English. Now, it's all a blur. We have English in town who want to fight Cromwell, who is also English. How does that make sense?"

"It doesn't. Trying to work that out will make you more flummoxed than you already are," said Sean, wisely.

"So, what have you heard?" probed Conor.

“That Cork has been taken. And that Bandon gave up without a fight. Cromwell seems to be a relentless force.”

“Bandon?” remarked Conor. “That’s not far at all. We must prepare.” However, for the first time in his life, it felt like a chore, not a challenge.

“You do what you’ve got to do, Conor. Your aunt and I, well, we’ll just stay put and let what happens, happen.”

He considered his strategy and soon realised that, although it stuck in his craw, Conor had to accept the Royalist military as his new allies. After all, they were helping to protect his home village from the Parliamentarians, who were supposed to be an even more destructive force. But, it didn’t mean that he now trusted them or anyone from either side. The paradox that, to an outside observer, it would look like he was fighting for the English King, had not passed him by. Conor visited the surviving members and new recruits of his unit, all hidden in various safe houses or shelters in the woods. They parleyed, concluding that they couldn’t fight two armies. The only available choice, for the present, was to side with the soldiers in town. A course of risky action was decided upon.

“They’ll listen to you, Conor. Only you can persuade them,” it was agreed.

Conor approached the garrison stationed in Dun na Sead. He looked up at the fortified walls, remembering when he climbed all over them as a child, before the castle had been requisitioned by English soldiers after his grandfather could no longer afford the lease. He noticed two guards on the roof, aiming their arquebuses at him. His familial home occupied by foreigners. *One day,* willed Conor, *one day we'll have you back*.

"Who are you?" barked the Redcoat sentry at the door.

Conor eyed the trooper, a sworn enemy, who he now had no alternative but to confide in. This went against his character. His mind fought his feelings of doubt, guilt and misgiving. *I just don't have any other option*, he thought. *Oh well, here goes, no guts, no glory. In God, we hope.*

"Conor O'Driscoll," he declared. The soldier seemed visibly shocked. Conor raised his eyebrows and smiled. *Good*, he thought, *he's heard of me*.

"And how can I help you?" the guard asked respectfully, recovering himself.

"I want to see the captain, to discuss how we are going to defend Baltimore against Cromwell."

"Wait here. There's a conference going on about that very matter. I'll let the captain know you're here." Conor was left outside, exposed. After a long wait, the soldier returned.

"Please come in," he said politely to the increasingly anxious Conor.

"Thank you," replied Conor, walking through the door of his ancestral fort.

Before he had taken two steps into the hallway, Conor was seized by two of the tallest and widest musketeers he had ever seen. Another soldier pointed a musket at his head, whilst a fourth swiftly tied his wrists behind his back. *I knew I shouldn't have trusted them,* Conor thought, gritting his teeth. *Am I to be captured in my own castle?*

"What's going on?" he enquired.

An upright man in full military uniform walked through a door from an adjoining room, mopping his face with a white linen handkerchief.

"Mr Conor O'Driscoll, finally. How nice of you to call round," welcomed Captain George Upstart of the Royalist, soon to be Parliamentarian, English army. He surveyed his captive slowly from head to toe. "So this is what you look like. You aren't nearly as significant as your reputation suggests," he said offhandedly. "The way you're talked about I thought you'd have two horns and a tail at least."

"Why have I been tied up?" demanded Conor.

"Well, we don't want you escaping now that we've got you, do we?"

"What's going on?" Conor repeated, "I've come to plan a defence against Cromwell with you. We're on the same side, aren't we?"

"That's probably a slight exaggeration but yes, we were temporarily, dear man, we were," replied Upstart, tucking his hanky into a breast pocket. "I won't subject your poor little bogtrotter brain with the details, but my fellow warriors and I have decided that discretion is the better part of valour, and would like to keep our lives intact. Therefore, I have already sent a message to Cromwell to say that, rather than fighting him, we will join him instead. In fact, we have requested that he send a few of his finest to help clear up the troublemakers in this area."

Fuck, thought Conor*, I'm fucked!*

"Surprise, surprise," smiled Upstart. "Now, what are we going to do with you? I imagine Cromwell will be ever so happy that you, Conor O'Driscoll, are safely in custody. You really have been a thorn in our side. Now let me think. Cromwell would undoubtedly hang you on the spot when he finds out exactly who you are and what you've been up to. But then again, seeing as I will probably get a medal for capturing you, I might be able to do you a favour."

"What's that?" asked Conor begrudgingly.

"I could always tell him that you gave yourself up, that you have seen the errors of your ways. That you want to give up fighting and place yourself in the righteous hands of the English," Upstart said, flamboyantly.

He's got one part right. I've had enough of fighting, thought Conor.

"Of course, I can't promise anything," Upstart continued, "but he may spare you your life. Take him to the dungeons," he ordered.

Cromwell dealt with Conor's immediate confederates with simple efficiency; some were shot, many were taken prisoner. Other more menial rebels scattered to lie low and evade capture. The Lord Protector of the Commonwealth of England, Scotland and Ireland and his men rested at Dun na Sead, cared for by the new extension to their army. No wine or pies were consumed at dinner that night.

"Tomorrow morning, Upstart," said Cromwell, before retiring to bed, "I will decide on the fate of the papist vermin. I am grateful that you have brought me up-to-date with all of them. That O'Driscoll character deserves my full attention. It's a shame that November the fifth has been and gone. We could have added some flavour to bonfire night by actually burning some Catholics alive. However, I'm considering all options. I've a good mind to invoke all the English laws for the correction of dangerous rogues, vagabonds and sturdy beggars for the whole of Ireland. Get rid of the heathen lot; maybe transport them to the colonies rather than hang them, as an act of mercy. Good night."

You? Merciful? thought Upstart, shuddering as he speculated as to what might have happened to him if he had not surrendered. He needed a drink and was pleased that Cromwell turned in early.

The following morning, Cromwell inspected his twenty or so political prisoners. To all except one, he offered the following, "Leave the country without your family or possessions and live in a neutral country. You can select either Spain, Austria or Poland. You will not return for at least seven years and only then if you promise to behave and are given permission from the English authorities. Either go or be hanged. Your choice." They all chose Spain.

"And that leaves you, O'Driscoll," said Cromwell, staring at his detainee disdainfully. "I should just hang, draw and quarter you or put you on a breaking wheel. You have done enough damage to warrant that, don't you agree?" Conor wanted to survive. He agreed, nodding his head, engrossed by the pronounced wart on Cromwell's lower lip.

"But, I've heard that you have changed," continued Cromwell. "Rather convenient, changing your ways, as soon as I turn up."

Conor hated himself but he choked up, "I have your Excellency. I have seen the light."

"The light that the Puritans bring to the world," beamed Cromwell. "Very well, I will spare your insignificant life, but you will be banished from this realm for as long as you live. You will never be pardoned for your part in this war. You are a rogue and a dangerous one at that. Therefore, I have decided that you will be barbadosed."

"Barbadosed?" queried Conor, baffled by the word.

"You, Conor O'Driscoll are condemned to be transported to Barbados."

"Where's that?" Conor enquired, relieved that he had escaped the noose.

"The West Indies," answered Cromwell. "Too far away to cause me any more trouble. You can make up for your treacherous ways with hard labour in the scorching heat of our sugar plantations, and help England make a grand profit."

The West Indies? cogitated Conor, *I know someone there.*

Conor, with just a small bag of clothes, was crammed into a slave ship setting sail from the port of Bantry. The cargo bay was full of Irish men, women and children, separated by flimsy wooden panels. It was a terrible trip; no hot water, no soft edges, no silver service and worst of all, no personal space. Conor lay down in the stinking hold and bemoaned his life. *My battle against the English is over,* he decided as the ship left his homeland. *Nobody's ever heard from John. I hope he's still alive and trying to return with the seal. It looks like I've got to give up the idea of reclaiming our land. All that effort for nothing. I must look after myself now and fight for my own existence. I wonder if Nevis is near Barbados.*

XXX

When Conor failed to return home, the O'Mahoneys didn't worry for the first few days. Conor often went missing unexpectedly on what he called 'a bit of business' forays. However, concern arose after they received a visit from a friend. English soldiers had been overheard boasting in the local alehouse that Conor O'Driscoll had been arrested and sent to Barbados with an instruction never to return. This came as a mighty blow to Bridget and Sean who now felt they had lost all three of their children, although only one was completely biologically theirs. Heartbroken and feeling purposeless they aged and deteriorated rapidly. Within twelve months of Conor's sailing, they died a week apart. If they hadn't they were due for eviction and beggary, having developed rent arrears for the first time in their hard working life. The small farm and cottage was reclaimed by the English landowner.

Chapter 14 – Tamana, Mali

Spring 1651 – Summer 1662

Mahmood sat back in his wicker chair under the shade of a mango tree, in the hazy heat of the afternoon. His hair and beard had turned a light grey, similar in colour to the smoke from his pipe. He was reminiscing; vaguely watching and listening to his nine-year-old grandnephew, Jomo, playing music with another boy and two girls of his age.

xxx

Flashback to 1642:

When Anais and Mahmood arrived at Tamana, she had not been herself; totally abstracted from grieving John's sudden death, and being pregnant in strange surroundings. Mahmood handled the situation with compassion and tact and led her to the chief of the village.

Boubacar, the forty-year-old cheiftan, with a calm air about him, greeted what he thought were strangers at first, in a traditional style; full of interest, offering food and drink. When he established that Mahmood was a long lost local and Anais his niece, the welcome became even more embracing; all smiles and assistance.

"Who is the oldest person in the village?" asked Mahmood

pushing his mostly eaten bowl of nyiri and soup away, demonstrating that he was full and wanted no more.

"That would be Binta," replied Boubacar, "she must be around your age."

"Binta," repeated Mahmood, "I haven't heard that name for a while. I had a relation called Binta..."

As Mahmood soon found out, his cousin Binta survived the war that Mahmood had always believed to have been a cattle-rustling raid all those years ago. It transpired that it had nothing to do with stealing cows at all, but was actually a lesson in religion.

xxx

Flashback to 1599:

A strict puritanical version of Islam had been sweeping the countryside, and Tamana village was caught up in the wave of militancy. In the minds of the militants, all ancestral worship had to be wiped out and replaced by a misguided, intolerant, authoritarian form of religion. Two marabouts visited the village many weeks before any military presence, peacefully spreading the word according to the Qur'an. They achieved some success, but it wasn't enough for the leader of the local army, Alpha. He became irritated at the slowness of the conversion of the village. If diplomacy or coming to a mutual compromise was the ultimate aim, he was the wrong man for the job. Believing in his profuse delusion that he knew best, made him over-zealous, outwardly extremely pious and excessively cruel. Impatience and a complete lack of compassion and understanding were his strongest personality traits. To a neutral observer, the similarities between Alpha and Cromwell were obvious; they were comrades in that harmful group; deluded, egotistical men.

"But we cannot force these people to revert," argued the marabouts. "They need time to learn more and seek change within their own conscience," they explained, to no avail.

"Nonsense," retorted Alpha. "They are pathetic and you have weak ways. We will teach these idolaters a lesson." The education resulted in six dead, including Mahmood's parents and six villagers taken and sold as slaves, including Mahmood and Dalanda. "I think I've helped nudge your cause forward. Now you can carry on being missionaries," Alpha had said pejoratively, leaving to continue his trail of fright throughout the country, his bloodlust appeased, temporarily. The marabouts were not to be put off but had to tread carefully. Their first difficult task was to try and redevelop trust within the village.

"They are not real Muslims," they explained to the suspicious villagers. "They are hypocrites; thugs with guns. They pretend to be Muslims but they prefer power to piety." Slowly they advanced towards their objective. The moderate Orthodox interpretation of Islam, the well-balanced one, made sense to most prudent residents and many of them converted, some just on the surface and others on a much deeper, spiritual level. A small mosque was built out of mud and wooden staves. Within a few years, the village was living peacefully under the leadership of Boubacar's father. He developed a reciprocal understanding with the local imam. Ancestral worship could continue so long as it wasn't overtly displayed.

xxx

A return to 1642:

Both Mahmood and Anais were uplifted by the mood of the villagers; friendly, accepting and generous. They shared a common religion and similar points of view. Mahmood had a heart-warming reunion with his relative Binta, who kept calling him Yaya, resulting in him having to explain to both her and Anais that he had chosen to change his name when he reverted to Islam. Binta reassured him that his parents' bodies were recovered and buried according to tradition. She and her husband, N'faly, lived in their tidy mud and straw hut at the edge of the community, overlooking cattle pastures and pens and the vast expanse of the surrounding Sahel. Not having been blessed with any children, they had more wealth than others and owned a spare hut which became a place to put things in that might come in useful one day. This clutter was removed and the hut made comfortable for Anais to live in.

Temporarily, Mahmood slept in a cattle shed, while he arranged for a smaller, separate hut to be built for his use. Anais settled into her adobe abode, grateful to have a place to herself. She needed space to put everything in perspective, before the baby arrived. One day, her hut became a maternity ward. With assistance from her female neighbours, Anais bore a boy. When all the mess had been removed and the baby suckled on a bursting breast, Mahmood visited.

"I want to call him Jomo, what do you think?" Anais asked, tired but relieved that the child was healthy.

"A fine idea," Mahmood concurred. "What about a surname?"

"I don't think it's fair to call him Jomo O'Driscoll, too many O's. He'd be teased with a name like that."

"I agree," Mahmood said. "To avoid questionable answers, how about giving him our name, Khodja, seeing as we accepted the name of my ex-owner, your father, many years ago? He will then have a link back to his maternal grandfather."

"Good point," approved Anais, "and when he's older, I will tell him his father's name." Anais held the aqiqah for her son, Jomo, a Fulani name meaning Burning Spear, seven days after his birth. It was similar enough, in her opinion, to feel he was being named in John's memory.

Jomo was lighter skinned than Anais but only just, and still darker than some of the others in the area. The Fula people are characterised by paler skins and straighter hair than other sub-Saharan African tribes. He had a more prominent nose and slightly smoother hair, but nobody asked any questions. All the villagers needed to know was that Anais was recently widowed, her spouse, Jomo's father, having died during the journey from Algiers. Within his first six months, Jomo received two short cuts on his cheeks, identifying his clan and tribe. Anais refused to allow her grief to take over and by devoting her life, love and time to Jomo, he thrived.

"You have your father's eyes and mouth," Anais murmured to her infant as they gazed at each other. Her dark brown, almost black, irises focussed on Jomo's lighter chestnut eyes, flecked with emerald green shards. Jomo grew steadily and solidly.

Mahmood took up cattle raising, helping out with Binta and N'faly's herd of Red cows, their chickens and goats. He was content but there was something missing, especially in the evenings.

xxx

When Jomo was five-years-old and everything was running smoothly on the farm, Mahmood decided he was no longer needed by anyone. The time had come.

"I'm going to do the Hajj," he announced to Anais after dinner one evening.

"Really?" Anais exclaimed. "That's wonderful."

"Yes, I think it is. It's now or never. I'm getting older and it's always been a dream of mine. I'm going to be away for a while."

"When are you leaving?" she asked.

"In two days. I've fixed up a lift to Timbuktu and from there I'll chance my luck. There must be others going. I shall join a group of pilgrims." Mahmood paused then said, "But I'm also thinking about visiting Algiers before I return."

"What? Why?" Anais probed. She had no desire to see her birthplace again, nor her controlling father. Filial feelings were weak.

"Well, I'd like to see the Pasha again. He treated me well enough and I think he would like to know about his grandson." He kept silent about the other reason. Jomo had given his great-uncle a tight hug before Mahmood boarded the boat to Timbuktu. He was away for the best part of two years. They all missed each other.

xxx

On Mahmood's return, people buzzed with excitement as he guided the cattle cart bearing his luggage, consisting of two large bundles wrapped in hemp sacking, through the village. He was the first villager to complete the Hajj. Respect. The imam, who originally came from Morocco and had attended twice in his lifetime, celebrated his return from the pilgrimage. Mahmood, unintentionally, had raised his status in the area. There was a warm family reunion before he started to unpack. Anais was intrigued as she watched the bundles being offloaded.

"What's in those?" she enquired.

Mahmood tapped his nose.

"Come on, tell me," she implored.

"Don't get too excited," he said. "Most of it is for me but packed in the middle is a surprise for you and Jomo." Mahmood slit one of the bundles open. Lots of small packages slid out, which he moved into his hut.

"What's in them?" Anais asked bluntly.

"You haven't changed, have you? Straight to the point as usual. It's kif, and a few other things."

"So, you have been to Algiers then?"

"Yes, and these," Mahmood said, as he withdrew two differently shaped parcels, "are for you and Jomo." Jomo was delighted that his great-uncle had returned; full of questions just like his mother, especially about the Hajj.

"All in good time," Mahmood said gently. "I will answer all I can when I have a moment. But first, let's see what you think of this," he said as he handed Jomo his surprise. When he opened it, Jomo's eyes shone and Anais could swear that the green flecks flashed.

"A new instrument," Jomo said, excitedly. "Thank you, Uncle, but what is it?"

"It's called an oud, and it's actually not from me. It's a present from your grandfather."

"Will I ever meet him?" asked Jomo as he, without having to be told, rested the oud awkwardly in his arms and started to strum.

"Inshallah," was Mahmood's reply, marvelling at his grandnephew's first attempt at playing the musical device, even though it was still too big for him. Then Mahmood turned to Anais and presented her with a smaller package.

"And is this from you or my father?" she asked as she unwrapped it.

"Your father."

She cried as she stared at the gift, and ran her fingers over the finely crafted Kabyle necklace, covered in blue, green, yellow and red stones, set in silver.

"It's beautiful," she said as she secured it around her neck. The colours contrasting against her glistening dark skin were comfortable on the eye.

That evening, Mahmood bit into a delectable dawamesc, a cannabis edible made with kif, pine and pistachio nuts, sugar, orange juice, cinnamon, cloves, cardamom, nutmeg and musk - an Algerian delicacy. He had brought the recipe and ingredients back with him. Whilst chewing and savouring the delightful tang he prepared his new sebsi, then lit up. *That's what was missing,* he thought, relaxing. *I might introduce some of this to the villagers. See what they make of it. I could start trading in it if they like it, begin a business.* He had smiled to himself, as the images of being the first importer of kif to the region went through his mind. There was no law against it.

xxx

A return to 1651:

Mahmood shifted in his chair. The children had just finished playing an enchanting song. Jomo had changed instruments during the performance from oud to kora, while the other boy skilfully produced the beats and background tones on two different sized djembe drums. The girl's voices harmonised perfectly. The rhythm and repeated melody had touched him. Mahmood was pleased with the way Jomo had grown up; strong willed, able to compromise and a serious studier of the Qur'an, Jomo was also a remarkable musician.

xxx

Flashback to 1645:

Mahmood remembered the first time Jomo had seen a kora. *He had just stared at it. He could only have been three or four at the time,* thought Mahmood as he recalled how, after feasting his eyes on the instrument for two or three minutes without moving, Jomo looked at his great-uncle and asked, “Can I touch it?”

Mahmood spoke to the owner Ahmed, the local griot, whose home they were visiting.

“Of course, just be gentle with it,” Ahmed said, sweeping his hand to encourage Jomo. “Do you know what it is?”

Jomo shook his head.

“It’s a kora. It’s like a woman: beautiful, mysterious, surprising, difficult to fully understand but worth every minute trying to,” explained Ahmed as Mahmood smiled at the young boy’s look of incomprehension.

Jomo had approached the kora, taking in the intricately decorated half-calabash with its antelope skin stretched tightly across it. He lightly fingered all twenty-one strings, heeding each note. Then he strummed them all together, listening intently as he waited for the resonance to end.

As the vibrations faded Ahmed enquired, “Would you like to learn how to play it?”

“Yes, please sir,” Jomo answered immediately, revealing shiny eyes and a striking smile. “May I, Uncle, please?” he beseeched, looking at Mahmood.

“I don’t see why not. But you had better ask your mother, it's her right to make the final decision. I'm sure she will give you permission,” Mahmood replied encouragingly.

Mahmood and Ahmed discussed terms in the event that Anais allowed Jomo to learn, then Ahmed fetched another, smaller kora. “You can begin your lessons on this,” he said to Jomo. “When you are older, you can transfer your skills onto the larger one.”

Anais was delighted with her son's new interest and quickly gave her consent. Jomo found that he had a natural talent and to Ahmed’s astonishment developed quicker than any previous pupil. This was all before the oud of course. Mahmood had mentioned Jomo’s musical ability to the Pasha. The oud was a very thoughtful present. As with the kora, Jomo quickly became intimate with the oud’s complexities, mastering its workings and creating entrancing music.

xxx

Anais watched her child grow from boy to teenager. She had a busy life. Content to settle in the country of her mother’s ancestors, she not only found purpose in raising her son but also in village life. Apart from caring for Jomo, she facilitated clean ups, games for the children, visits to the sick and disabled and made sure that those who were responsible, did their duty. Anais showed indifference if a man displayed a special interest in her, remaining faithful to the memories of John. At times, she yearned to hold him once more. *Have I let you down?* she wondered, thinking of how she had promised John that they would go to Ireland after staying at Tamana. But that would have been with him. Guiltily, she recalled agreeing practically on John's deathbed to take the seal to his homeland and somehow give it to Conor.

She hadn't even enquired about the possibility of doing that on her own. No one round here had a clue where Ireland was. It meant having to visit Segou for that information and even then, there was no guarantee that anyone there would know. She did want to meet John's family, and introduce Jomo to them, but she procrastinated and any decision to act on these thoughts was deferred. *I should have done it before, as soon as Jomo was old enough to travel. Now I don't have the energy, I'm too old,* she decided. *Or am I just making excuses?*

When Jomo reached the age where living in such close proximity to his mother was immodest, a new hut was built for him. One day, Anais sat him down and said, "I think you are mature enough now to know about your father."

xxx

Jomo hadn't asked about his father for years. When he was younger, he thought of Mahmood as a father figure, but the first time he called

Mahmood "Dad" he was informed otherwise.

"I am not your father, I am your great-uncle; but you can call me Uncle."

"Then who is my father?" said a rather direct three-and-a-half-year-old, looking at his mother and blurting, "You are my mother, aren't you?" suddenly anxious that his whole life was about to implode.

"Yes, of course I'm your mother, darling," Anais replied, biting her lip. "Now, about your father. He died before you were born and I will explain it all to you when you are older and can understand. For the moment, all you need to know is that Mahmood and I love you very much and we are always here for you."

"My father died," Jomo stated unemotionally, seemingly quickly accepting the news. But the question arose again in his mind a few times.

"Who is my father, Mum?" Jomo enquired again some months later.

"I've already told you. I will tell you all about him when you're older and the time is right. Now don't ask me again," Anais said forcefully, slightly agitated.

Having been rebuffed on several occasions, Jomo had given up. If his thoughts started to drift in that direction, he would compose music in his head. Some classic pieces were the result of those meditations.

"You are sensible and considerate and I am pleased with you, my son. It is now time for me to tell you about your father, who you are and where you're from," continued Anais, conscious that she had rehearsed this speech many times. Jomo held his breath in anticipation. Anais told him the complete truth. It was a lot to take in. They both grew tired, emotions drained.

"So, there you are, Jomo. That's the whole story. You probably won't remember it all, but we can talk again."

"Where is the seal?" asked Jomo.

"It's here, it's safe." She touched her gris-gris hanging round her neck. "I will give it to you tomorrow when we're refreshed. I'm tired now."

Jomo struggled to control his thoughts and feelings; he was shocked. He couldn't imagine what a white man looked like, or the location of Ireland. What he did take away from the conversation, was that his heritage belonged to both aristocracy and slavery. The handing over of the seal ceremony took place the next day. Anais untied her gris-gris, a two-inch by two-inch pocket of cowhide, sewn together with goat catgut, which she had made to house the seal after John's brat had eventually fallen apart. Carefully, she withdrew two small pieces of parchment with Arabic writing on them. Then came the seal, still wrapped in its original green velvet pouch.

"I am giving you these things," Anais said in a serious tone, "including the gris-gris. These pieces of paper have helped me stay strong in difficult times. I hope they have the same effect for you. The one is a hadith about how mothers are at least three times more deserving than a father. It's helped me to remember my mother, who always had the power to endure. The other is Surah 1: al-Fatihah from the Qur'an. The prayer has a way of easing a troubled heart." She placed the gris-gris and papers on the wicker table.

"This is the seal," she said, handing the small bag to Jomo, who emptied the seal onto the palm of his hand and looked at the design.

"There's a ship on it but I've never seen one like that," he said, thinking of the dhows and pinasses that plied the river.

"Apparently, your great grandfather was something of a sailor," responded Anais.

"What are these words? What language is that?" Jomo asked curiously.

"It's called Latin. All I know is that the words mean *My Hope in God*."

"That's good," Jomo said approvingly.

"Your father told me that the seal is the only proof that his family had to show that they used to own land in Ireland. It appears that the land was unlawfully taken over by a tribe called the English. As I told you, your father was Irish and the two tribes have been at war. I'm giving this to you because you are the rightful heir, if there is indeed any land to be had. You are the only known direct male descendant, unless of course your father's elder brother, Conor, has a son, which I have no way of knowing. He's probably dead as well. It seems that he was out fighting the English all the while. But your father was a peaceful man."

A relaxing silence fell between mother and son. Jomo was deep in thought. A sense of accountability was growing, a dawning that his mother was placing trust in him, treating him like a man.

"Have you ever been to Ireland, Mother?" he asked.

"No, I don't even know where it is," Anais replied, sighing. "There have been times when I've considered taking you, so that you can meet your father's family, but with one thing and another, it hasn't happened. I'm sorry. I feel very guilty about that."

"Don't worry Mother, it wasn't meant to be," said Jomo softly, slightly embarrassed being in the presence of his mother's open honesty. "Is Ireland far away?" he asked.

"I don't know. All your father said was that it took about a month to sail across the sea to Algiers from his homeland."

"A month on water!" exclaimed Jomo. "It must be miles away. The sea must be even bigger than the Niger in full flood." He sat, thoughtfully, for a moment. "Do you think I should go there?"

"That's for you to decide; all in good time. As you mature further, you will know whether it is right for you. Whatever your decision, you must ensure that you are being true to yourself and nobody else," Anais replied, feeling a weight slipping from her shoulders.

"Does this mean," Jomo asked, holding up the seal, "that I, I mean we, could own land in this country called Ireland?"

"I don't know. Maybe, maybe not. Your father said a lot of things but one thing I do know is that he believed it was extremely important to keep it safe. I have done that and now you must carry that burden."

Jomo nodded slowly, took another look at the seal, winked at the cormorant and said, "You're mine now, I'll protect you. Maybe I'll take you back to where you came from when I'm older." He placed the seal and papers back into the gris-gris, tied it round his neck and patted his chest. A comfortable weight. "Thank you," he said, hugging his mother. "I love you."

Jomo grew unwaveringly towards adulthood and continued to develop in all areas. He was learning the Qur'an by rote with the imam, flirting with the idea of studying to become a marabout. Slowly but surely, he mastered the Arabic language. The music he played, as a pupil of Ahmed, was initially Arabic-Islamic in tone and nature. However, the ageing griot, ever the traditionalist, disapproved when he first heard

Jomo experimenting with different styles of playing, accompanied by the drums. He didn't quite feel the results of the fusion between the kora and West African beats as Jomo did, but knew he couldn't stop experimentation. When he heard Jomo exploring musical boundaries with the oud, Ahmed shook his head with a grudging respect.

The farm ticked over. Mahmood aged healthily with bright but baggy eyes, drooping shoulders and long, white, matted, curly locks that swung down to the small of his back. He had always wanted to grow them, but his life in Algiers dictated that he wore a kufi all the time, so was forced to depilate his head. His popularity increased after he shared a little kif with some friends. A few took to it like birds to flight, others refused to try it and the rest were ambivalent. Those who enjoyed the effects used the plant sensibly, in moderation, respecting it's physical, mental and spiritual qualities. They agreed to take over the biennial cannabis run to Algiers. Recent discussions concluded that it would be worth branching out to Morocco as well. Mahmood didn't care. All that mattered was a steady supply. Anais continued to be industrious and positive.

xxx

It was late summer and an ordinary Friday. After the Jumu'ah prayer, Jomo and two friends went fishing as usual. The River Niger was the lifeline for the whole region, providing people with opportunities for food, water, trade and transport. The young men strapped cloth bags around their waists and carried their nets over their shoulders. They agreed that their favourite spot was too shallow so they decided to walk further up river to a deeper pool. Although it was a decent walk, they were more likely to catch something there.

Out of sight from the village, they eventually reached the perfect place; an eddying deep patch of water on a corner of the river constrained by vertical sides of red mud. In order to fish, the friends had to climb into the flow onto a shallow submerged silt bank, then face the embankment with their backs to the main course. The water was knee deep, moving slowly, the air warm, alive with insects. Apart from the bugs, the only sound was a liquid murmur which was gentle on the ears. The trio steadied themselves on the sandy bottom and cast their nets into the dark green pool. There were no results from the first attempt.

"Equal so far," said Jomo quietly, referring to their competition of who would catch the most fish, the biggest and the largest number of species. They threw their nets again and this time each caught a fish or two. These were quickly placed into the bags. The fishermen concentrated. The game was on.

Seeking to execute some panyaring, three two-manned canoes came around the bend in the river. Coming downstream, there was no need to paddle, only steer. A muscular man with a circular face and skin as dark as coal sat at the front of the first canoe. He was the leader of the small group and couldn't believe his good fortune. It was the perfect opportunity. With his hands, he noiselessly signalled to the other members of the flotilla. They knew the meaning and each canoe quietly coursed its way to one of the three anglers, all facing in the opposite direction. The main man aimed for Jomo. There was no warning. All three were taken in the same way at the same time. A sharp blow to the head with a paddle from behind, a rope quickly placed over the torso and pulled tight, pinning the arms. Two were unconscious as they were heaved onto the canoes and gagged. Jomo was too dazed to react but managed to groan rather than shout for help as his brain had intended. His reward was another bash to the head, a gag tied round his lolling mouth and a helping hand into the canoe. With their cargo aboard, the abductors turned the vessels round and paddled furiously upstream. The fishing nets drifted to the depths, asphyxiating any caught fish trapped by fibre from freedom.

When darkness fell and there was no sign of Jomo, Anais started to fret. Mahmood was sat outside his hut, smoking.

"This is not like Jomo," she said anxiously, fanning a small fire in readiness for cooking. "He always brings the fish back before he goes anywhere else."

"Perhaps he's had no luck," suggested Mahmood.

"Then he would have come and told me, wouldn't he?" she said, growing impatient. "He knows I'm waiting to cook whatever he catches."

"He's probably just been delayed somewhere, a woman maybe."

"Do you know something I don't?" she asked.

"No, just surmising."

"Well don't, it's not helpful. I want to know where he is. It's not like him," she repeated.

Mahmood said nothing, but when Jomo didn't return that night nor the following morning, his nonchalant tone changed. He followed Anais to the homes of Jomo's friends. They hadn't returned either.

"Something's definitely wrong," said Anais, shaking her head. "Where did they go fishing?"

The families and other villagers searched the locality. Not a trace. Had the jinn taken them, or the crocodiles? Anais became withdrawn. She caught Jomo's voice on the breeze, saw him from behind and heard his music. For hours, she would stare vacantly at the opening to their yard. She lost weight and questioned God.

Is this one test too far? What is all this innocent suffering for? she pined, aching from within.

Mahmood became depressed and disillusioned. Even the kif provided no relief. It was a week later that the headline news from drumming messages, spreading from village to village repeatedly warned, “Watch out, slavers about.” Previous rumours that there was a growing slave trade spreading inland from the coastal regions had become a reality. Upon hearing this, Anais grieved again, broke down and ululated. Unknown voices came from deep within her and she imagined her ancestors joining in her lament. Her consciousness swayed betwixt the world of pain and release.

Finally, with her emotions liberated and feeling completely spent, she cried, “It is written. My mother, my uncle, my husband and now my son, enslaved to the north, enslaved to the west.”

Tamana had turned out to be the knee in a slave trader’s dog leg. Anais and Mahmood lived out the rest of their years in Tamana, bereft of energy, despondent and spiritless. Death brought them peace; they died within months of each other, neither finding out about Jomo’s fate.

Chapter 15 – Journey to Fort James

Late September to early December 1662.

What the devil happened? Jomo thought as he came to. He opened his eyes and saw the side of the canoe. He was lying on his front, head askew, on the floor, tightly gagged but breathable, arms and legs tied. Wincing with a headache he never forgot, he glanced up and saw the river bank passing by and a darkening sky. He heard the grunted efforts of people paddling the boat. Jomo tried to look down to check his gris-gris but his head refused to budge, a lead weight. He closed his eyes, prayed then began to mull things over. *I've been kidnapped,* he deduced. *By whom and why, I have no idea. There's nothing I can do about it at the moment.* It pained him to think that his mother would start worrying as soon as he was late with his fish delivery.

Night fell. Jomo had fallen asleep with the rhythm of the paddles and had awoken when the canoe came to rest on a sandbank in the river. Each captive was handled onto the seasonal strip of land. Only one prisoner was unbound at any given time and four of the six captors would surround them, preventing any chance of escape. When it was Jomo's turn, he rubbed his wrists, ankles and head, then checked for the feel of his gris-gris.

"Don't worry," said Jomo's assailant. "We wouldn't touch that. We know your amulets are very powerful."

"Who are you?" asked Jomo.

"I will tell, but first eat and drink. We're cooking your catch."

Jomo was hungry and welcomed the roasted fish. In the light of the fire he noticed that his kidnappers were from a different tribe. They were darker skinned, had rounder faces and flatter noses.

"So, who are you?" he repeated.

"I am Poosun from the Mande people. We live beyond Bamako and inland. Don't worry, we're not going to kill you. We want you alive and well."

"What for?"

"To sell you as slaves," Poosun replied. *Slaves,* thought Jomo, *like my ancestors.*

"Are you a Muslim?" he asked bluntly.

"Don't bring religion into this," barked Poosun. "This is a purely for profit enterprise. Business. Cowrie shells and lots of them."

"How come you took us?"

"Pure luck. We heard that there were undefended villages in your area and it turned out to be true. We've been camping here for a few days. It took time to find you."

"What happens now?" questioned Jomo.

"We'll take you further up the Niger then travel cross-country to the Senegal River," explained Poosun. "We sell you there. You'll be taken further by another trader."

"Where do we end up?"

"On the coast," Poosun answered.

"The coast," echoed Jomo. "I've never seen the sea."

And that's what happened. Jomo and his friends endured another uncomfortable two-day river cruise before disembarking for a gruelling foot march. The body snatchers kept their prisoner's wrists bound and legs chained to one another. Never in a position to slip away unnoticed, they completed the arduous journey, a five-week slog of unrelenting exercise with just enough sustenance to maintain the body's functions. To stay positive, there were times when Jomo had to compose music in his head, melancholy but soothing. He hoped to play the pieces one day.

At the Senegal River, Poosun bid them farewell, showing off two leather bags of cowrie shells. Jomo met his second captain slave-catcher, a wiry weasel of a man who introduced himself as Paavo. He had a rifle in his hands and a pistol tucked into his loin cloth. The trio were transferred across the river where they joined a group of about thirty other captives, some of who were women and children. For the next part of the journey, the adults were fastened in a coffle again, but this time it was with Y-shaped wooden logs secured around their necks, the children chained by the wrists to the timber.

As Jomo was being secured, he took the opportunity to ask where they were being taken to.

"Overland to the Gambia River," answered Paavo, checking the security of the shackles.

"Where does the river take us?" Jomo queried.

"Nosey, aren't you? You're going to Fort James. That's where I'll sell you to the English." *The English?* speculated Jomo. *If the English are there, then maybe Ireland is nearby. After all, they have been fighting each other.*

"I've heard of them," he said. "They're white, aren't they?"

"White and greedy," Paavo added.

"Is Fort James near Ireland?" Jomo asked innocently.

"Ireland?" replied Paavo, stumped at the name. "I have no idea."

"Why the English?" Jomo probed.

"They've taken over the fort and are hungry for slaves. There's huge competition between the English, French and Portuguese for the likes of you. That's why we've had to come so far inland to trade, they're running out of quality slaves by the coast."

Jomo raised his brows and said, "I've never heard of the French or Portuguese. Who are they, other tribes?"

"You could say that," Paavo conceded. "They're white and greedy too."

"Do you get paid in shells?"

"Not anymore, I've moved up in the trade. My remuneration is comprised of gewgaws and guns. Much more useful. With guns we can take land, with the gewgaws we make our women and children happy."

"Have you seen the coast?" enquired Jomo, bewildered by all this information.

"Of course."

"What's the sea like?" quizzed Jomo.

Paavo shook his head pityingly at the naive but understandable questions. "You'll see soon enough. Just do as you're told and all will be revealed," he said, starting to walk away.

"What happens to us at the coast?" Jomo called after him.

"You get on a ship and sail far away," was the reply.

Jomo just didn't understand.

Guards watched the progress; whips or guns in hand, over-demonstrating their powerful position. Jomo took it all in his stride; the physical effort, the mental challenge of staying calm. It was just God's will, wasn't it? He had a lot to think about. *It's all so strange. The English are white and I am the son of a white man. I can prove it too,* feeling his gris-gris swinging against his chest. *Maybe they will listen to me and help me out of this situation, even if I am half-Irish.*

It was a relief when they reached the river, even more so when the yokes were removed from their necks. One by one the captives were placed in two pirogues, both about forty-feet-long, singly hollowed from the trunks of a likondo tree. They sat two abreast, all facing forwards, with Paavo's oarsmen stationed every four seats. Jomo, wrists tied behind him and ankles tightly bound, made himself as comfortable as he could. He had become separated from his friends. They were in the other boat. Sitting beside him was an ill-looking, old man with his head bent forward, resting his chin on his chest. Directly in front of him was a woman and on her left a girl child, no more than five-years-old. Nobody talked, all were mentally restrained. Even the children were quiet. Paavo managed his men and off they paddled down river towards Fort James.

The group hadn't travelled far when Jomo's neighbour suddenly cried out and fell forward, knocking his head on the gunnel and sliding down between his seat and the child's. He was motionless, his face contorted in an image of agony with closed eyes and his skin had taken on a deathly pallor.

"Hey, get up," urged Jomo with instant solicitude. But there was no response.

Jomo shouted to the paddlers attracting their attention to the incident. The boat was banked. Paavo and one of his men checked the fallen man for a pulse, agreed he was dead and unceremoniously heaved the body out of the canoe and chucked it in the river.

"That's a few trinkets less, unless we can find a replacement along the way," grumbled Paavo. They returned to their posts quickly, pushed off and paddled away. Jomo watched the corpse float a short time before it sank abruptly, as if it had been grabbed by something underwater.

Four days of sitting were broken up by three nights of rough camping, eventually bringing the company to Fort James. The geography had changed from the wild jungle to grassy, sparsely wooded savannah. When the fortification came into sight around mid-morning, Jomo was overwhelmed by the colossal size and shape of the building. The four bastions, one at each corner, housed large cannons. Originally constructed by colonising Courlanders out of locally quarried stone blocks on an island in the river, the stronghold looked incongruous, flanked by banks of flat land and a couple of small villages made up of mud and straw huts. Jomo stared up at the fort, in wonderment, suddenly feeling uneasy at the uncertainty of what would happen to him once he entered there. He looked away, catching the eye of the woman in front of him, who was also observing the scene; their eyes locked, an intensity ran between them, sharing the common apprehension of what awaited them.

xxx

Jomo had tried to make conversation with the woman at the beginning of their voyage. He felt a sudden surge of empathy when he had heard her and the child sobbing, leaning against each other for support.

"Don't cry, sisters, try to be brave," he said softly. The woman's head turned at the sound of his voice, just enough so that Jomo could see her eyes, full of sadness and despair. She said nothing but her snuffling ceased momentarily, as did the child's. Before she turned back Jomo asked, "Are you all right?"

With a sniff, the woman shook her head and faced forward again, resting her head on the child's next to her. Jomo's mind had wandered. Looking around, he spotted the bold contrasting colours of the Pied kingfisher patrolling the water and the Black heron with its unique way of standing still in the shallows, opening its wings like an umbrella creating a circle of shade below it, producing a perfect view of any fishy treats. The darter confused him as, at first sight, he thought it was a snake. Suddenly the bird dived, resurfacing with a fat fish in its beak. Jomo smiled, thinking that the catch was too large for the bird, but then witnessed it flip the fish twice, until hunter and hunted were eyeball to eyeball. Opening its mouth wide and extending its neck, the bird swallowed the prey whole. Jomo shook his head in disbelief, thinking that had he not seen it for himself, he would never have imagined that a darter could swallow a fish at least three times wider than its slender neck. He scanned the forest canopy, brushed with a kaleidoscope of effervescent green hues, reflected in the shards of his eyes. Taking in the beauty of his surroundings, he ruminated on his situation. *A rubbish position in paradise*, he thought.

"I'm sorry," a female voice said in his vicinity, causing him to alter his vision.

Jomo looked directly in front of him, and saw that the woman had managed to turn half her body round, twisting her head so that she could almost look at him properly. Her eyes were soft, deep and brown, bloodshot from crying. High cheek bones, pert flat nose, cornrowed hair, one skin tone darker than Jomo.

"Hello," he said and smiled.

"What have you got to smile about?" she asked.

"Well, if I take my mind off the fact that I'm a prisoner, I can concentrate on the other fact that I'm in a stunning place with a beautiful woman," he replied, surprised at his own boldness.

"You're a dreamer then," she said. "Don't think I'm being rude but this is an uncomfortable position," and had turned back to face forward.

"I'm Jomo. What's your name?" he asked.

Her shoulders dropped a little. "Salina."

"Where are you from? How did you get into this mess?"

"I am a Susu, from south of the Senegal River," Salina replied. "We've had a severe famine and my father had to borrow shells to pay for the family food. To clear the debt, he gave me to his creditor who sold me to these slavers. In one go my father rid himself of his arrears and a mouth to feed. I was supernumerary, old enough to make it on my own. How about you?"

"Clubbed over the head while I was fishing," Jomo said cackling crazily. "That sounds funny now."

"Your brain's been mashed," she snickered. There had been a pause. The child was silent but snuggled up closer to Salina.

"There, there," Jomo heard Salina say to the child. "I know it's upsetting but you can be with your mother again when we stop." To Jomo she had then said, "You've provided a nice little distraction, but what's going to happen to us next?"

Jomo sighed, shrinking inside with the actuality of their circumstances. "I don't know for certain. But if the slaver is to be believed we are all going on a long sea journey," he replied, sullenly.

xxx

Salina was similarly awestruck by the imposing fortress.

"Those men up there, they're white aren't they, or pale anyway?" voiced Jomo. Red-coated armed soldiers, their brass buttons reflecting sunlight, were patrolling the three-storey watchtower under an English version of the British flag, the Union Jack, with its combined crosses of Saint George and Saint Andrew, barely fluttering in the weak breeze.

"Looks like it," replied Salina, with eyes wide open as she tried to take everything in.

As their canoe manoeuvred past a full-rigged Guineaman anchored in the river, they both noticed a float of crocodiles at a point off the island where the water abutted a stone defence wall. Suddenly three soldiers appeared at the top of the wall carrying the naked lifeless forms of a black man and child. They dropped the bodies into the water where a feeding frenzy immediately followed. Dread entered Jomo and Salina's hearts as they moored alongside a low-lying jetty and were forced to disembark. The captives, again bolted and chained together by the ankles, limped up a stone causeway in through a heavy wooden gateway and into a courtyard. The men were separated from the women and children.

In two groups, they were roughly pushed down some steps and ushered into different dungeons carved out of the rock. Squeezed in, body touching body, heavy air, no ventilation, calls of nature, stuck together, breath shallow, suffocating. Jomo shuffled in near the back of the male queue and found himself staring at the white men standing around, armed, sweating and looking churlish. If he hadn't beheld it, he would never have believed that blue-eyed people existed. Scarlet clad wardens were posted at the entrance of the lockup.

"I'm the son of a white man," Jomo said to one of the guards, who burst out laughing.

"I've never heard that one before," he guffawed. "Hey, guys," he shouted to his colleagues, "one here says he's the son of a white man." They laughed as well.

"But I can prove it, I'm half-Irish." That line brought the house down. Jomo tried to explain that he had the seal as evidence but his hands were tied behind him so he couldn't reach for it. They weren't listening anyway.

When they stopped laughing, the closest guard said, "that's nothing to be proud of, lad. Irish aren't white, they're Irish. They're even lower than you darkies in the pecking order," pushing Jomo forward towards the prison door.

Jomo was clueless as to what the man was talking about, but quickly realised the animosity the English had for the Irish. *No wonder they're at war with each other*, he thought.

"Anyway, Sambo," the guard continued, "you'll be in good company soon. You're bound to find some Irish where you're going. We send them to the West Indies as well."

"Where's that?" asked a bemused Jomo.

"Across the sea," came the reply. "Far away. Do you want to know exactly where you're going?" Jomo nodded.

"You're one of the lucky ones," the guard said sarcastically. "You'll only be here for one night. There's a slaver standing by that's almost full. It's been waiting here for three weeks to fill up the empty spaces and you lot should just be enough. You'll be joining the ship in the morning. It's Nevis bound, the Queen of the Caribees. Now, get in there."

The guard shoved Jomo through and slammed the door, locking it. Jomo was glad he didn't suffer from claustrophobia. He hadn't seen his friends. It was no use craning his neck, there were too many bodies to look over. He noticed many different tribal markings in the room; the crowd was made up with members from a variety of clans and tribes. The music he had composed played in his head.

"They can't do this to us," he mumbled.

"Hipi," said a Wolof man, as Wolof and Fula-Irish-Arab skin were forced close together. "Open your eyes. We are enthralled, they can do what they want with us." Jomo gritted his teeth. He wondered how Salina was faring.

Chapter 16 – Bridgetown, Barbados

Spring 1652 – Winter 1663

Conor survived his one-way crossing to Barbados. Some didn't. The bloody flux from contaminated water was the main problem. He had certainly suffered from loose bowels and at first had thought that that was it, but he didn't experience any of the accompanying symptoms of fever and nausea. *Must just be the slop we get to eat*, he had thought.

Prior to landing, the survivors were ordered to wash with buckets of sea water and actual soap. They were fed fresh fruit and vegetables, supplied by small boats from Bridgetown's harbour. Conor had particularly enjoyed the salubrious effects of the acerola cherry; addictive, with its abundance of vitamin C replenishing his undernourished body. Now, Conor and his surviving fellow travellers were being marched to the town's main square. He overheard the captain talking to a boatswain.

"From now on, it's pure profit," the captain said, excitedly.

"How do you mean, sir?" asked his subordinate.

"Cromwell paid us handsomely to bring this bunch of losers here. That, in itself, has covered the cost of the trip. Now we'll sell their labour to the highest bidder and what we get is ours to share amongst the crew.

You'll get your share. Call it a bonus."

"Thank you, sir. A bonus for a bosun sounds good," the boatswain punned, laughing at his own humour.

"Pity we lost some to that barrel of dodgy water," bemoaned the captain, "or we'd be getting more."

I'm up for sale then, thought Conor. The market place was bustling with people. Standing on the large wooden stage, Conor looked around. The crowd was mainly made up of white men, with a few black men and women amongst them. Sweeping his eyes over his fellow merchandise he saw a bedraggled, degraded bunch. A woman caught his eye. She was standing fully upright staring straight ahead with a determined look on her face. Some children were blubbering, holding onto their mothers ragged frocks. The sun was burning high when the captain spoke before the auction.

"Gentlemen, here is a fine group of Irish to help you with your plantations. They will be sold as indentured servants. Seven years for the adults and longer for the children, depending on their ages. Now, who will start the bidding at ten pounds for this woman?"

Conor's turn came; he was sold for fifteen pounds to an English sugar plantation owner, Ken Lishay, who also bought the captivating, intently focussed woman Conor had noticed earlier. As the paperwork was signed, Conor noted for the first time that his boss was carrying a whip in the belt of his trousers. Lishay directed his new workers to the back of a horse-cart, showing them where to sit. A poker faced black man was already sat there looking bored, resting a thick wooden stick on the floor between his legs. *Bodyguard,* thought Conor. Another black man was in the driving seat up front ready to encourage the horse to take them to the Lishay estate.

As the wagon started to roll, Lishay began talking. "Come on you two, don't look so down in the dumps. Count your blessings, things could be worse." He paused for effect. "What's the matter? Cat caught your tongues?" Lishay rattled on when he didn't get a reaction. "I'm chomping at the bit to hear your stories. Come on Conor, why are you here?"

Conor looked at Lishay, disparagingly. "For a holiday," he said drily.

Lishay and the woman burst out laughing. The black man didn't twitch.

"I love it," giggled Lishay. "Your wit is as quick as lightening. Now, seriously." Conor told Lishay he had been in debt to an English planter and been made homeless. He had been transported having been found guilty of vagrancy.

"And what about you, Mary, dear?" enquired Lishay. Mary looked as if she was about to speak then sighed and remained silent.

“As you wish, have it your way. All in good time. I am patient and patience is a virtue, so they say,” he cackled. He was already getting on Conor’s nerves.

Always oblivious as to what anyone thought about him, Lishay droned on, “now then, let me tell you what you need to know. You are mine for seven years. Don’t step on anybody’s toes or there’ll be trouble. At the end of those seven years, you’ll be free. I’ll cut to the chase. You look after me, I look after you. When your contract ends, you will be granted the freedom dues depending on the custom at that time. It used to be ten pounds but it's in the process of being reviewed. Probably will be a whole heap of sugar. Trust me, it’s the real deal. Your job, Mary, is in the kitchen at the Big House working for my cook. Yours, Conor, is in the fields under Matlock's watchful eyes.” Lishay pointed at the impassive black man. “He’s your next in line so don’t try to pull the wool over his eyes, he’ll report anything to me. He’s salt of the earth, docile and trustworthy.” Lishay patted Matlock on the head as one might to a pet dog.

Conor nodded at Matlock, who didn’t react.

“All the way from Ireland, then?” carried on Lishay. “Well, we don’t get persistent showers but when it rains it pours, then it’s sun galore.”

When Conor thought Lishay wasn’t noticing, he leant towards

Mary to try and grab her attention, raising his eyebrows as if to ask if she was all right. As Mary nodded back at Conor, Lishay noted the interaction and said, "Come on, spill the beans. Don't act as thick as thieves." Neither responded.

"Oh, you're so boring," sulked Lishay.

I think the shoe is on the other foot, thought Conor. At the plantation, Lishay took Mary to the Big House while Matlock took Conor to the servant's village area.

"Do you talk?" asked Conor, as they approached some wooden huts.

"Of course," replied Matlock.

"What do I have to do?"

"Today, you've got to build your own hut," explained Matlock. "Here are the pieces and there are the tools. I'd get on with it, there could be some rain tonight."

"What about tomorrow?" enquired Conor.

"Up before sunrise then straight to the fields."

Before the final rays of the purple edged, crimson sunset disappeared beyond the horizon, Conor managed to get the roof on. *I'm worn-out*, he thought as he sat down for a moment, admiring his handiwork and the colours in the sky. He watched as a line of black men and women returning to the camp walked past him. They filtered off into several huts a little way off. *Slaves*, he thought to himself. *They look as tired as me... and as hungry... Where can I get some food from?*

A smaller group of white people followed the black workers. They filed off to a closer section of huts. There was a definite boundary in the living quarters, an invisible barrier, between the black and the white villages. Conor's place was on the edge of the white accommodation, closest to that provided for the Africans. After a short while, a white man approached Conor, who was busy testing the strength of the join between the roof and the sides of his new home.

"You want some grub?" the man asked in a Scottish accent.

"To be sure," replied Conor enthusiastically, in his contrasting Irish brogue.

"Oh, you're Irish? Hard luck."

"What do you mean by that?" said Conor strongly, hackles raised.

"No offence meant. It's just that..." the man swithered then said, "I'm Angus, by the way, and you are?"

"Conor."

"Well, Conor, welcome to paradise," Angus said, without a hint of satire. "As I was saying, it's just that the Irish, you know Catholics, are hated by the English. They tolerate us, the Scots, probably because we're Presbyterian. But I'm just warning you, be careful, that's all. I don't have an issue; there's good and bad in all of us, but the English hate you guys. Scran?"

I'm used to that, thought Conor. "Great. Thanks," he said, "I appreciate the warning, not that I take religion seriously anyway. That Lishay chap seemed reasonable enough. Very boring though."

"Boring beyond belief. But a ruthless bore, you'll see," responded Angus gravely.

"What do you mean?" asked Conor.

"My advice is to have as little to do with him as possible. You can't trust him. You never quite know what he's going to do next. I'm sure you'll find that out sooner or later." It transpired that Angus had recently arrived in Barbados from England. He was transported as a prisoner following defeat at the Battle of Worcester during the English Civil War, fighting for the Royalist cause. He hated Cromwell as much as Conor. Angus' prime reason to fight for the king was to prevent Christmas being banned by Cromwell. Conor elected not to challenge Angus about some of his countrymen crawling behind the English military and taking up some of the land stolen from the Irish. As they had a common enemy in Cromwell, Conor allowed Angus the benefit of the doubt. He knew the Scottish people were canny operators and not the prime movers in the invasion of Ireland.

Conor decided that, for now, he would just do what he was told, keep his head down and not reveal his own opinions on religion. He had made his decision about a Supreme Deity relatively recently. There can't be a God because if there was one, the English would have left Ireland by now. He joined a field gang of white serfs, drudging six days a week, from sunrise to sunset, with two hours for lunch, planting, weeding, burning, hacking, cutting, clearing and loading sugarcane. The sun burnt, peeled and re-roasted Conor's pale skin. He toiled in the uniform of the slave – a loose fitting shirt and breeches. He occasionally wore his kilt to cool his body temperature, but the skin suffered. Red blotches surfaced, died and resurfaced all over his face, arms and, especially, his legs. Shortly after arriving, and having just gotten used to working with his group, Matlock ordered Conor to move over and assist the Africans in another field one day.

"Three are sick, and they need more help," Matlock had explained. For the next few months, Conor worked alongside black men and women. He admired their stolid strength.

"Here," said one of his co-workers. "If you cut the cane at an angle, it's easier to slice. Trim it lower down too, just above ground level." Conor followed the advice; it was true.

"Thanks," he said. "What's your name?"

"Kofi, and yours?"

"Conor."

"Where are you from?" asked Kofi.

"Ireland. You?"

"Guinea, Africa."

"Oi! You pair, stop your prattle and work. Or I'll whip you 'til you do," shouted a white overseer.

Conor and Kofi went silent immediately. When the occasion presented itself, they cautiously exchanged a range of conversation, and over time became friends, helping each other when possible and necessary. One evening after work, Conor crossed the boundary between the two villages to visit Kofi and share some food with him. Matlock had noticed and advised him not to make a habit of it; Lishay discouraged social contact between black and white labourers, paranoid that they would join forces and rise against him. If Lishay caught them, they could be flogged. He was the only authority who decided who you could fraternise with, even if you wanted to start courting. Neither group of workers could freely engage in relationships; permission had to be granted for everything. Conor and Kofi were forever vigilant when they met outside work hours to socialise. On one such occasion, they were discussing their situation.

"We're slaves, right?" said Kofi.

"You are, but I'm not a slave. I'm a servant. They don't enslave Europeans, only Africans. I'm free after seven years and I've already done three," responded Conor.

"Maybe that's true. But you look like a slave from here. You do the same work, same hours, same clothes, same food, same hut."

"Yes, but Lishay doesn't own me for life, only the next four years," said Conor.

"If you live that long," Kofi said ominously. It was the truth. As many as twenty percent of all labourers died from suicide, disease, exhaustion or cruel violence. Everyone knew someone who had been buried. There were rumours that certain masters forced servants to work harder than slaves, with the hope that they would die from their exertions before claiming their entitlements.

"I'll live and get my freedom," said Conor confidently. "You can't do that, can you?"

"I could if I wanted," Kofi shot back.

"How?" asked Conor, interested to hear.

"I could escape and join the Maroons in the hills," explained Kofi.

"Who are they then?" Conor was intrigued.

"Escaped slaves," answered Kofi. "They hide away and live off the land."

"Is that real freedom though? Always having to check over your shoulder to make sure you're not being hunted down?" tested Conor.

"It would be hard, I agree, but it would make me feel better. Or

I could pay for my freedom, but I ain't got no money nor any means of getting some," said Kofi, despondently.

"Or you could get a boat and sail back to Africa," suggested Conor, half-jokingly.

Kofi considered this, and shrugged. "Will you go home when you're freed?" he asked.

"I can't, I'm banished."

"So, you will only be free here? On Barbados?" Kofi exclaimed, incredulously.

"I guess," said Conor solemnly. "At least I can have a life."

"Is that what you call it? How exactly do you think you're going to do that?" asked Kofi, putting Conor on the spot.

"Lishay will give me my freedom dues when I leave and I'll set myself up. Not sure what I'll do yet, but whatever it is will provide," Conor said, expectantly.

"You'll get a whole heap of nothing; I've seen it before," responded Kofi emphatically. This was also true. Dependant on their masters complying with the laws of the land, some freed Scottish and Irish servants weren't rewarded for their time in service and trying to seek recompense through the legal system was a bureaucratic trial of patience. Even more so when the case usually came down to the plaintiff's word against a plantation owner, who, being English, was always considered to be the honest party.

Conor worked on but started to feel depressed with the repetitive nature of his days. It was planting time. Furrowing acres of land using a spade or controlling the ox plough, followed by laying cut canes in the rows and covering them with soil, was monotonous. The bending, twisting and turning racked his back and each morning he woke with stiff joints. *What am I doing with my life?* he thought, stretching his arms. *I need a plan. I'll finish my time here and see what I get from Lishay. If I'm given enough, maybe I can buy a boat, set myself up as a fisherman and earn enough to pay for Kofi's freedom. What if he's right and I get nothing? I'll find work and save, save, save. Then release Kofi and pay for our passage to Nevis. See if Patrick's still about and just chance my luck.*

Conor felt better the next day, having made some decisions. It was a Sunday too, a day off in the growing season, not the harvesting. He pretended to be attentive during the mandatory Anglican service, but was moved to actually participate when the hymns were sung. Those black voices were a treat to hear; strong, fervent and soulful. Conor had felt quite spiritual listening to them. He was on his way to the Big House which he had only ever seen from a distance, but never visited. Matlock had asked him to fetch the weekly ration of meat for the servant village. Every Sunday felt like an early Christmas and Eid party to the Christian servants, the Christianised Africans and a Muslim minority of the slaves. Even if it was usually chicken, or occasionally pork, allowed in Islam when survival is at stake, it made a welcome change to the dull loblolly they were fed during the working week.

Conor knocked at the kitchen side entrance, drawn to the stately grandeur of the building. *Reminds me of Dun na Sead*, he recollected, catching himself out with a flurry of feelings. Home and the seal! He hadn't thought much about the seal for ages, or John for that matter. *All of that's a problem for the future*, he decided, bringing himself back to the present. Conor was startled when Mary, the colleen, opened the door. They hadn't seen each other since the day of their arrival. She had gained weight, a light tan and a cook's uniform.

"Hello," he said, taken aback as he was reminded how attractive she was.

"Oh, it's you," was all she said, as if she had been expecting him.

"It's Mary, isn't it? Conor, in case you had forgotten."

"I couldn't forget you, could I? You were the first person to make me laugh for months," she replied. "Here for a holiday! It still makes me smile."

"Good," he said smiling. "How's it been for you?"

"Well, apart from the fact that I shouldn't be here, it hasn't been too bad. The work's pretty painless and I've been treated all right. I can't say that for the young black women here, though. Lishay is a lecherous slime ball and uses them like playthings. How he can call himself a Christian is beyond me."

Conor shook his head sympathetically. "I'm here for the meat, by the way."

"Oh, and here I was, thinking you'd come to see me."

Conor felt himself flushing and his facial blotches reddened.

"I wished I had," he said, grinning, conscious that there was a feeling of flirtation in the air. "I'm curious; you never did say why you were here."

"Similar to you really, only the reason for my vagrancy is different. I had a fiancée who was always fighting the English. But he got caught," Mary revealed. "They sent him to Poland, I think. I wasn't allowed to go and was lost without him. My family disowned me because I'd been living with him. So, like you, I was homeless. The authorities picked me up off the street along with a few others I had been living rough with."

"I told a lie," said Conor.

"What do you mean?" asked Mary, intrigued.

"I wondered if Lishay was testing us when he asked the question. I assumed he knew the truth so I made up a story to see if he reacted. When he didn't I realised that my reputation hadn't reached this far from Ireland. I wasn't a homeless vagabond. I was one of those Irish who fought against the English as well; I could have fought alongside your fiancée."

"How come you're here and not in Poland then?" queried Mary.

"Apparently, I'm a dangerous rogue so I've been banished here for life."

"After my seven years, I'll be free to go home, if I can get the wherewithal."

"Well, at least we can be here together for the next three years," Conor stated.

"Be here together?" she said, raising her eyebrows.

"If I was free and able to do so, I would invite you to a romantic dinner," he said enticingly. Mary pretended to be shocked.

"But I am a betrothed woman," she gasped, hiding a smile behind her hand. Conor put his hands up.

"I wouldn't want to offend your honour. But truthfully, do you still feel engaged?" he asked, looking her in the eyes.

Mary looked back. "No I don't," she acknowledged soberly, "and now I know that life's too short."

"If we get permission, maybe we could meet again and carry on this conversation," said Conor, hopefully. "Only if you want, of course."

"I would like that," she responded. "I'll have to ask Lishay first and see what he says. If we get the go ahead," she said slowly, her eyes glinting, "you can try and offend my honour then. We'll see exactly how dangerous you really are. Matlock will let you know if I'm allowed but I can't foresee a problem. You can trust him completely, you know. He has hidden depths. Wait there, I'll get you the meat, it's chicken today."

Conor returned to his village with a spring in his step. Approval for relationships was granted to Lishay's labourers, according to his whims, and all of them were highly regulated; including when, where and how often couples could meet. There were different rules for the two groups of workers. If a servant became pregnant by another servant, it would contravene her indenture contract, resulting in her being evicted to become destitute, an easy route to prostitution. However, if a female servant engaged in coitus with a slave, and this was sometimes encouraged as a breeding programme for the next generation of slave stock, the resulting child would belong to Lishay, to keep or to sell. The babies from slaves impregnating slaves became another cheap way of adding to their numbers.

Before Mary had an opportunity to speak to Lishay, an event occurred that resulted in her never seeing Conor again. That very week, smallpox entered the Big House via a white overseer, who had been infected by a prostitute in a Bridgetown brothel, who had in turn been infected by an English sailor, who had been infected by who knows who or where. The white overseer sneezed over one of the black maids, who sneezed over Mary, who sneezed, vomited and grew flat-topped red spots full of pus all over her face and body. Having only just found a glimmer of hope on the Lishay estate, the possibility of an amorous liaison in her lonely existence as a servant, Mary died, alone, a month later. Conor was disconsolate when he heard the news.

Conor was over two-thirds of the way through his term when he finally saw the alleged, capricious side to Lishay. He had heard some nasty rumours about his boss's ability to suddenly lose his temper and become viciously violent but hadn't actually witnessed it. One lunchtime it happened directly in front of him. Unusually, Lishay had visited his workforce at that time of day. The regular number of guards wandered around the area, each armed with a whip and wooden baton.

"Something's not quite right," Matlock said to Conor, who was trying to swallow some loblolly.

"Why do you say that?" asked Conor through a claggy mouthful.

"Just a feeling," replied Matlock. "Lishay's in a strange mood." They watched Lishay as he talked to a subservient, unassuming male slave, Tim, a few huts down from Kofi's. There felt like some tension in the air but then Lishay seemed to share a joke with Tim, who laughed as Lishay began to walk away. "Maybe I was wrong," admitted Matlock. Then, without warning, Lishay started shouting, unravelled his whip, returned to Tim and forced him to the ground.

Standing over his slave and addressing his lunching workers, the master roared, "You will all watch to see what happens when you break the rules," and started flogging him. "Don't," thwack, "bite," thwack, "the," thwack, "hand," thwack, "that," thwack, "feeds," thwack, "you," thwack. Lishay screamed each word with every blow of the whip, a full seven times, and then added one extra lash to even it up. Sweating profusely and breathing heavily, Lishay left Tim writhing and beckoned Matlock over. Conor, shocked, watched them in discussion. Some slaves began to help move Tim to his hut. After a short time, Lishay walked off and Matlock re-joined Conor.

"What was that all about?" asked Conor.

Matlock sighed. "I knew something was up. Tim's been accused of looking at Lishay's wife. He didn't, who would? She's got a face like a busted toad. But that's not the point. Lishay can turn. He's been looking for any reason to beat poor Tim. If he can't find one, he'll make one up. Now he's achieved two things in one; flaying Tim and reminding us."

"What of?"

"By making us watch he has reinforced our place in life, accentuating his dominance over us, maintained by fear. You never know what to expect from him and we're powerless to do anything about it," replied Matlock, sombrely. Conor looked away, apoplectic with the injustice of it all.

Conor's final day arrived and he went to receive his freedom papers and reward for time served. Lishay gave him a clean set of second hand clothes and a hoe. It was the new custom of the country, he explained to a dejected Conor; freedom dues were no longer bound by law. Handing Conor his identity pass, Lishay dismissed him with a final comment, "good riddance to bad rubbish."

Conor shook Kofi's hand on the way out. "I wish I could stop thinking that I told you so," said Kofi.

"I'll survive and make enough for us both. I'll be back to see you," reassured Conor.

"Where are you going to go?"

"I'll try a few other places first, see if I can get work. Or I'll join some others. I'll sort something out," Conor replied wistfully.

Nobody wanted to employ a freed Irishman. African slaves were cheaper, for life, more acclimatised to the weather, more efficient and therefore, more profitable. Conor joined a group of ex-servants, a mix of Scottish and Irish, in the Martin's Bay area. They were people on the edge, living in ramshackle shelters. Despised by other white people on the island, and ignored by the slave labourers, who had enough of their own problems to deal with, they eked out a form of survival from untamed land and seafood. Conor had lived rough for years, but this was something different. It was literally back to hunter-gatherer mode. No fishing, no eat; no foraging, no eat; no digging, no eat. The chelonian egg laying season provided a short abundance of sustenance. On good days, a Hawksbill turtle was scooped from the sea or a raccoon or iguana would be caught; mostly though, it was an effort to find enough calories to sustain himself. Malnutrition set in amongst the group, some died. Survivors carried on, everybody contributing to just hang in there. And most did.

There were moments when Conor questioned whether he was better off being free, poor and starving as opposed to being indentured, poor but with a full stomach. After a few years, when he had struggled enough, he reached his bottom line. He had exhausted any possibility of finding full time work. Reality had killed the idea of earning enough money for himself and Kofi's freedom. He had occasionally found hope with a few weeks' worth of labouring during the busy harvesting period but it wasn't permanent, and he knew he wasn't accomplishing anything. It was time to move on. *Plan B,* he thought. *I'm going to get out of here*. Conor confided his thoughts with his Redleg neighbour, Angus, who he had worked with at Lishay's place.

"How will you leave the island? You've got no money to pay for a passage. Can you swim?" Angus joked.

Conor ignored the sarcasm. "I'm going to steal a boat, want to come with me?"

"Steal a boat? Are you sure you know the front from the back?" laughed Angus.

"I can sail and navigate the stars. I was doing it from the age of five, all round Roaring Water Bay, back home."

"Oh, I see, sorry. You're serious then? Come with you? Nice idea. Are you going to Ireland? I could hitch a ride there and make my way to Scotland. Now that Cromwell's dead and the King restored, I've been thinking of going home, somehow," Angus said dreamily.

"Well, good luck on that one. I can't go home, I'm banished. They'll never let me back. I expect they'd think that even at my age, I'd carry on where I left off. Mind you, it's probably true; I would if I had the energy."

"Where will you go then?" asked Angus.

"Nevis," Conor answered. "I've got a cousin of mine living there. At least I hope he's still there... and alive."

"Where's that?"

"Don't know yet, but I'm going into town to find out," replied Conor.

Conor trekked over the island to Bridgetown, ignoring jeers of *smell the Redleg* and *bakra man* from some of the small-minded people he passed. There was another reason to visit; he needed to investigate the types of boats moored nearby. After carefully observing the harbour for a while, Conor made his way to the main street. Outside a hotel he heard a raised but familiar voice. Lishay! A drunken Lishay! Conor decided to confront him. *He owes me and what have I got to lose?* he thought. Lishay was with a group of white men. Matlock watched from nearby, catching every word.

"Cost me an arm and a leg, but I'll bet your bottom thaler he'll work like a dog." Lishay was loud, bullish and verbose. *Bragging about a new slave, no doubt*, thought Conor as he approached. Matlock caught his eye and raised one eyebrow in recognition.

"Hello Lishay, remember me?" interrupted Conor. Lishay stopped talking, turned and gave himself time to focus his rheumy eyes. He burst out laughing.

"Well, here's a blast from the past. The turf-cutter who came for a holiday," he said derisively. "Having a good time, Paddy?"

Conor ignored the insults. "Not really. I'll come to the point. You never paid me my freedom dues."

"I beg to differ," Lishay riposted then paused. "Having said that, I can't remember off the top of my head," he slurred.

"I'll remind you. You gave me some old clothes and a hoe."

"Oh yes, it put me out of pocket too," laughed Lishay.

"I could take you to court," cautioned Conor. "The law says I should have had four hundred pounds of sugar."

"That's the new law, you are up with the times," Lishay remarked sarcastically.

"I've heard that they'll backdate it if they find an injustice."

"Are you threatening me, Irish? You know what they say about you lot. The Negroes are just smoked Irish, and the Irish are inside out Negroes, only good for slavery and fighting," mocked Lishay. Conor glared at him, weighing up what the consequences might be if he just broke Lishay's nose there and then.

Before he decided, Lishay suddenly changed tack and lessened his tone, "Come now, come now. Listen, I'm in a good mood, don't spoil it. I've been making money hand over fist, so let's come to an arrangement before this gets out of control. I will give you three carolus, no court, no questions, end of matter, agreed?" Conor couldn't believe his luck and accepted the gold coins, equivalent to three pounds. "You don't look a gift horse in the mouth, do you Irish?" Then as he turned back round to his friends Lishay said boisterously, "now get back to the gutter where you belong." Conor walked over to Matlock.

"Smart work, Conor, you caught him at exactly the right time," Matlock said. "You know your law. Kofi misses you."

Conor talked quietly with Matlock about his plans. Matlock listened, expressionless. "I've seen a boat; it's the perfect size, with oars and a sail. That's all I need. It's near the end of the moorings, quick to take. Security is lax. Nobody steals boats here, so no-one watches them. I can be unhooked and away in minutes." Conor spoke quickly, he was beginning to live it.

"Why are you telling me all this?" asked Matlock breaking up his deadpan face.

"Mary said I could trust you."

Matlock nodded. "Her death was tragic. She knew I only made it appear that I was informing Lishay of everything," he said.

"She was a sad loss," agreed Conor, "I was hoping to see more of her." He hesitated, remembering then sighed, shook his head and carried on. "I want to take Kofi with me, but I don't want you getting into trouble if one of the slaves goes missing."

Matlock grinned, "I appreciate that." He dithered, considered what he'd heard and then said, "I've got a better idea. Not only will you take Kofi, but me as well. Is the boat big enough for three?"

Conor hadn't considered three. "We'll make do, of course" he answered. "The only trouble is, I don't know which direction Nevis is in. I'm going down to the quayside to find out."

"No need," said Matlock. "I know where Nevis is."

"How do you know that?"

Matlock smiled. "There's a lot you don't know about us Africans.

We're smarter than the English think. They may rule us with guns, whips and fear but we use our minds to outwit them. I get information from lots of islands. We have a network. We call it the Underground and it stretches all the way from Guyana in the south to Virginia in the north. News travels slowly but surely, and sometimes surprisingly quickly."

"That's outstanding," approved Conor, "but how do you send messages from island to island?"

"Via freed slaves who work on the fishing boats that ply their trade between islands. They pass on what they know to friends working at the ports," explained Matlock.

"What a clever system," praised Conor, "so where's Nevis?"

"North-West."

"Any idea how far or how long it takes?"

"You should get there within a week," replied Matlock. "This is a good time to go; the hurricane season is over and the weather is likely to be fair."

"We," corrected Conor.

"Actually, I only want to go as far as Martinique. It's on the way to Nevis. I've got a relation there, Cyrus; he's part of a group of Maroons. You can drop me and Kofi off there. I'll then point you in the general direction for Nevis."

"Why Kofi as well?" queried Conor.

"Where else would he go?" said Matlock, countering the question.

"With me."

"With you?" exclaimed Matlock, raising his eyebrows, unusually flustered. "How do you think he's going to survive with you? He'll be an escaped slave and, no offence, but you hardly look rich enough to afford a slave by your side. He can't hide the fact that he's branded and without papers."

"I hadn't thought that far, to be honest," said Conor, sheepishly.

"No, well, wake up. Kofi will be fine with me. Cyrus knows how to survive, he'll look after us."

They agreed a plan and set a date; Sunday night in two weeks' time. That was by far the calmest period at the plantation. Everyone went to bed early for the start of the working week. Matlock was a trusted slave who had the authority to rota himself for sentry duty that evening and would have a key to the gate. Conor revisited the harbour for another recce, reassured himself with his observations and then celebrated his new-found wealth with a few drinks. Overhearing the word, "Irish" in a backstreet inn he listened intently. Two Englishmen were talking.

"Got in from Montserrat last week," one was saying. "Dangerous place I reckon."

"What's that?" asked his companion.

"Dangerous place, Montserrat."

"Why?"

"Aren't you listening? That's what I said, all the Irish. They're all over the place like a swarm of irksome mozzies."

"Why dangerous?"

"Well, they're damned papists, aren't they? Like the French. There's trouble with the Frogs on Saint Kitts. If the Irish join up with them, which they've done before, we could lose old Kitty, Nevis *and* Montserrat." Conor's ears pricked up even higher. It was a timeless moment. The names Saint Kitts and Nevis echoed in his head. And now another one, Montserrat. *They can denigrate the Irish all they like*, he thought, finishing his rumbullion, the traditional Caribbean drink he had discovered on his liberation*, we'll have the last laugh. Montserrat, is that another island? I'll have to ask Matlock.* It felt good to hand over a cash coin; to receive and feel change in his pocket once again, his own money. He treated himself to a peppered steak dinner and a quadroon drab for the night before returning to Martin's Bay the next day.

"I want to give you a double crown," announced Conor to Angus after bringing him up-to-date, without mentioning Matlock or Kofi. Informing the authorities about escaped slaves could be a lucrative business. Although Conor trusted Angus, he knew that people can act uncharacteristically when in dire straits. He decided that Angus didn't need to know every detail.

"That's kind of you. That can go towards my passage home. I wish you the best of luck," said Angus, shaking Conor's hand.

Contrary to Murphy's Law, some plans actually do go to plan. The boat was big enough, but only just. The jetty was devoid of human presence, and anyway, even if there had been one or two, they wouldn't have questioned a white man with two slaves, going for a night's worth of fishing, unless they owned the boat that they were taking, of course. In the soft glow from the half-moon, the free and the escapees each carried a small bag with a few belongings, food and a cow's bladder full of fresh water. To a casual observer, it looked like they were moving lobster pots. Conor checked for the Plough; for the last few nights he had been recalling his sailing skills and observing the movement of the star cluster, Ursa Major, low in the night sky scene, to ensure that he could accurately pinpoint the direction of north when needed.

Conor was excited as he carefully stored their supplies. Taking back control of his life with the aim of a hopeful reunion with Patrick, was uplifting. He looked at his crew as he rowed quietly away from the jetty, before hoisting the sail. Matlock was watching Bridgetown recede with a wide grin on his face whilst Kofi was sobbing with joy.

Lishay was furious when he found out that two of his slaves were missing, presumed escaped. The loss of Matlock hurt especially.

"Didn't I favour him?" he grumbled to his wife. "The worm that turned. Honestly, you give an inch and they take a mile." He had notices printed and distributed around the island:

Wanted by the Lishay Plantation: A twenty-five-pound reward for two runaway Negro male slaves. Both marked KL on top of right arm. Number 1 – named Matlock, black complexion, woolly hair, 6-foot-tall, quiet but intelligent, well-built, in his 40's. Most likely in the company of Number 2 – named Kofi, very dark colour, short wiry hair parted on left side, about 5 foot, 6 inches tall, stocky build, high cheek bones. Whoever apprehends or provides information for their capture shall receive fifteen pounds for Number 1 and ten pounds for Number 2, including any reasonable expenses - Ken Lishay.

Lishay looked forward to their arrest, anticipating the pleasure of watching them flogged for their disobedience. *They'll get more than their just deserts*, he gloated, not realising yet that he had been thwarted. When the news reached Angus' ears, that the two slaves had scarpered, people he had worked alongside and spent time with, he remembered Conor's friendship with Kofi and guessed correctly that Matlock and Kofi were other pieces in Conor's jigsaw of an escape plan. Keeping his thoughts to himself and proving completely trustworthy,

Angus had smiled ruefully with a joyful jealousy, pleased for everyone involved and envious of their rebellious achievement.

The boat owner, a local butcher, did a double take when he went to go sailing and fishing with a bottle of rum for some downtime on his one afternoon off, two weeks after Conor had slipped the boat from its moorings. Baffled and angered, he asked around but nobody knew anything about the missing vessel. In fact, some of his interviewees just laughed. It didn't help that a few months previously he had returned from his time off, inebriated and staggered up the jetty, failing to fasten his craft properly. Fortunately, at that time there were witnesses and one jumped into the water to retrieve the drifting skiff. The butcher shook his head and vowed to give up drinking after he drank his fill, blaming himself for his own stupidity. The vanished goods were never linked. The downside on Lishay's plantation was that no slave was ever given a position of trust again.

Chapter 17 – The Middle Passage

December 1662 – February 1663

Jomo exulted being in the fresh air. He wasn't sorry to be leaving Fort James after bearing the worst night's sleep of his life to date. Crammed together in the dungeon, impossible not to be touching another sticky, sweaty, unwashed body, the captives had eventually managed to co-operate in lying, sitting, or leaning against each other. Now on his way to a completely unplanned, unwanted change of life, Jomo was shuffling along the jetty, chained again by one leg to another male slave; one in front and one behind, wrists tied at his back, stumbling towards the waiting rowing boats ready to transport the unfortunates to the sailing ship secured to the river bed. The women and children were in a separate line. He tried to spy Salina, eventually spotting her towards the rear, looking back at him. He nodded and smiled. She shrugged her shoulders in response. He saw his two friends a few spaces behind him. They acknowledged his look.

Most of the prisoners wore loin cloths, some were naked. Jomo noticed that a small proportion had gris-gris hanging round their necks. He hoped they were Muslims. A sailor went to snatch a talisman off a man in the line in front of Jomo. There was an immediate commotion, arms and legs flailing, chains tautening and men being knocked off balance.

"Leave those things alone, Nobby," another sailor shouted. "They'll fight for their lives to keep them. I saw a man break his own leg once to try and retrieve one, nasty business. It's not worth the effort. You can rip off his cloth though, he won't be needing that." His colleague, Nobby, nodded, tore away the flimsy material but left the amulet alone. Jomo glanced at his, a solid weight on his chest. Jomo knew what was coming his way. He decided to try and remove his own short dhoti, an attempt at obtaining a small amount of independence in a powerless place, but he couldn't loosen it from the front with his hands fastened behind him. Then he heard a scream and a yell and an "Ow, ow, ow!" *What now?* he thought.

It was branding time. Jomo winced but didn't make a sound as the red-hot iron sizzled the flesh on his right shoulder. He looked down at the letters on his burnt skin. *BRIS* - short for Bristol, the name of the ship he was bound for. His final piece of clothing was forcibly removed.

Jomo never talked about his experiences on that ship; what he saw, heard, felt, smelt and tasted. He saw sick or incurably diseased Africans thrown into the sea for insurance purposes, and opportunists escape by diving overboard, only to be eaten by sharks or drown. He heard the crying, moaning and sobbing. He felt the complete degradation, the animosity of the European crew commanded by English officers and the loss of his home. He smelt the faeces, the urine, the vomit, the body's decay and death. He tasted the food. 'Foul' doesn't start to cover it. How the white chef managed to make okra, rice and black-eyed peas so bland was an enigma. Jomo lost weight. When salted beef was seldom offered, he asked if it was halal.

"What do you mean?" asked the cook.

"When you kill the animal, God's name should be spoken at the time the throat is cut," Jomo explained.

"What the hell has God got to do with it? Sometimes we cut the throat but we shoot and club them to death as well. What's the difference?" was the disinterested reply.

Jomo realised that halal food would be infrequent, if at all, and so said an extra prayer of gratitude for any meat he received. He stuck to fish whenever possible. Jomo was disgusted with himself when he silently rejoiced after one of his nearest, fettered neighbours died of dysentery and was removed. It meant he could stretch out more. He had no proper contact with his friends, they were at the other end of the hold. He never saw Salina, chained in another part of the vessel. It was every man, woman and child for themselves. Basic survival. In his most lugubrious moments, Jomo prayed and fingered his gris-gris with his one free hand. The music he mentally composed was bluer than the Blues.

The best part of the journey was the end. After ten weeks of cruising in a manner where even the lowest form of economy class would be considered extremely posh, the ship dropped anchor a short distance from land. Magnificent frigate birds with their red throats swooped and soared, Brown pelicans cruised, skimming just above the waves. Jomo and the other survivors were taken up on deck, washed and fed fresh snapper, boiled chicken, vegetables, Irish potatoes and mangoes.

"Got to get you lot looking as fit as possible for the slave market in a few days," said the cook, slapping another spoonful of mashed yam onto Jomo's plate. The hold was cleaned and disinfected while Jomo enjoyed the warm sea breeze, the sun on his face and the view. He saw a single peaked, small island rising from the azure Caribbean Sea like an erection in a blue tin bath. The human cargo was returned to the dark prison but its mood had shifted upwards. Two days of wholesome nourishment later, Jomo noticed a small amount of substance showing on his skeletal, wasted body. During that time, he heard women and children on deck. He presumed they were getting the same treatment. Jomo strained to hear one voice in particular amongst them; hoping Salina had survived, but assuming the worst.

Chapter 18 – Nevis, West Indies

July 1627 – February 1663

Patrick O'Mahoney, supporting a purple-veined, bloated, sot's nose had survived for over thirty years on the island of Nevis, enjoying equal measures of highs and lows. He loved the place; the sapphire sea, the Indian gold sun, the various hues of jade amongst the foliage and the amber rum. When tobacco was profitable, he made good money, but the market had dropped away with competition from Virginia. Out of financial necessity, the plantation owners turned to sugar to try and make wealth. An influx of Jews had moved to The New World, finding new homes following another enforced migratory diaspora, this time from Spain and Portugal. They brought their sugar growing know-how with them to the area. The Sephardims were an important ingredient in the success of the sweetness trade and well rewarded for sharing their knowledge. To make more than just a living, Patrick needed extra land, but that was out of the question since the big plantations were taking over the smaller plots. He agreed with Hilton to grow cane on his leased land and, in effect, worked for him, seeing as his sugar had to be processed at his former master's mill. Patrick had a share of the profits, which was enough and he had a little savings. He was also paid for looking after Hilton's horses. At his age, he was content with that.

Patrick lived in his simple two-roomed hut with a female slave. He had bought her over ten years ago when he was wealthy enough to afford a house keeper; someone to cook and wash for him. It raised his status in the neighbourhood as well. However, Patrick had been lonely, having failed to make any close friendships. Most of the acquaintances he mixed with during his first year on Saint Kitts had remained there when he moved to Nevis. Work was his life. The routine of toiling from dawn until dusk to make a living meant that most of his free time was spent preparing meals and sleeping; any time left to relax was focussed on his devotion to the company of rum. He didn't fit in with the English set and the few other Irish servants he met in Vic's tavern in town on his Sundays off were just drinking mates, not people he could have any meaningful conversations with. Thus, loneliness had enveloped him. He understood why he hadn't heard from his cousin John when news of the raid on Baltimore was reported in one of the three letters he eventually received from his parents. He continued to correspond once a year but after a period of ten years with no response, he stopped writing and assumed they were dead. The snippets of information that came his way about his homeland sounded like chaos, for the Irish anyway. *I'm better off here*, he had thought. *What have I got back home? Less than nothing.*

Over the years, Patrick fantasised about the women on the

island, both black and white, but a religious-induced guilt and a lack of confidence in communicating with the fairer sex had prevented him from taking any direct action on his dreams. He had never developed a sense of humour to hide his inadequacies and so, instead, started befriending the local rum, the powerful, popular by-product of the sugar industry. It was cheap, delicious and dangerous. By the time he bought a slave, he was heading down the perilous alcoholic's path.

Before she struck Patrick's eye that day at the slave market, Bolanile, as she knew herself, had just bid a sad farewell to her cousin Kodou, who had been bought by an English planter. To Patrick, she seemed no threat, nothing complicated; she was middle-aged with a face characterised by her gentle, calm composure. She reminded him of his mother. He bought her cheaper than expected, with few other bids.

"What's your name?" he had asked.

"Bolanile," she replied.

"Eh? I can't cope with that. I'll call you Bridget. At least it starts with a B. And you must always call me Massa," he added, trying to get used to his new status.

"Yes Massa," she said obediently while thinking, *that's what I'll be, plain B.*

"That's good. Let's get home."

But when they arrived at his cabin, Patrick didn't know what to do with her. He hadn't thought things through properly. He poured a slug of rum and showed B the run of the place. Not that there was much to run. They worked it out. B quickly understood Patrick's situation, perceiving that he was full of maudlin self-pity, and tried to make life easier for him. Firstly, she took control of where she slept, in his bedroom, while he moved into the only other room that combined as a kitchen-cum-living area-cum-dining room. Patrick rarely slept in his bed anyway, often too drunk to move from his chair. Rudimentary washing and toileting facilities were outside. B regulated and decided when and what they would eat and which clothes he would wear. Soon Patrick couldn't understand how he had ever coped without her. She even heaved him into a sleeping position when he was intoxicated.

One day, whilst sipping a light one before dinner, Patrick said to B, "you can stop calling me Massa, Bridget. From now on, I am Patrick, but only when it's just the two of us. Do you understand?"

"Yes, Patrick," she replied submissively.

He grinned. "Thank you for looking after me so well. You seem quite happy here, is that true?"

No, I'm not happy being here, you drunken rum-soak, B thought to herself. *Don't fool yourself, Mister, just because I put on a compliant act in front of you.* "Of course, Patrick," she responded faithfully.

Patrick sighed contentedly into his glass. He had a nice thought.

"Is there anything I can do for you?" he asked.

"Yes," returned B, immediately. "Would you be kind enough to give me permission to visit Mr Opran's plantation? I have a relative there that I would like to see. We came from the same village. She was sold to Mr Opran before you bought me."

"Well, his place is just down the road. Personally, I don't see why not. But I'll have to speak to Opran first, he'll have to agree to it. What's her name?"

"I know her as Kodou but that might not be her name now," B said pointedly. "However, if it helps, she can be identified by the same tribal marks as mine, the three short perpendicular scars under each eye. There weren't any other women from our tribe for sale that day."

"I'm sure we'll establish who she is," responded Patrick warmly. "Is that all?"

"I was also wondering if I could have a piece of land to grow vegetables on. It looks like you used to have a patch for ground provisions, but it's all overgrown," said B.

"You're right," Patrick said, exhaling deeply. "I did, but I've been concentrating on the sugar and the horses. I don't seem to have had the time..." he drifted off, staring at all his hopes in his glass.

"That's what's been taking up your time," B stated confidently, pointing at the tumbler. Patrick looked up, felt the rebuke and knew it was justified.

"You're right again," he said, shrugging.

"I'm sorry Patrick. You are drinking too much. It must be said. No-one else is going to tell you."

"You're right, again and again. You are so honest, like my mother," murmured Patrick morosely, vaguely wondering if he should be spoken to in that way by a slave.

"Well, I'm not your mother, am I?" retorted B, beginning to feel that she was being too familiar in her position. She quickly changed back to her original subject before Patrick decided she was speaking out of turn. "Tell you what, Patrick. Why don't we have a competition, vegetable growing? Let's see who can grow the best callaloo."

Patrick let his thoughts dissipate and agreed with some enthusiasm. He slightly reduced his drinking, but still lost the first contest.

xxx

Patrick clopped his horse to Opran's plantation, the largest one on the island, with a work force to match. Simon Opran, the Big Boss, took a hard line against slaves meeting other slaves. What was in it for him? Patrick tried to persuade Opran by arguing that keeping slaves content would lessen the chance of an uprising. Opran called him soft, but Patrick persisted and offered a bottle of rum as an incentive. After

Opran had raised it to two bottles it was agreed that B could visit her relation there one Sunday afternoon. The slave that B knew as Kodou was identified by her tattoos, and now went by the name of Chloe. Patrick gave B a hand-written pass stipulating a strict timetable of travel allowance between 2pm and 5pm. It enabled her to spend just over an hour visiting and get home before her curfew. Lateness would incur an unstipulated punishment. Patrick hoped she never tested that, he wasn't the punishing kind. However, he wouldn't be a proper slave owner if he didn't imply a threat. If there were no problems, she could go every Sunday and bottles of rum would pass hands. Not being someone who deliberately caused trouble, weekly trips became habitual for B, as did Opran's toasting of Patrick's good nature, a sign of weakness in Opran's eyes. He, not being an excessive drinker, never had to buy another bottle of rum.

Feeling more motivated than he had been for a long time, Patrick started a fitness regime and restricted his alcohol intake by halving his consumption. From now on, it would only be one bottle per day. The change helped him produce a plethora of fine cane crops. Hilton congratulated him. It was a decent profit for all concerned.

"Bridget," Patrick called out one day, having counted his money for the umpteenth time, concluding with a smile on his face, "get ready to go into town. I'm going to buy you some new clothes. There's a slave ship in today. We'll take a look at that market first. It's always interesting to see who's buying what." *For you maybe*, thought B, recalling her own low feelings during her first day on Nevis. "And remember to walk behind me in public."

"Yes Massa," B said, reverting to role in a second. Patrick frowned but said nothing as he donned his straw hat and went outside.

Chapter 19 – Slave Market, Nevis

February 1663

A decent crowd had gathered in Charlestown's market square and a tremor of excitement and anticipation reverberated amongst the spectators, as the slaves were brought up in chains, from the dungeons below ground. Men were the first to show; Jomo's friends in the leading bunch. The ship's captain introduced himself and encouraged the onlookers to sample the goods. Some of his crew assisted, while the enslaved were inspected by interested parties; touched, prodded and checked. The bidding was brisk; these being strong young men, the cream of the crop. Competition amongst the plantation owners was fierce for this type. Prices of twenty-one pounds each were agreed upon in no time and off they went to their new homes and lives. Patrick was at the back of the mass, watching with B behind him. He saw Simon Opran bid a couple of times, then seem to lose interest.

As Jomo was led up the steps at the rear of the last group of men, he squinted against the piercing sun. When his vision finally adjusted, he looked across the crowd. Naked and feeling vulnerable, he was determined to stand straight and firm. His fellow captives were bought and he was left standing on his own. *Here we go*, he thought, as his mouth was forced open by the strong hands of a sailor, to allow a finger to examine his teeth. *I wonder what I'm worth*, wishing he could clamp his jaw on the invasive digit. The bidding started at fifteen pounds, which would have been a bargain. A few offers came in and the price rose to twenty-one. Then there was a pause. Just as the auctioneer was about to hammer his gavel, Opran submitted an advance of twenty-two pounds. A murmur spread around the square. Another planter cried out a higher price, immediately raised by Opran. They duelled, climaxing in Opran's winning bid of thirty. The crowd began to disperse. Most had only attended for male workers.

As Jomo was about to leave centre stage, the first group of female slaves was brought into view. He recognised Salina who was second in line. He nearly tripped over, reacting as if he'd seen a spectre; but it was Salina, looking as beautiful as the first time he had seen her. She was malnourished, frightened, but alive. Their eyes met as he was led away. B saw the look and knew immediately what it meant. An idea quickly formulated in her head.

"Excuse me, Massa," she said reverently behind Patrick. He turned round and saw a gleam in her eyes and earnestness on her face.

"Yes?" he said, peering down at her.

"I was thinking that now I'm getting older and finding things more difficult, it would be nice to train a younger slave into my role. If you bought one, I promise to help provide for her upkeep. She could share my room and I'll feed her from the produce I grow. It wouldn't cost you anything apart from the purchase, and imagine what the other planters would think of you... owning two slaves," B said, stressing the word 'two'.

Patrick weighed up the idea. "You seem to have thought this through. I wasn't thinking about buying a slave, but you've presented a good argument. Do you have one in mind?" he asked, looking back at the group of naked African women.

"I do. The second one looks like she would work hard," B replied.

Patrick looked at Salina; young, pretty, innocent. Something paternal stirred in him. He was surprised to feel consternation when an overweight, white, balding, greasy, grey-haired man of about Patrick's age, whilst inspecting the women, placed a hand on one of Salina's breasts and his other on her buttocks. His motives were obvious. Salina recoiled at the unwarranted touching and, unknown to Patrick, had jerked her head back to avoid the groper's fetid breath. *It's time to do something decent in my life*, thought Patrick when he heard the lascivious leach start the bidding at five pounds for Salina. A couple of other men declared an interest but the pervert was keen and took the price up to eight pounds. *That is not going to happen,* Patrick decided, astonished at his strength of purpose.

"Eight pounds and ten shillings," he offered. From then on it was between him and slick-head. The gavel fell in Patrick's favour on eleven pounds. Salina wondered what was in store for her as she became Patrick's property.

"What's your name?" he asked, filling out the paperwork.

"Salina," she replied quietly, almost whispering.

"Speak up girl!" he demanded.

"Salina," she repeated, clearly.

"Sally," he said, mishearing, "that's easy enough. Even I can manage that name. I'm Massa and this is Bridget. You are in her hands now. But first things first - I promised Bridget some new clothes, but you are needier than her. She's the one that encouraged me to spend all that money on you, so it's her own fault that she's going to have to go without."

Two batiste dresses, a pair of pants and shoes later, the three of them arrived home. Patrick went to check the cane and horses, whilst B introduced Salina to her responsibilities. The two formed a bond immediately, quickly building trust between each other as they spoke openly about their lives to date.

"Why did you ask Massa to buy me?" Salina enquired.

"Because I saw something in you. I knew I needed to help," B replied, enigmatically.

Salina questioned, "What did you see in me?"

"I saw that moment between you and the man ahead of you... that chemistry."

"What... who?" stressed Salina, nonplussed.

"You know exactly who," B stressed.

Salina went silent, as a shy smile appeared on her face. She looked up at B's own suggestive, amused look.

"So, what are you trying to say?" Salina asked.

"You and that man... you have a thing for each other," B responded.

"I think he likes me," nodded Salina.

"And you like him. Who is he?"

"His name is Jomo," Salina replied, "we came from Fort James together."

"I know where he is. I can get a message to him. Only if that's what you want, of course."

Salina's eyes lit up, "please! How?"

B explained that Jomo had been bought by the neighbouring plantation and that she visited a relation there every Sunday.

"You have been so kind to me," said Salina with tears in her eyes. "I will repay you one day, have no doubt about that."

Chapter 20 – Montserrat, West Indies

Winter 1663 – Spring 1665

Conor's seafaring abilities had become rather rusty and during one tack he forgot to shout the warnings, *ready about* and *lee ho*, causing the boom to bounce off Kofi's raised head. No real damage done; they all laughed. Setting course in a general north-westerly direction, the boat slid comfortably through the water, guided by a strong breeze and the light from the clear semi-circle of the moon. They had to make the first island, Saint Lucia, with her easily identifiable twin peaks before dawn. Conor had no navigational aids to help him during the daylight hours. Matlock informed him that so long as they reached Saint Lucia during the night, they could travel on by day as the island of Martinique would be visible.

"Have you heard of Montserrat?" Conor asked Matlock, as they all tucked into some of the beef jerky and water they had brought with them.

"Of course, it's another island. You've got to pass it on the way to Nevis. Why?" Conor explained what he had heard at the inn.

Matlock laughed, "You white folk. You're all at war with each other. The Spanish, the Dutch, the English, the French; you're all just greedy bastards."

"Don't count me in with that lot. I'm Irish, but that's definitely true about the English," responded Conor. "They call themselves Great Britain now. G.B... Greedy Bastards is better. So, what do I do after Martinique?"

"Head north, keeping the islands in view on your right. You'll pass Dominica, then Guadeloupe. After that, your next stop will be Montserrat. However, you will have to travel by night because it's too far away to see by day. Steer slightly more to the west and you should hit Montserrat. If you miss it, you'll bump into Nevis," explained Matlock, not bound by the technicalities of a nautical manual.

The night went peacefully. Conor was bedazzled at the beauty of the sunrise as they floated past Gros Piton and Petit Piton on the south coast of Saint Lucia. From there, they entered the waters of Martinique. Matlock kept look out, trying to pinpoint the spot where, according to his information, he could safely swim to shore, avoiding French patrols and the reefs. Suddenly, he became animated. The coastline looked deserted as had been foretold and there was a noticeable gap in the breaking waves where, due to tidal rips, the coral formed a natural channel that was safe to swim through. Quickly, Matlock and Kofi tied their bags tightly round their heads, shook hands with Conor, climbed over the side and swam off. Conor sailed on, trying to put the acute sense of loneliness and the loss of his crew, out of his mind.

Keeping to the leeward side of the islands was easy. In his mind, Conor went back to Roaring Water Bay, fighting the white horses and swirling currents in his small dinghy. This outing was tame compared to that. At night, he anchored up and managed to get a few hours' sleep. Dominica came and went with an impressive display of whale tail bashing.

"Come on Captain, let's see what we've got," he said aloud to himself, checking the provisions. There was plenty of beef and fish jerky to sustain him for another couple of days, and one cow's bladder, still full of fresh water.

According to Matlock, the island of Guadeloupe was on Conor's starboard side. It was late afternoon and Conor was waiting for the first stars to appear. The only other boats he had descried on the journey so far were a couple of canoes, manned by native Caribs fishing, as well as three large sailing ships on the horizon, heading away from him. While he bided his time, a turtle bobbed its head above water. It was a fully mature Leatherback, at least six-foot-long, with huge, glazed orbs the size of cannonballs. Conor admired the calmness of the creature as it gulped and sank into the depths. Conor decided to stop off at Montserrat, if he managed to land there, to see what jobs were available. He needed to earn some more cash. It crossed his mind that if there really was a large Irish community on Montserrat, he may even find someone he knew. If it all seemed hopeless, he would head straight to Nevis, and try to track down Patrick. *Could he really be alive?* thought Conor, shaking his head, *even after all these years?*

Darkness falls quickly in the tropics, and with no clouds to obstruct his view, as soon as Conor identified north, he set off on a west-north-westerly course under a moon, now two-thirds full. It was a special feeling being alone at night. The sensation of insignificance when surrounded by uninterrupted water and open firmaments was immense. As dawn rose, an island came into view. Gliding closer, Conor noticed the smoking summit of the Soufriere Hills volcano.

"Is this Montserrat or Nevis?" Conor asked a man sitting on a bollard on the jetty, where Conor had just moored.

"Montserrat," laughed the man. "Is that the answer you were looking for?"

Conor smiled, tired but pleased that the plan had worked so far. "Well, I was hoping it was one or the other, and not somewhere else."

"You're Irish," identified the man. "You've come to the ideal place. There are loads of us here. Where are you from?"

"Munster, originally, but today, Barbados."

"I'm from Leinster myself. Have you come from Barbados all by yourself?"

"Yes," Conor lied. After all, lying can be a form of justice.

"I've heard of it done before in small boats but I've never met anyone who actually managed it. Nothing short of miraculous. Pleased to meet you, I'm Hugh," he said, extending his hand.

"Conor," and they clasped firmly.

"I'll bet you could do with some breakfast and a drink after that trip. Fancy joining me? I've got half an hour or so," said Hugh, sociably.

"To be sure," replied Conor, swaying slightly. The land seemed to move.

"Steady on mate, looks like you've had a few drinks already," laughed Hugh.

"Only sea legs," grinned Conor, steadying himself.

The pair walked to a harbour-side tavern that was already busy serving fried fish and boiled lobster in the mid-morning sunshine.

"So, why are there so many Irish on Montserrat?" asked Conor, sampling the local spirit. *Better than that Barbados fire water*, he thought, feeling the sensation of the smooth kick in his throat, before tucking into a plate of mixed seafood.

"We've been here from day one, working as servants for the English. But the Irish population increased dramatically a few years ago, mainly due to religion," replied Hugh. "When we started to outnumber the English, Catholics felt safer to come here from other islands escaping persecution from the Protestants, the Anglicans and Baptists. Those quiet ones, the Quakers, are no problem. They know more than anyone how it feels to be harassed for your religious beliefs. Those killjoy Puritans are the worst. They're so extreme in their views. They hate us with a vengeance, even refusing to acknowledge that we're fellow Christians."

"I felt some of that on Barbados," recalled Conor. "What did they do to you?"

"Stopped us from practising mass," explained Hugh. "We weren't allowed to congregate and if we were caught holding an Agnus Dei, we'd be fined. The restrictions increased last year when they brought out the new *Book of Common Prayer*. Anyone found using different prayers would be imprisoned. We're better off here; many of the English plantation owners have left and been replaced by wealthy Irish Catholics from the merchant class. They employ indentured servants and some slaves, but most of the people you meet here have been banished in one way or another; either as a victim of Cromwell's campaign in Ireland or as an African slave. Those of us who are free mix together, friendly-like. We can do our own thing, more or less. There's less formality, if you know what I mean."

Conor reflected on how much of an impact Cromwell had made and scanned the room, noticing a few black but mostly white men eating and drinking together, talking and laughing. Freed slaves decided to stay on, or make their way to Montserrat because they had a commonality of experience with the Irish.

"It certainly feels more relaxed here," he said.

"It's relaxed at our level," Hugh expounded. "But the island is governed by the English, and there are always tensions between them and the French. A word in your ear," Hugh lowered his voice and moved closer to Conor, confidentially, "there are some Irish who join forces with the French when there's trouble. Personally, I keep out of the way."

"That sounds like good advice," said Conor. "There's no way I could fight in this heat. So, where have the Irish come from, apart from Ireland obviously?"

"All over the place. Saint Kitts, Nevis, Louisiana. I came from Antigua, myself." *From Nevis?* thought Conor. *Could Patrick be on Montserrat?*

"I've never heard of Antigua," he said, "but I know about Saint Kitts and Nevis. How far away are they?" asked Conor.

"No real distance. On an exceptionally clear day, you can see Nevis from here. Why do you ask?"

Conor explained his familial interest. "Although, Patrick would be in his mid-fifties now."

"Patrick O'Mahoney," iterated Hugh. "I've not heard of him. But,

I don't know everybody on the island. I'll ask around. Now I must be off. I hope we meet again."

"That sounds good, thanks," said Conor, shaking Hugh's hand before he left, and ambling up to the counter.

"Two more?" asked the landlord.

"Just the one," Conor ordered.

"I haven't seen you around these parts before," noticed the barkeeper, looking at Conor properly. "Are you new here?

"My first day," replied Conor.

"In that case, welcome to Plymouth, I'm Dennis." He poured out a measure of liquor and handed it to Conor. Conor introduced himself, paying and taking the glass.

"I hope you don't mind me being nosey, but what brings you this way?" Dennis enquired.

"Not at all," responded Conor. "I might just be passing through," and went on to explain some of his past including his current aim to find Patrick.

"I know lots of Patricks, and a few O'Mahoneys, but not a Patrick O'Mahoney. So, you're a West Munster man. I'm from Ulster originally. Before I left, I was told you can go to hell or Connaught. I'm not sure which is better. They sent us to grow potatoes on rock, the English pigs."

"It sounds like we share the same opinion of the English,"

laughed Conor. "What brought you here?"

"I heard about the Irish on Montserrat and thought, *'where there's Irish, there should be an inn'*. I worked my passage on a supply ship and set this place up."

"Good idea," approved Conor, sipping his rum.

"Might you be looking for work as well?" asked Dennis.

"That I might," replied Conor.

"Well," said Dennis. "This place gets quite a few people going through it and someone may have heard of your cousin. I'm looking for a general hand here. My last one left two days ago. Joined a bloody slave ship, reckoned there was more money in it. There may well be, but a whole lot more sin too. Anyway, I can offer you a job, if you're interested, food and accommodation included. Nothing fancy, mind you. I'll pay you three shillings a week and you can ask anyone about your Patrick. If he's around, someone should know."

Conor agreed, shook Dennis' hand and the deal was done. *This is more like it,* he thought, testing his comfortable enough, but somewhat hard, bed that night in a small room upstairs. *I must write to the Redlegs sleeping rough on Barbados and tell them about this place. I've got a job, a boat and a bed. Everyone should have a bed at least.* Conor settled into his new role easily; serving, bottling up, rolling casks, socialising. He became adept at barbecuing fish, a cooking technique learnt from the natives. Hopes of finding someone who knew Patrick dwindled over time. He grew tired of asking people and getting no closer to an answer. Hugh had passed by a couple of times, but he had no information. It took six months before he heard about a man called Patrick O'Mahoney, but it turned out to be a false lead. The news reported that the individual, a twenty-year-old newcomer to Montserrat had died; poisoned after naively drinking a pint of rum distilled in a lead casket.

One morning, Conor woke up with a tightening in his chest and began to pant and sweat. After a wash, he felt better. At work, however, the symptoms came on again, without any notice and then diminished quickly, leaving him dizzy. He ignored them, taking a rest on a stool. *It's probably indigestion*, he thought, *or just age. I'll be sixty next year; this old body is definitely changing.* Conor enjoyed the tasks and social life. After a year, during which he witnessed the ownership of the island change from English to French then back to English hands, he knew he was getting too comfortable and needed to refocus on his original plan; go to Nevis and try to trace Patrick. Deal with it once and for all, stop thinking about it and just do it. One morning, as Conor opened the doors to the public, he decided to inform Dennis that evening of his intention to resign and move on. Mid-afternoon, a fat, white, ageing, balding, greasy, grey-haired customer came in. Conor hadn't seen him before and without any expectation asked his usual question.

"Damn right I do," replied the man flatly, sweaty and breathy. "Patrick O'Mahoney's your cousin, you say? I haven't heard or thought of his name for a while. But I'll never forget it. I made that bastard's acquaintance a year or so ago."

"What do you mean?" asked Conor, blanching at the pong of halitosis, suddenly more alert and handily ignoring the slight on his family.

"I was over on Nevis on a business trip," the shrew-like man explained. "Before I came back, I stopped at the slave market to see if there was any worthwhile stock. One of the women aroused my interest, but that deviant O'Mahoney outbid me, the dirty swine."

"What age would you say he was?" queried Conor, furrowing his brows at the insults.

"Too old for that girl, well over fifty," the rodent replied, without an inkling of irony. *That could be him*, Conor thought, surprised to hear that Patrick was buying female slaves at his late stage in life. Conor was heartened by this information, even if he did have his doubts about the offensive informant.

"That's interesting," he said, "let me buy you a drink."

That night, Conor handed in his required two days' notice. Dennis was pleased for him, but not entirely happy to be losing a reliable member of staff.

"If it all goes wrong, you can always come back," offered Dennis.

"Thanks," said Conor, "but I think my place will have been filled. You can expect a couple of willing workers from Barbados in the next few days. Two of my friends from the Redleg community are on their way and I recommend them. I hope you can employ them."

"With a reference from you, I'll see what I can do," responded Dennis, genially. They shook hands and Conor went to check the necessities on the boat. He liked what he hoped would be the final part of his plan, celebrating his sixtieth birthday next Saturday with Patrick. *Pray God he's still alive,* he wished.

Chapter 21 – Opran Plantation, Nevis

Spring 1663 – Spring 1665

When Jomo reached the Opran Plantation, he was welcomed with another lava-hot branding; this time on his left shoulder – *S. O*, unmistakeably identifying him as the property of Simon Opran. Weary and in pain, Jomo decided to try and take an easy course for this next part of his disrupted life. *Do what they say, don't question a thing, just don't forget what they do, or what you have to do; keep the faith and survive*. A further aim was to take the opportunity, if one came his way, at trying to find his white family and pass on the seal. He was informed about his lack of rights, as if he didn't know already; shown how to build his hut; where to cook and obtain food; what to wear; and equally as important, where the communal latrine was. A heavy presence of white male guards populated the estate, many with dogs. The Cuban Bloodhounds, large and broad with short muzzles, were encouraged to be wild; trained to tear the flesh off black bodies if they came within reach. Loyal only to their handlers.

On his first evening, Jomo prayed outside his new hut. He had no idea which direction the qibla was, so he guessed, assuring himself that in these vile circumstances it would be understood if he was facing the wrong way. Kneeling and bowing in supplication to God, he recited the Salat al-Isha in perfect Arabic. There were observers.

"We've got ourselves another one of those Mohammedans... worshipping a false prophet," said a shaven-headed, thickset overseer with a vivid scar that traced from the left-hand-side of his mouth, down to his chin, making him look more sinister than he already was. He was talking to an equally bald colleague, holding a dog tightly by a leather lead and choke chain collar.

"Shall I make him stop?" the dog handler said, itching for some action.

"No, leave him, it's his first night and I don't need any aggravation at the moment. If he's at it tomorrow, be my guest."

"I thought he was one of them when I saw that thing round his neck. Have you ever seen inside one?"

"Yes. Just the once," said Glum-face. "I lambasted a runaway a couple of years ago. He died so I cut it off his neck. Very disappointing. There wasn't any money, only a piece of paper with scribbles all over it and a small stone."

"I wonder what they mean," said the canine carer.

"Supposedly some spiritual thing. Who cares? It's only hocus pocus. We all know that Jesus was the last prophet." The guards walked away; the dog followed at the heel, obedient, forever alert. Another pair of eyes had seen Jomo pray and approached him as he rose from his knees.

"Salaam alaikum."

Jomo looked round. "Alaikum salaam," he returned, looking into the whites of two eyes. They shook hands; a short, gentle clasp, as if checking that the other really exists.

"What's your name?" asked Jomo's visitor.

"Jomo, and you?"

"Ibrahim. It's good to meet you, Brother. Be careful praying in the open. They'll whip you if they catch you again. Settle yourself in over the next few days. We have Sunday off. We'll talk properly then."

Jomo started to learn the routine the next day. Not much to remember really: up before sunrise; quick breakfast of last night's leftovers; off to the sugarcane; toil; back for lunch comprising loblolly, kidney beans and potatoes; return to the fields; more exertion; clock off at sunset; wash; dinner of potatoes, plantain and occasionally meat; and then to bed, exhausted. On Sunday, after attending the obligatory Anglican church service, Jomo and Ibrahim sat a short distance away from their huts, in the shade of a gommier tree, known by the original inhabitants of Nevis as the canoe tree. Growing straight and true, the trunk was perfect for carving a stable, functional vessel. The pair were watching a small group of Carib-Indian slaves who lived in their own style of huts, round rather than square, nostalgically reminding Jomo of the dwellings in his home village, Tamana. Rope hammocks swung nearby from sturdy branches. Jomo was paying special attention because the Caribs were practising their fire making skills with an animal gut bow drill and two pieces of wood, a method Jomo had not seen before.

Ibrahim disturbed Jomo's concentration, "These Christian priests - all they do is proselytize and try to make us idolaters. They justify our slavery to show us the light, the way to salvation, so they say," he commented.

"Would it make life easier to convert to Christianity?" asked Jomo.

"I doubt it. Some say it's a way of helping you get your freedom and those are the ones that have converted, on the outside anyway. I say it's sheer oppression."

"True. This is oppressive."

"Jomo, I need to know what kind of Muslim you are," Ibrahim said urgently. "Do you mean it?"

"I believe in one God and that Mohammed was his final messenger. Why?"

"Good. I was a trainee marabout in Saint Louis, Senegal and..." Ibrahim started to explain.

“A marabout! That’s a noble occupation,” interjected Jomo, approvingly. “How did you end up here?"

“I was kidnapped and shipped to Saint Kitts three years ago by the French. Opran bought me there and brought me here. But the point is, there have been slave marabouts in these parts for years, and their time has not been wasted.”

“What do you mean?” Jomo asked.

“I will come to that. But first, and this is serious now, if you believe in Allah and Mohammed then you put faith in the Qur’an, correct?” challenged Ibrahim.

“Of course.”

“In that case, you will know that, as a Muslim, God permits us to defend ourselves if we are attacked or being oppressed. Would you say we’ve been attacked?”

“Definitely,” replied Jomo, feeling the raised scar on the side of his head.

“Would you say we’re being oppressed?” pressed Ibrahim.

“Absolutely. They’re trying to coerce us.”

“So, would you say we had grounds for an armed jihad to stand up against our oppressors?” probed the inquisitor.

Jomo deliberated, then said, “I hadn’t considered such a jihad but yes, as Muslims, we do have grounds.”

"Then we must fight back anyway we can. It is our duty unto Allah," said Ibrahim, passionately.

"How do you propose we fight?" asked Jomo, wondering what he was getting himself into.

"I don't know all the details yet but there's a plan afoot. That's what I mean when I say that the marabout's time has not been wasted. I'm continuing the work they started here. We have friends on Nevis, and other islands. The marabouts started a network called the Underground. You don't need to know too much at this stage, but I want to know if you are a friend who will join the cause."

"If it helps me get out of this situation, I'll do anything," assured Jomo. They watched a black woman walk past their huts and enter another one, two doors up from Jomo's.

"That's one of them," whispered Ibrahim, "that's one of our friends. She gets a special pass to visit her relative, Chloe, every Sunday. We can give her messages to pass on to other friends in the Underground."

"She's not from this plantation then?" asked Jomo, intrigued.

"No, the next one up the road," Ibrahim disclosed.

XXX

B recognised Jomo talking to Ibrahim as she walked past them without making eye contact and went into Chloe's hut.

"Things have changed," she announced. "Old rum-soak has bought a new, young slave girl, Salina."

"What for?" queried her cousin. "Don't tell me he's getting lustful in his old age?" They both laughed.

"No," said B. "I talked him into it for one reason only and I need your help."

B gestured to Chloe, and tugged her over to the entrance of the hut. Peeking out just slightly, B directed Chloe's gaze over to the two men sat under the tree.

"Him," continued B. "The one talking to Ibrahim. You should have seen the look between Salina and that man... Jomo, when they were at the slave market. It was pure passion.

Chloe sighed. "Talking of passion, that Ibrahim's so handsome."

B giggled. "You still after him, are you? Well, I wish you luck with that. Salina's a lovely person and I want to do something good whilst I can. Will you tell Jomo that Salina is fine and not far away?"

"Of course I will," replied Chloe.

xxx

Jomo duly received the message. His heart leapt.

"Can you send a message back?" he asked Chloe.

"Yes."

"Please tell Salina I am thinking of her. That's all."

Chloe smiled, "I can do that."

xxx

The slaves worked, rested, conversed and plotted. Messages were received and answered, some of a subversive nature, others of concern and a few of love; all full of meaning. It was yet another sizzling hot day as Jomo hacked at the cane. He was no longer the bony, thin figure that had left the slave ship. His muscles were honed and toned from the physical graft. He ate everything and anything, tasty or otherwise. Not far from Jomo, a co-worker tripped on a piece of stubble, falling awkwardly, banging his head on a stone. Mistakenly, he rubbed his temple before standing up and received a bite of leather on his cheek, expertly flicked by the scarred overseer.

"Get up, you lazy dog! Get to work!" He ordered.

The tip of the whip had opened a small gash. Instead of scrabbling to his feet, the slave checked for blood. This mistake was followed by another strike, stinging the left leg.

"Get up, I say!" The supervisor reinstructed vociferously. The man tried to rise, but too slowly. As Scarface drew back to deliver for a third time, he saw a person's profile out of the corner of his eye, rushing towards him unexpectedly. In a flash, the figure caught the casting arm and held it rigid. The whip fell limply to the ground. The overseer tried to release a knife attached to his side but Jomo was too quick and, without thinking about the consequences, punched the sadistic bully unconscious, with his other fist. *Oh no, I think I've overstepped the mark here,* thought Jomo, as he heard a dog's growling nearby.

"Whoa, boy, stop where you are or I'll let Ripper tear your throat out. He's got a taste for blood!" shouted another guard, gruffly. Jomo complied and was escorted to Opran.

"It was unjust," Jomo remonstrated in his defence.

"Unjust? Nonsense," said Opran, dismissively. "There is nothing unjust in punishing laziness. It says so in the Bible."

"He wasn't being lazy, he just tripped over," Jomo argued.

"My witnesses say otherwise. He was clearly lying down on the job. You attacked my overseer with no provocation. That must be punished... fifty lashes. Take him away."

The overseer, nursing damaged self-esteem and a sore jaw, was positively orgasmic as he carried out the punishment mercilessly, throbbing with power. Later, barely conscious, Jomo was dragged and carried to his hut by Ibrahim and Chloe. They bathed him, spread soothing Aloe Vera juice over his bloody mass of peeled skin and mopped his brow. Chloe brewed up her own concoction of boiled leaves from the Bitter-rush and Leaf of Long Life plants, a brew to reduce fever and improve energy. A home-made spirit, Mobbie, was fed to him daily.

It was rough and gasp-inducing but also invigorating, able to dull the agony. This was bush doctoring at its best. Jomo was off work for a week and a half.

"That was not a clever thing to do," admonished Ibrahim when Jomo had recovered enough to listen beyond the pain.

"I know," admitted Jomo regretfully, "I forgot myself."

"That is not the kind of jihad I had in mind. You've got to learn to ignore what you see," advised Ibrahim. "The time will come for direct action. There's a committee discussing a rebellion of slaves led by the Muslims. The uprising is to take place simultaneously on different islands. That way, the *authorities* can't get help from anywhere; they'll all be too busy defending themselves. We must be organised."

"Is it going to be soon? I can hardly fight in this state," said Jomo, resisting the urge to scratch his itchy healing back.

"I don't know but we must be ready for when we get the signal."

"What's the exact aim of the revolt?" asked Jomo.

"To kick out the white ruling classes and claim the land for ourselves. Overcome the injustice of slavery. If enough of us are in on it, we can win. We outnumber them five to one."

"Now that would be a proper jihad," acknowledged Jomo.

xxx

When B heard about Jomo's actions and punishment, she informed Salina. They talked and concocted a scheme. A couple of Sundays later, B feigned an illness.

"Patrick, I'm feeling unwell and won't be able to visit my relative today," she moaned. "Would you be kind enough to give Salina my pass so that she can let her know?"

"I would, but I'm afraid I can't," replied Patrick. "I will have to clear it with Opran first. I will speak to him this week if your sickness persists."

The women had been expecting this response. B kept acting out the symptoms of headaches, hot flushes, some of which were bona fide, and a cough. Patrick mentioned the situation to Opran who saw it as an opportunity to extract an extra bottle of rum from Patrick. It was eventually agreed that Salina could visit in B's place until B was better. The following Sunday, Patrick wrote out the pass.

"You keep resting Bridget, conserve your strength," he ordered.

"Thank you, Patrick, you have been most generous," she responded.

I do buy the best, Patrick thought, *honest, trustworthy, grateful and worth their volume in rum. I'm still buying less liquor than when I was a total drunk. Women's troubles, no doubt, at her time of life.*

xxx

Having been waved through the gate by a sleepy watchman, Salina recognised every step of the way once inside the Opran Plantation; B had described it perfectly. Jomo knew Salina might be coming that Sunday. It had all been pre-planned. When she saw the dogs with their handlers, her insides contracted. She wasn't prepared for that. Neither Patrick nor Hilton owned dogs.

Jomo was sitting down outside his place, cleaning and trying to smooth his cracked fingernails, when he saw Salina walking towards the huts. He saw a guard with a dog approach her.

Salina froze. She couldn't look at the animal. Her knees started to shake.

"Who are you?" sneered the guard, holding the dog firmly.

Salina explained and showed her pass. The guard read it slowly, making her wait, knowing that the dog was petrifying her. He looked her up and down, then gave the dog three inches of slack, which it took immediately before being choked back. Salina nearly fainted when the dog lunged, and the shock caused her bladder to leak. The guard smiled when he saw the dripping result of his actions.

"Go on then. Clean yourself up, you're filthy," he said brutally. She forced her wobbly legs to move and walked away.

Jomo had stood up, ready to act impulsively again, but relaxed when he saw Salina moving on. He sat back down before attracting attention, fuming at the guard's behaviour. Salina walked past. Their eyes met and for a second they were transported to a beautiful place. Reality returned with a jolt. Knowing they couldn't be seen together on her first visit, even with Chloe, a routine had to be established. Relying on Patrick's gullibility, B pretended to be sick each Sunday for a while with Salina always taking her place. They accepted that at some point in the future B's fake illness might become suspicious. Before that happened Salina's visits would have to end or, at best, be less frequent. Salina walked up to Chloe's hut and knocked the door, desperately resisting the desire to look back at Jomo. Chloe let her in.

Jomo wondered what was being said. With a sharp stone, he had whittled Salina a small panpipe from two pieces of locally grown bamboo. Tying the canes together with twine, he plugged the bottom ends with chips of wood. Gently blowing over the tops of the pipes, he produced two notes. Played quickly together, the whistling music sounded like the notes of the house martin's song. He had given it to Chloe to pass on to Salina. He hoped she liked it. When the time came, Salina left Chloe's hut, took out the panpipe from her pocket and blew over it as she walked past Jomo's yard. It chirped perfectly. The connection was made.

For the next few Sundays B's symptoms strangely grew worse on Saturday evenings. Patrick noticed that she improved during the week and took care of all her duties and hoped, for her sake, that the maladies were over. B was touched and amused by his open attentiveness when she started acting out her weekly ailments. The Sunday came when Salina and Jomo finally met face-to-face again. Chloe always either stood or sat between them. To an outsider it seemed perfectly normal, a group of slaves, having a social on their day off. To the insiders, it was far from ordinary. Meeting tortured Salina and Jomo as much as it pleased them. It became a routine. Sometimes Ibrahim joined them. They all talked, not of their recent pasts, but of what was happening in their shared realities of now.

"What's this white man like?" Jomo asked Salina. "The only ones I've ever met have been evil bastards."

"He's easy enough. He wouldn't hurt a fly, really. He's all bark, and even then, not very loud," replied Salina.

"Is he English?"

"No, he told me he was Irish."

"Irish?" queried Jomo, raising his voice in surprise.

"Shhh!" hushed Ibrahim.

"Sorry," said Jomo quietly. "It's just that I wasn't expecting... oh, I'll tell you in a minute. First though, what's his name?"

"Patrick O'Mahoney, why?" responded Salina.

Jomo pondered this in silence. This was the closest, as far as he knew, that he'd come to an actual Irishman. His mind started to fill with suppositions and conjectures.

"You'd better prepare yourselves," he said to them all, "you're going to find out who I really am." Jomo explained his background, including the seal still hanging round his neck. It was now protected by finely woven hemp, in place of the cowhide that had disintegrated on the ship, corroded by sweat and sea water. Whilst on board, Jomo managed to scrounge some old, tarred jute sacking and create a poor but useable substitute. This had now been replaced by clean cloth. The two slips of paper, with Islamic messages on them were long gone too, mushed to soggy pulp during the voyage. The soft, velvet pouch had survived somehow, although the seams were rotted and the plush worn thin. Jomo ended his tale by asking Salina if she would do something for him. Salina was dumbfounded and fascinated in equal parts by Jomo's story. The information sunk in slowly and she took her time to gather her thoughts about Jomo's question.

"So, you want me to ask him if he knows of a John O'Driscoll from Baltimore, Ireland? Is that correct?" she asked, slightly apprehensive at the idea.

"Yes please, nothing more, nothing less," Jomo said, honestly. "I know it's a slim chance but I don't know what else to do. He's Irish and so was my father. It's worth a try, isn't it?"

"I suppose so. I won't get into trouble, will I?" she said anxiously, biting her lip.

"Tell him I asked you to ask. If there's any difficulty, it will come back to me then."

"In that case, I will," she agreed, wanting to help Jomo in any way she could, but also somewhat relieved. "I'll be back next week."

"It won't be too soon," he said smiling. Returning a loving look, she left, memorising the question all the way home. *Can't do any harm, can it?* thought Jomo, watching Salina's back receding. *He should understand why I'm asking. I am half-Irish after all and I can prove it.*

xxx

The Muslims had their secret ways of meeting and exchanging information. Most of them were literate and handwritten coded Arabic was a sure-fire way of outmanoeuvring the authorities. If the scraps of paper, relatively secure in a gris-gris, were intercepted by suspicious officials, deciphering them was impossible. To the inevitable questions, plausible answers were offered, such as, *it's part of the Qur'an* or *it's my daily prayer*. These were accepted in a patronising way, and the duped officer would hand the 'innocent' message back to the carrier. News and ideas passed along the network from island to island. During his recruitment drive for freedom fighters, Ibrahim explained that nobody had foreseen that they would become slaves. That's what was preordained, what God had willed, but no-one knew the next part of the script. There was no reason why the plot couldn't turn in their favour.

"If we succeed, we'll be freed," he had repeated to the hopeful jihad warriors, "but if we don't try we can only blame ourselves for our plight." Ibrahim knew he could count on at least fifteen of the Muslim slaves; not the largest of armies. Most non-Muslim chattel had taken to Christianity and were being encouraged to learn how to turn the other cheek. No blame there, it was shoved down their throats, convinced that it would lead to their freedom. *You're not going to brainwash me,* thought Ibrahim. He was relying on several slaves, or hopefully even all of them, to swell the ranks when the time came. Not because of religion necessarily, but out of a desire to be free. *When will it happen?* he wondered.

XXX

It took until Thursday of that week before Salina found the time and confidence to pose Jomo's question to her master. Fortunately for Patrick, he was sitting down, enjoying a pre-dinner swig as he waited for his food, when Salina asked, "Excuse me Massa, do you know of a John O'Driscoll from Baltimore, Ireland?"

Gobsmacked and silent, after a few seconds Patrick managed to utter, "Say that again, but very slowly."

Salina was troubled when she noticed the shock on Patrick's

face. Slowly, and less confidently, she repeated the question. Patrick floundered a little, and took a sip to compose himself.

"Yes, I do know of a John O'Driscoll from Baltimore, Ireland. Now you are going to tell me exactly how you have come by that name."

Salina told him. "That's all I know," she ended, keeping it simple.

Patrick was at a loss as to what to think. He refilled his glass and knocked it back in one.

"I'd better pay a visit to this Jomo," he said in a down-to-earth manner. "Meanwhile, I abrogate your Sunday pass until I've got to the bottom of this. That goes for Bridget too. There'll be no passes for either of you." Salina was distraught as B tried to comfort her.

"If what Jomo says is true and he can prove it, all will be well," B consoled. She didn't bear to consider what would happen to them all if it wasn't and he couldn't.

With his mind still boggling with the mystifying turn of events, Patrick finished his work before sundown the next day and visited Opran's plantation. A black butler answered his knock at the door.

"Is your master at home?" enquired Patrick.

"Yes sir. It's Mr O'Mahoney, isn't it?"

"It is," smiled Patrick, enjoying being recognised and treated with respect.

"Please enter and wait in the hall. I shall inform the master," said the butler. Simon Opran greeted Patrick who explained the purpose of his visit.

"That's strange. I've had trouble with that Jomo before but he's a damn good worker," said Opran. "Let's go and find out what this is all about. They'll all be coming in from the fields now the light's beginning to fade."

Jomo had just arrived at his hut when he saw the two slave owners walking together, coming his way. He grabbed a piece of dried coconut from inside, then sat out front, chewing. The despotic overseer with dignity fully replaced was following on behind his betters, the ever-present whip tucked into his waist. Patrick and Opran approached Jomo and stood over him.

"This is Jomo," said Opran to Patrick. "Now then, boy," he barked at Jomo, "you've got some explaining to do. And you had better do it well or else you will be leathered worse than the last time." The middle management thug stared at Jomo, tapping his sjambok silently with a lopsided smirk on his face. Jomo ignored him.

"What do you want to know, Massa?" he asked.

"Go on Patrick, he's all yours," encouraged Opran.

"Do you know who I am?" questioned Patrick.

"No, Massa," although Jomo had guessed.

"I am Patrick, Sally's master."

"Are you Irish, Massa?"

"Yes. Is it true that you asked her to ask me about John O'Driscoll?"

"Yes, it is. Do you know him, Massa?"

"You tell me how you know that name, first," said Patrick.

With a sharp piece of twig, Jomo released a chip of coconut lodged in a tooth. "John O'Driscoll was my father," he said, bluntly. Patrick didn't know whether to laugh or cry. He was speechless.

"Your father?" he eventually spluttered. "Are you mad? He's my cousin. Who is this joker, Mr Opran?"

"If you've made this up boy, you're in big trouble," warned Opran. "You had better explain yourself fully, immediately." And so Jomo divulged just about everything but excluded the seal. He wasn't going to reveal that straight away. When he finished, there was a resounding silence. Patrick, staring at Jomo, took a moment to think. *Can life truly be this uncanny? Can I believe this boy? What are the chances?* The short dusk had disappeared and he could no longer see Jomo properly in the darkness, illuminated only briefly by the small cooking fires around some other huts. He needed to see him in the daylight to check for any family resemblances. *This is ridiculous*, he thought. *But what choice do I have? It's such an odd story, you couldn't have written it. If Jomo is telling the truth, then that would make him my second cousin... or second cousin once removed... or something like that.* He felt light-headed at the possibility. Patrick awoke from his trance, and looked around as he became aware of the silence. Opran seemed to have lost interest in Jomo's account and had wandered over to talk to the overseer. Patrick went up to them.

"You must have more important things to do, Mr Opran," Patrick said. "Don't waste your time here. I don't think there's going to be any trouble. Please, feel free to leave me with him."

"If you're sure," Opran shrugged. "Let me know what you decide about this matter. If it turns out to be a complete fabrication, I shall have him thrashed within an inch of his life, again. And if you've got anything about you, you should horsewhip that slave girl of yours, too."

"Yes, yes, I will, I will," said Patrick, glad to see the two depart.

Jomo was waiting to see what Patrick had to say. He'd been astounded to hear that his father was Patrick's cousin. *What a piece of luck*, he thought. *It was worth a try. I hope no harm comes from this now.* He looked over to see Chloe cooking by a fire. A young child, no more than four-years-old, was helping her by stirring a pot. He assumed that Chloe was trying to overhear as much as she could. He saw Ibrahim standing outside his hut smoking some native tobacco. Ibrahim raised a hand but it wasn't at Jomo, it was to Chloe, who waved back. Finally, Patrick returned.

“Jomo, as you can imagine, this has taken me completely by surprise. You seem to be sincere, but I’m sure you understand it's difficult to believe. I must see you properly, in daylight, to detect any family likeness to John. Otherwise how can you prove you are telling the truth?”

Jomo, realising it was all or nothing, opened his gris-gris and pulled out the seal. “This,” he said, holding it up in his hand, “is the only thing I’ve got. It’s my father’s seal.”

“John’s seal? The O’Driscoll seal?” clamoured Patrick.

“That’s what my mother told me,” replied Jomo calmly.

“Let me see it.”

“Will you let me have it back?” challenged Jomo.

“Don’t forget where you stand in this world. If I want to see it, I will and there’s nothing you can do to stop me,” Patrick retorted, glowering.

Jomo placed the seal nervously into Patrick’s open palm. Parting with the object felt like he was handing over his identity. He doubted about letting it go, but as Patrick had made it clear, there was no choice. Patrick examined the seal as well as he could in the shallow light. He saw the outline of a ship, but he wasn’t sure what he was looking for. He must have seen the seal many times in his youth, but had never taken the time, nor thought it necessary, to study it properly and no memory came leaping in to help.

"I don't know," Patrick said, shaking his head with mild exasperation. "What day is it today? Friday. You'll be in the fields all day tomorrow, so I'll come back on Sunday and see you and this in the light of day. I can make an accurate assessment then. We'll take it from there. Here." He handed the seal back and Jomo replaced it in its special space.

"There's something else," said Jomo, slowly.

"What now?" spat a stressed Patrick.

"I know that my father had an older brother," revealed Jomo.

"Oh, do you indeed? And what is his name?"

"Conor," was the reply.

Patrick was, yet again, totally startled. His mind faltered to comprehend the level of information this slave knew about his family. "I'll... I'll see you on Sunday," he stammered, shuffling off. *Incredible*, thought Patrick as he went to find Opran to inform him that he would be back on Sunday and that all visits from either of his slaves were cancelled for the time being. He walked home completely perplexed.

Chapter 22 – Charlestown, Nevis

Friday, Spring 1665

Conor moored up in the early evening at the jetty in Charlestown's harbour. The smooth crossing on a light south-westerly wind from Montserrat had been uneventful apart from yet another chest spasm. Dismissing it, Conor had focussed on the direction of the boat, keeping the singular peak of Nevis in sight all the way. The mountain slowly grew larger as he approached, cotton wool clouds, hovering around the invisible summit. He had noticed the steep, thick wooded hillsides, levelling to gentler slopes lower down, cleared for agriculture.

Conor wandered into town. The first hostelry he found was called *Vic's*. The smell of fish caught his breath as he entered, but not from cooking odours. The clientele, all white men, whose overalls reeked from old and fresh fish scales, sat drinking at tables. He went up to the counter where a smooth-skinned, thin-faced black man was serving. After ordering and receiving a large splash of rum, Conor started talking to the server. He came straight to the point.

"I'm new in town and I'm looking for a cousin of mine who I believe lives here on Nevis. His name is Patrick O'Mahoney. Have you heard of him?"

"The only Patrick I know is Hilton's man," replied the barkeep. "Hang on a minute, I'll ask. Hey! Admiral!" he called out, raising his voice above the general hum of conversation, attracting the attention of an old weather-beaten man sitting on his own at the end of the countertop. "Gentleman here asking about his cousin. What's Patrick's surname, the fellow who worked for Hilton? He used to frequent here regularly but hasn't been in for a while, you know who I mean?"

"Is it worth a drink, Vic?" replied Admiral, his shiny eyes twinkling. Vic looked at Conor who nodded.

Admiral took his cue and said, "That would be the Irish one, O'Mahoney."

"Infallible as usual. Thanks Admiral, you can go back to manning the mainsail now." Vic returned his attention to Conor. "It's just a nickname, Admiral. He's a retired sea captain and most of the time relives his past. He knows just about everybody on this island though, and he never forgets a name. I think we've found your cousin," he said.

"Can you tell me where he lives?" asked Conor, feeling a surge of excitement.

"He's got a place on Hilton's land about two miles from here, up Fig Tree way," was the reply. Vic gave a very thankful Conor the directions to Hilton's plantation. He decided to visit Patrick the next day, Saturday, his birthday. He bought Vic a couple of drinks and spent a convivial evening in the company of Admiral who regaled many "let me tell you the about the time I..." stories. Admiral couldn't believe his luck that he had found a new willing ear. At closing time, Conor bought a bottle of rum to share with Patrick, booked himself into a room and slept deeply.

Chapter 23 – Patrick's Place, Nevis

Friday evening - Saturday night, Spring 1665

On returning home from his meeting with Jomo, Patrick's mind was a cacophony of thoughts. He needed something to drink. *No I don't*, he argued with himself. *I need someone to talk to. No, actually, I need a drink and someone to talk to.* In the end he did both, opening a bottle of rum and confiding in B and Salina. After all, Salina had started this business in the first place. He tried desperately to work out how he could establish whether the seal was real or not. One possible way was to send it back home to a member of the family, get it checked out and returned. *How long would that take? Who would he send it to? What if it got lost?*

On Saturday morning, Patrick had a slow breakfast, feeling grumpy, tired of thinking. Needing time to deliberate by himself, he went into his front garden and sat in one of the chairs shaded by the breadfruit tree, staring in the general direction of the road. He eventually closed his eyes. B and Salina kept out of the way, keeping to themselves as they tended the vegetable patch. Four inches to the right and the breadfruit would have knocked Patrick out. As it hit the ground, Patrick woke from the thud, jerking back to life. It was mid-morning. He looked at the glossy emerald fruit, considered how lucky he had been, and decided to move. He picked up the chair and sat down again under the shadow of the lignum vitae tree. A fluorescent turquoise hummingbird whizzed around from flower to flower.

Blinking his eyes to refresh them, Patrick looked back along the road. There were a few people walking, some carrying cane on their backs, a child crossing, a cart rolling, pulled by an ox. One of the pedestrians was a white man, the only white person on the road, coming in his direction, ambling slowly.

XXX

"Happy birthday, Conor," he said to himself that morning, on waking up. He felt a tingling in his chest, but put it down to excitement. *Finally, hopefully, nearing the end of my quest*, he contemplated. With his bag packed, rum bottle secured inside it and full of an egg and saltfish breakfast, Conor set off along the cart-rutted road in the direction of Fig Tree. The trail turned into a steady climb, the sun blazed and Conor started puffing with effort. He took off his jacket, rolled up his sleeves and rested for a few moments, before continuing. When he reached the top where the track began to level off, he paused again to take a break and mop his brow.

XXX

Patrick was focussed on the white man, fully awake now. For a moment, he forgot all his worries. He watched as the fellow stopped and dabbed at his forehead; empathetic at how hot and tired the man must be, having forced himself up that hill many times, when his horse was lame and couldn't be ridden. Remembering all the occasions he had lost his breath on the incline, Patrick decided to fetch the stranger a drink of water. He stood up, walked over and climbed the steps, entering his shack to fill a glass from the pitcher inside. When he returned, he saw that the chap had stopped outside the entrance to his yard.

xxx

Conor inhaled sharply when he saw Patrick. *Sweet Mary, mother of Jesus, that's Patrick, by Christ! His nose has grown considerably and he's aged like me, but it's still Patrick.*

"Patrick? Patrick O'Mahoney? Is that really you?" he shouted. "It's Conor."

Patrick dropped the glass and it fell onto the soft, dusty mud; emptied but unharmed. He trembled and steadied himself on the post at the top of the steps.

"Conor?" he exclaimed, incredulously. "Conor O'Driscoll? Good Lord in heaven, I don't believe this!" The cousins came towards each other and embraced with a tight hug. They held on, one supporting the other as emotions rose and fell by degrees. Finally, they released. The pair were tearful, but elated.

"It's my sixtieth birthday today, and we're going to celebrate. Me and you, my long-lost cousin," said Conor, as his joyous feelings calmed. "I've got a little something to help us do just that," and he pulled out the rum from his bag.

"We'll need more than that," said Patrick, laughing. "I've got plenty. Come on in. This is totally insane. Bridget, Sally, come here," he called. B and Salina came running. "This is my cousin, Conor O'Driscoll. He's just blown in on the wind. He is John O'Driscoll's brother. He will be able to say whether the seal is genuine. You can both have the rest of the day off once you've prepared us a dinner; it is a day to remember. It's his birthday and we have much to catch up on."

"What's all that about John and the seal?" asked Conor, excitedly when B and Salina left.

"Oh, you're not going to believe what I've got to tell you. Let's get ourselves settled for the long haul. Be prepared for some bad news first."

Patrick dealt with John's death to begin with, introducing Jomo to the conversation and the information that John had died of a fever in Africa.

"At least he wasn't incinerated in the raid," said Conor.

They talked, drank, drank and talked and had the craic as only the Irish can. When Patrick asked about his parents, who he believed were deceased, Conor informed him that they were getting old but still alive at the time of his banishment. Considering that that was thirteen years ago, it was reasonable to presume they had died.

B and Salina made them a special meal, not out of generosity but in the hope that it would alleviate any punishment they might have to face if the future turned sour. They knew that men with full stomachs were a happier bunch.

"I hope this Conor can prove that Jomo's telling the truth," said B, mixing the marinade for the meat.

"I have complete faith in Jomo," replied Salina, as juice ran down her hands from the ripe mango she was peeling. *I have to*, she thought.

It was late afternoon when Conor and Patrick sat down to eat. Their mouths salivated at the mingling smells of goat curry, rice and peas and fried plantain. A bowl of fungi and fish stood steaming on the table next to a side dish of dasheen, a sweet potato and coconut mix. Silence reigned while their taste buds singed and sang. A fruit salad fused, waiting to cool down their palates.

"Wow," said Conor, through a mouthful of gravy soaked rice, finally slowing down his hand to mouth actions. He released a long, deep throaty belch. "Excuse me," he gurgled. "This food is delicious."

"They definitely know how to cook," agreed Patrick, unfastening his belt.

"Talking of them," said Conor, more seriously, "there's something I need to clear up. I met a character on Monserrat a few days ago who'd heard of you. He told me you were on Nevis but said some nasty things, insinuating that you were a womaniser. What gives with the two slave women?"

Patrick stopped chewing and scowled. "Who was this man?" he asked.

"Just a stranger in the place. Coincidentally, he came in on the day I'd decided to resign anyway. I asked everybody if they knew you and he was the first person who did. He said he'd come across you at the Nevis slave market some time ago and you had outbid him on who I presume is Sally."

"Was he about our age, obese, balding, greasy and grey-haired?" pursued Patrick.

"That just about sums him up, but you missed out the putrid breath," Conor replied.

"Thankfully, I never got that close to him," said Patrick. "That dirty bastard is one of the reasons I did buy Sally. He had his hands all over her when he was checking the women. You could tell what he was after. I saved her from him. Bridget put the idea in my head so that she could train a new girl to do her work as she got older. And as for Bridget, well, I just wanted a house-keeper and some company."

"That makes more sense," said Conor. "Wish I hadn't bought him a drink now. So, changing the subject, tomorrow we solve this mystery with the mysterious Jomo, eh?"

"Absobloodylutely," affirmed Patrick.

"What's the plan then? If it's not the seal, it's simple. It proves that Jomo is a sham and this Opran gent can do what he wants with him. Agreed?"

"Agreed," responded Patrick, "but I won't take any action against Sally for this. After all she's the innocent one. She knew no better. She didn't mean any harm."

"Fine, that's your decision. Now, what if by a very slim chance it's the real seal?" They both paused from eating for a moment as they thought it over.

"Then he's got to be telling the truth, hasn't he?" Conor said, revealing his thoughts as he refilled his mouth. "How else could he be in possession of it? Stolen it? He knows my name, and obviously John's, and where we come from. The seal's got a ship on it, you say, well, the original one does too. And don't forget, John was supposedly taken to Africa. Could it actually be true?"

"If it is, that would make him your nephew."

The pair eventually called it a day when Conor accidentally wasted half a bottle of rum, swaying his arm and missing when trying to fill his glass. They agreed that they had both had enough and slept where they were, on the ground, resting against the lignum vitae tree. Two hours later, they managed to crawl up the steps to the hut and inside, having been rudely disturbed by biting insects.

Chapter 24 – Opran Plantation, Nevis

Sunday, Spring 1665 – Summer 1665

Jomo sat outside his hut, whittling patterns on a piece of wood undecided what he wanted to carve while enjoying the feeling of release after the tedious Christian church service. He wasn't nervous. *I'm the only one who knows the truth*, he thought*, I've done what I can, it's now in the hands of God. Do I look like my father? Allah knows best.*

The other individuals in this scenario were anxious for different reasons. B and Salina worried about disciplinary action if it all went wrong and Patrick and Conor fretted about the consequences of Jomo's claim being true. Jomo had informed Chloe and Ibrahim of the developments. Although she wasn't involved directly, Chloe fussed because it was in her nature, she could worry for the world, a futile occupation; while Ibrahim was concerned for Chloe.

XXX

At Patrick's place, there were two hangovers.

"We've got the cure for this," groaned Patrick to a bleary-eyed Conor. "We'll have a Nevis Negus each. Then instead of riding, we'll walk. The exercise will do us good." The pick-me-up of port and lemon juice combined with sugar, cinnamon, pimento and nutmeg, cleared the haze before they set off to Opran's plantation.

xxx

When Jomo saw Patrick and another white man walk up the path to Opran's door, he was disappointed not to see Salina with them. *Why isn't Salina with Patrick, and who's that other man?* He brooded. *Is she ill or hurt? I hope she's not in trouble.*

He waited, watching them enter the Big House, whilst also noticing the way that Chloe nervously twisted a rag and walked in and out of her hut. She couldn't keep still. After a short while, Patrick and Conor emerged, and walked towards the slave camp. They arrived at Jomo's place.

"Now," said Patrick. "First, introductions. Jomo, meet Conor O'Driscoll, John O'Driscoll's brother. Now, stand up. Let's have a close look at you."

What! thought a surprised Jomo, rising to his feet. *My uncle? This gets better and better*. He blinked his eyes and then stared at Conor. Neither said anything. Jomo started feeling like a zoo animal, locked in by slavery, inspected by curiosity and also suspicion.

When Patrick first met Jomo in poor light, two days previously, he initially thought that Jomo looked like any other African man. *They all look the same, don't they?* he assumed. But today, he had a reason to scrutinise on a deeper level. There was something familiar about the face, if you considered each individual aspect. Whilst being studied in silence, Jomo decided to try and break the ice.

"My mother told me you were always fighting the English," he said, still locking his gaze on Conor, "she thought you would probably be dead."

Conor did not respond, but a sudden visible pulse on his neck revealed heightened stress. He ground his teeth. Conor's instincts informed him of Jomo's true heritage. He recognised parts of John in Jomo immediately, aside from the skin colour. The nose, the mouth, and the colour of the flecks in the eyes were all John's. Conor's sense of reasoning seemed to desert him momentarily as he thought, *this can't be, can it? But it is him, a young black John, by Christ! Isn't it?*

"What do you think, Conor?" asked Patrick.

"Let me see the seal," responded Conor agitatedly, ignoring the question.

As Jomo removed the dilapidated velvet pouch from his gris-gris and handed it to Conor, he said, "My mother also said that if you were dead, I was the heir to the chiefdom of the O'Driscoll clan. Unless you had any sons, of course. Do I have any cousins?"

Paying no heed to Jomo, Conor emptied the contents onto his hand. He knew instantaneously that the seal was authentic. He was transported back to the last time he had seen both the seal and his father. Forthrightly he felt a surge of family nostalgia and tears pricked his eyes. Batting them back, he inspected the seal closely, noting the fine carving of the ship and cormorant with *Spes Mea in Deo* whittled onto the scroll. Turning it over, he saw the two finger grooves. He placed his right thumb and index finger into the slots, imagining the grip of his grandfather. Apart from a small amount of water discolouration, there wasn't a mark on it, it had survived intact. Just then a sweeping pain crossed Conor's chest and he lost consciousness, crumbling to the ground in a heap. That put a stop to the proceedings. In the initial confusion that followed, Jomo retrieved the seal from Conor's clasp. There hadn't been time to ask about Salina. To begin with, Conor was carried to Opran's house where he was allowed to stay in a spare room. The doctor was called and forbade visitors. Conor recovered partially and within a week, was well enough to be moved to Patrick's place where B and Salina tried to nurse him back to health.

On Conor's first night back, the doctor visited and performed a blood-letting procedure which had no positive effect apart from making Conor believe he was being cured. When the physician left, Patrick approached Conor's crude, improvised bed of floor cushions, thin blankets and a worn, holey mosquito net. B and Salina went about their chores, silently.

"How are you feeling?" Patrick asked.

Conor grunted, "Felt better," he said, "but glad to be alive."

"It's just as well that you are. I still need to know what you make of Jomo and the seal."

"It's real, and so is Jomo; he's telling the truth," said Conor without hesitating. "I'd better say this before I have another attack. I might not outlive the next one. I believe he's John's son. The seal is definitely ours and his story fits. Jomo is my nephew and, after me, heir to the O'Driscoll clan."

"So, you don't have any children then?" asked Patrick.

"Not that I know of," replied Conor, trying to smile but only succeeding in a grimace. "What do you think about Jomo?"

"I agree with you," said Patrick in accord. "He's not an imposter. What are we going to do?"

"You could take him to Ireland, introduce him to the family and maybe, just maybe, when we get rid of the English, he can claim our land back."

"Why don't you?" asked Patrick.

"I'm exiled, remember? Besides which, I probably wouldn't survive the journey anyway."

"Oh yes," conceded Patrick. "This is tricky. He's a slave and owned by Opran. He isn't free to do anything."

"But he's family," Conor pointed out.

"Only we know that. We need to speak to Opran. You're in no position to do it. I'll go."

xxx

Chloe and Jomo received no visits or news for two Sundays following Conor's collapse. On the third, they saw Patrick riding his horse, heading towards Opran's door. When Jomo saw that Salina was walking behind, he felt an immediate fluttering of excitement and comfort in his stomach.

"You go and visit your friends, Sally," said Patrick, tethering his mare, "I've got some business with Opran."

Now that Jomo's story had been confirmed, Patrick had allowed visits to recommence. Salina had taken B's place again, with B shamming her usual syndromes. She almost ran to Chloe's hut. *Calm down*, she thought, *decorum first*. As a pair, Salina and Chloe visited Jomo.

Salina told him about her ban and then said excitedly, "you're who you say you are, Jomo. They believe you. B and I overheard them."

"Thanks be to Allah," said Jomo, relieved. *Now what?* He thought, *I've found my father's family but now what?*

xxx

"I don't care if he is allegedly part of your family or if he is the great grandson of an Irish chief. Or even if he's related to an Arabian or African one for that matter. None of them count for much anyway," Opran announced forcefully. "He's *my* slave. If you want him you'll have to pay."

"How much?" asked Patrick.

"He's expensive, even more now you say he's royalty. A prize specimen, and I don't want to sell him. To you, one hundred and fifty pounds."

"A hundred and fifty pounds? That's extortionate!" complained Patrick, knowing that the sum was way beyond his means.

"Like I said, he's expensive."

"Are you open to a touch of chaffering?" enquired Patrick, hopefully.

"No. You have nothing to offer me and rum is certainly not a substitute for my property," Opran replied emphatically.

There was little else Patrick could do but leave.

XXX

Patrick ambled along the path to Jomo's hut, very downcast, and joined the three slaves. It was the first time he had met Chloe, who, before politely leaving them to discuss the situation, respectfully asked how B was coping.

“I’m sure she’ll recover soon enough,” Patrick told her, “but,” sighing and looking at Jomo, “she’s the least of my problems at the moment.”

“How’s my uncle?” Jomo asked, acutely aware that Patrick was distressed.

Patrick tried a smile, “you’ve heard, have you?” looking at Salina. “Walls have ears, eh? Listen, Jomo. He’s not brilliant, but welcome to the family. I’m afraid I can’t hug you, we’d both get into trouble, but Conor and I believe you.”

“So, where does that leave all this?” enquired Jomo.

“I don’t know,” Patrick replied, as he informed him of his conversation with Opran. As Patrick talked, Salina gazed at Jomo, who stared back, barely listening.

“Is there something going on between you two?” said Patrick, suddenly feeling that he was talking to himself. Both quickly averted their eyes, but it was too late. Even Patrick wasn't that naive. They’d been lost in the occasion.

“Oh dear,” said Patrick heavily, “that just makes things more complicated.” Now that he was family, Jomo felt confident to confide in Patrick his feelings for Salina.

“We’ll work something out,” Patrick said, feeling tired and worn out. “I don’t know what that is yet, but we will. Come on Sally, time for us to get back. I've got a lot more thinking to do."

As he started to leave with Salina, Jomo called, "one more thing!"

"More, oh no!" moaned Patrick, turning back.

"I just think you ought to know, I'm a Muslim and my father reverted to Islam in Algiers."

"What? Oh! Um... I don't know what to say," flustered Patrick. "I'm not sure if that's a good thing or not. Wasn't it Muslims who took John from Baltimore?"

"In name only, not heart and mind," replied Jomo.

Patrick and Salina were accosted by Opran before they left his land.

"I'll tell you what I'll do," he said to Patrick. "Contrary to popular belief, I'm not completely heartless. I'll give Jomo a pass for a Sunday once a fortnight starting next week, on condition that he does extra work on the other Sundays. He can leave after church but must be back well before sundown. So now you can have lovely family meals together," he added scornfully.

This made things a little easier. Jomo was prepared to give up a day off if it meant spending time with Salina. B recovered miraculously from her weekly ailments and started visiting Chloe again while Salina, Patrick and Conor, who was still bed-ridden, entertained Jomo, every other Sunday. On his first visit, Jomo noticed a stringed instrument leaning up against the wall in a corner of the room. He was intrigued.

"What's that?" he asked Patrick, pointing to the implement.

"A guitar. Have you ever seen one before?"

"No, but it looks similar to an oud."

"A what?" enquired Patrick.

"An oud," Jomo repeated. "It's an instrument that I played back home. Can I hold it?"

"Certainly," said Patrick. "I bought it years ago, intending to learn to play but never did. Help yourself but it's out of tune."

Jomo picked up the guitar and strummed. Two of the strings were very loose, one was too taut but the others sounded reasonable. Jomo nestled it in his arms. Twisting the pegs at the top of the guitar's neck he picked the strings, tuning them to D, G, A, D, G, C, by ear, the note sequence of an oud. Finger picking the open chord, he then moved his left hand up and down the fret board, changing keys as he went. In no time, he was playing a melody that seemed to enter the soul; real, raw and to the point. He had composed it in one of those doleful moments during his passage on the boat. Patrick was moved, Salina fell deeper in love and the music seemed to lift Conor momentarily.

Four weeks later, Conor relapsed. He had never recovered properly from his collapse. The doctor shook his head as he checked him over.

"There's nothing more I can do," he said, "I've tried everything there is to try."

Conor hung in there. He was still hanging in there, just, when it was Jomo's Sunday to visit. The three family members talked. Salina listened courteously, realising Conor's end was close. She had seen enough people in the final throes of death on the slave ship. Conor was fixated on getting Jomo to Ireland with the seal. He became very flustered.

"You've got to go to Ireland and petition our land back," Conor rasped hoarsely, "you're our last chance. Take my boat, do anything, but get there and claim the land back," he repeated over and over, his anxiety increasing.

"All right Uncle, I'll do my best," said Jomo, more to pacify Conor than with any meaning, "calm down, Uncle." Conor nodded feebly, grew tired and fell asleep. His body became weaker, his breathing shallower, until finally, death overcame. The last gap in the cholesterol congested coronary artery was sealed and the heart stopped. Conor was dead. There was no consecrated ground for Catholics, but the Synagogue was more broadminded than the Anglicans, so Conor was buried in the Jewish cemetery. After a religious political row with the Capuchin administration, the Society of Jesus had won the contract to nourish the

Catholic souls on Saint Kitts and Nevis. Consequently, the funeral was undertaken by Father James Stretch, a Jesuit priest, who had been administering to the spiritual needs of the thinning Irish population on Nevis.

When Conor died, so did the chances of him finding out that he had actually sired a son with a farmer's wife, one of his numerous trysts. Conor, during the aftermath of the Eiri Amach of 1641, and needing a place to lie low from the English, had asked a distant cousin, the farmer Flourence Driscoll, who lived in the depths of the Munster countryside, to provide a safe house. Flourence, who desperately dropped the 'O' from his surname to appear less Irish and so please the English, had been allowed to keep some land. Giving Conor carte blanche, including access to a newly installed illicit poteen still, Conor took more. Only his lover, Catherine Driscoll, knew the truth. She decided not to tell Conor. He was a flight of fantasy but much too unstable to consider as a long-term replacement for her husband, who she loved deeply. Often bored and feeling isolated she had allowed herself a moment of pure outrageous sensuousness, a one-off passionate event, fully committed to it with no regrets. The boy, christened Donal, was brought up as the farmer's son. Neither the child, nor anybody else for that matter, after Catherine died, knew that he was the illegitimate, biological heir to the O'Driscoll dynasty, except for the priest, known for his meticulous keeping of records and loquaciousness, to whom she confessed whilst he administered her last rites.

Chapter 25 – A Plan

Summer 1665

Life's routine continued as usual, except for the alternate Sundays which now became a time for Jomo and Salina to develop a loving, trusting, honest relationship. There was no place for mind games in their situation; it had to be the truth or nothing. Patrick let Salina and Jomo get on with it.

"There's something you need to know, Salina," said Jomo slowly, summoning up the courage to say what was on his mind.

"And what's that, my love?" she replied, gaily.

"You know Ibrahim?"

"Yes, of course."

Jomo exhaled. "He's planning a revolt," revealed Jomo reticently, struggling to look at Salina directly. "He wants all the slaves to rise against their masters, kill them or kick them off the land so we can take it over."

"Is that what you want to do?" she asked pointedly.

Jomo looked away. "Yes," he responded reluctantly, "and no," looking back. "Opran, yes, but Patrick, no."

"Have you agreed to join in?" she questioned, needing to

understand the full picture, conscious that Jomo was having difficulty opening up.

"Yes," he admitted softly.

"When's this going to happen?" Salina demanded firmly.

Jomo shrugged, "I don't know. He's been talking about it for ages. It's very hard to arrange. At some point soon, is all he says."

Salina lingered, trying to work out how she felt. Finally she said, "I shall lose you if you do that. I won't join in. What are you going to fight with anyway? Knives and clubs against the English guns and their ships' cannon? You'll never win, or even survive. It's suicide."

"You speak the truth," Jomo agreed, nodding his head, looking at her confidently again, "it does seem a desperate idea when you put it like that. But something must change. I don't want to live like this. I want to be free, so we can be together."

"How can we do that?" she asked.

Checking they weren't being overheard, Jomo whispered, "We could escape."

Salina's response was equally softly spoken. "How?"

Jomo pondered. "I'm not sure. Have you ever heard of the Maroons?"

"No, who are they?"

"Ibrahim was telling me that on some islands, slaves have fled into the mountains where they live off the land or raid the plantations," he explained. "Sometimes they are hunted down, but a few hold out against the odds. They're as free as they can be."

"Let's become Maroons then. There's a big mountain just there," Salina said, pointing at Nevis Peak.

Jomo raised his eyes. "It's a possibility," he acknowledged.

Over the next few fortnights, they discussed the pros and cons of escape. A plan developed. It was now a waiting game until an unforeseeable set of circumstances arose. They knew where to go, how to get there and what to take. They decided against leaving on one of their Sundays as the alarm would be raised as soon as Jomo didn't return at the allotted hour, restricting the amount of time they'd have to flee and find somewhere to hide. That was the obvious choice, but much too dangerous. They wanted to feel that they at least had a chance to succeed. It would have to be a situation that afforded them some breathing space. All they could do was prepare themselves for when and whatever that might be.

"Who can we tell?" asked Salina.

"We'll have to let Patrick know," answered Jomo thoughtfully. "He's family and I must inform Ibrahim. I suppose we should share the idea with B and Chloe as well. We can only trust that few."

They did. Patrick said he'd like to help but once they had

vanished he would have to report Salina missing, presumed escaped. There would be a bounty on their heads. They knew the risks. Ibrahim was disappointed but understood. B and Chloe were excited for them.

"How are you going to stay alive? You can't live on love," said B, forever practical.

"I know all the fruits, roots and herbs on this island now," replied Salina. "And we can catch animals and birds. We'll have to be careful with fires, maybe only have them when there's cloud about which is, luckily, most of the time. There's bound to be a mountain spring up there and plenty of material to build a shelter."

"You've got it all worked out, haven't you? I'm rather envious," said B intrigued.

"Come with us," suggested Salina.

"No, I'm too old now. I'd never make it even half way up. Besides, someone needs to look after Patrick. Although he's my master, I run the roost. I'm comfortable here and he needs me. I think all that's happened in the last few months has taken its toll on him."

Chapter 26 – Escape

Autumn 1666

A year passed by and no opportunities to escape arose. Neither slave had freedom of movement and Opran's maximum security measures were effective, day and night.

xxx

A Caribbean hurricane season rhyme: -

June, too soon (first month),
July, standby (for news of a storm),
August, you must (prepare),
September, remember (to standby),
October, all over (last month).

On a September Monday, ship's captains noticed white clouds building on the horizon.

On Tuesday, the clouds had turned grey, with a wide base.

On Wednesday, the horizon was invisible.

On Thursday, the winds increased, strong enough to bend the tops of the coconut trees.

On Friday, the rain started. Saint Kitts, only two miles away was out of sight, darkness triumphed and the coconut fronds were at right angles. On Saturday, the hurricane hit Nevis with full force.

xxx

Jomo knew this was the time to put the plan into action. Nature had provided an opportunity. Had God had a hand in it? *It is written*, he thought, as he picked up the bag he had already packed in preparation for this moment, everything light and useful. Dropping in a mug, plate, knife, fork and spoon, his daily articles, he walked out of his hut, both straining to stay upright in the storm. There was only one more thing he needed to get, well two, actually: machetes. He dashed to the store-shed where they were handed in, secured and guarded each evening. There was nobody around to challenge him; no guards were on duty, everyone was concentrating on protecting themselves from the weather. The screws in the padlocked latch had come loose in the wind and it took Jomo little effort to force the door open. He quickly grabbed two machetes, hid them in his bag, and ran.

The wind was harsh, the rain sharp. Lightening flared and fizzed as thunder rolled and clapped. Huts were torn apart, people panicked, not knowing what to do or where to go. Some folk just lay flat on the ground and crawled towards cover. Dogs howled and horses bolted. A tree cracked and fell, then another. All the boats in the harbour were smashed, driftwood forever. Coconut palms were bent double. When Jomo left the plantation, he thought nobody had seen him in the chaos. As fast as he could he raced to Patrick's place, hollering for Salina once he arrived. B came running out instead.

"Oh, it's so terrible, so terrible!" she cried.

"Yes, it's not very pleasant, is it?" said Jomo.

"No, no, not the weather, you fool, it's Patrick, he's been killed."

"What? Where? How?" shouted Jomo, the wind taking his breath away.

"He was out the back, calming the horses. They were so scared. One of them kicked him straight in the head. He's gone."

Jomo's first thought was, *I wonder if that makes Salina free now*. Then he remembered that Patrick was family, a Christian and a believer of the Gospel, up to a point anyway. "We must bury him according to his religion," he spoke decisively. "Where's Salina?"

"Sheltering inside. Why are you here? It's not Sunday."

"It's a perfect time to escape. It's bedlam out there. I need to speak to Salina." He went inside, the window shutters rattling noisily as the foundations shook from buffets of wind. He found her sitting on the bed she shared with B.

"Salina, it's our time. Come on, we must leave, this is it," he encouraged.

She nodded, set a determined face and picked up a bag. "I knew," she said, "I'm ready." B came in dishevelled and drenched.

"You two make off now and good luck," she urged.

"Come with us," Salina suggested again.

"No, I'll stay here and bury Patrick and see what happens. You guys go, go on, go. Visit sometime," B shouted above the gale.

"We can't go until we've helped to bury Patrick," bellowed Jomo.

"Of course, you can," argued B. "Patrick won't mind, he's dead. You're putting yourselves at risk if you delay any further."

Jomo conceded to B's logic and turned to leave. As he did, he spotted the guitar in the corner of the room. He leapt over and grabbed it. They both hugged B and set off uphill. The trek was an effort in good weather, but it was a huge endeavour in a hurricane. The runaways covered the cultivated land as quickly as possible, avoiding flying debris. It was a deluge. The rain stung where it could, the wind barged them, flash flooded streams criss-crossed the fields and ghauts raged with torrents. Tripping, slipping and hand gripping the pair made it to the tree line. They rested at the edge and looked back, sodden. The scene was one of mayhem and devastation. Roofs and sides of huts swirled around, shouts and screams echoed in the wind. There was a fire in the town, the wind tried to spread it, the rain failed to quench it. They had passed no-one.

"How are you coping?" asked Jomo, when his puffing slowed down.

"Don't worry about me, Mister, I'm just fine. You look after yourself," Salina replied, smiling, taking deep breaths; drops of rain mixed with perspiration dripping from her mouth.

"That's the spirit. Let's battle on," said Jomo, turning into the forest.

Salina followed. It was darker and quieter, but the trees still shook violently and shed their rain in thick heavy drops. On they went; up, up, up, swinging their machetes to hack at the vine-twined undergrowth, forever moving forwards and away. They had broken the back of the climb when they entered an area of low cloud. Visibility was further reduced and the woods were transformed into a misty murk. They paused to catch their breath again; sheltering as well as they could under a small grove of banana trees. Their sweat grew rapidly colder.

"What's the plan, Jomo? We're here now. Where do we stop?" said Salina looking around.

"Let's get to the top first," he replied, "then we'll have an idea of how far things are. But keep an eye out for something... maybe a fallen tree that we can build around, for a shelter." They looked at each other.

"I hope this will be the most unattractive that you ever see me," Salina said.

"You're beautiful to me," he responded. "The wet look suits you. Come here." They hugged and kissed.

"This is how freedom feels," he said, "exciting, eh?"

"Never mind exciting, you lovely man, let's find somewhere to get out of the rain. I'm freezing."

"You had better explain exactly who and why you are here, forthwith," said a deep, strong voice. Turning their heads in unison, Jomo and Salina saw a young black man standing within four feet of them, having just emerged from behind a tree. He was pointing a bow and arrow directly at Jomo's chest. Jomo covered his breast with his hand involuntarily, while Salina grasped his arm in fear.

"Please don't shoot! We mean no harm. We're escaped slaves," pleaded Jomo, feeling tense.

"Excellent," said the armed man disarming his bow, "two more."

"Two more?" queried Jomo, relaxing a little.

"My sister and I ran away four months ago and we've been here ever since. Come, let's get out of this rain. My name's Marcus."

"I'm Jomo."

"And I'm Salina," Salina said, not quite sure what to make of

Marcus.

They followed him uphill for another few minutes, a foggy trudge. Marcus was a few yards in front of them when he suddenly squeezed in between two closely growing trees. Vegetation closed behind him. Neither Jomo nor Salina were fully concentrating and although they came to the two trees, they still weren't sure in which direction Marcus had gone.

"He definitely came up to these trees, didn't he?" asked Jomo, looking around.

"I think so, but where is he now? There's no path or sign of him."

Marcus's face unexpectedly appeared through the foliage. "Boo!" he laughed. They jumped and looked puzzled. "Come on, through here. You're in for a big surprise." And his head disappeared again.

"After you," said Jomo.

At first Salina pushed her hand through the greenery tentatively. She felt a definite change in atmosphere, warmer and drier. Withdrawing her hand, she adjusted her dress and put one foot through slowly, feeling for the ground. She moved forwards but then her buttocks became stuck between the trees. She glanced back, a little embarrassed.

"Would you?" she giggled, motioning to Jomo.

"Yes, ma'am, anytime," he replied, pushing her gently, easing her through the gap. He followed. They had entered a fissure in the old volcanic rock, a cave of sorts. No light showed through the entrance where they had come through but further inside they could see a slight glimmer. Marcus gave them a moment for their eyes to acclimatise.

"Follow me," he said. "It's quite narrow to start with but it gets much wider. Mind your heads for the first few yards." Moving towards the light, keeping their hands in contact with the grey rock wall, the trio stayed bent down low. Occasionally they heard the hurricane but they were out of the wind and rain. The temperature was pleasantly temperate.

"This is bloody fantastic," said Jomo, having difficulty restraining his joy. "Whoever would have thought that this place existed?"

"At least it's dry, that's the most important thing," replied Salina.

The cave widened where the faint light rested. The illumination came from a hole in the roof some forty feet above. A few drops of rain fell through, thumping softly onto sandy ground.

"It's dark today because of the storm," explained Marcus, "but when the sun's out, this place really brightens up. Not much rain gets through. This is the worst it's been." He kicked at the damp patch. "The mountain sides are really steep up there, I've been. The rain just slides away. Leila? Where are you?" he called.

A girl, maybe eleven or twelve-years-old, timidly emerged from out of the shadows. Her light brown skin matched the colour of her long straight hair, tied in an unkempt plait. She didn't say anything.

"Leila, don't be shy. These two have come to join us. They've escaped, just like we did. She's slightly... how shall I put it... different. She can't talk, but she makes sounds. Once you get used to them, you know what she's saying. She understands everything though."

"It's nice to meet you Leila, I'm Salina and this is Jomo," said Salina, smiling, "we're not here to hurt you, we just want to help, and we need a little help too." Leila looked at Salina and broke into a wide smile.

"Huzzah!" interjected Marcus, "I haven't seen her smile like that for months." Marcus explained that they found the cavern by chance when Leila had followed a rat through the vegetation at the entrance.

"So, you're the hero," Salina said to Leila, who made a parrot-like squawking sound and unasked, approached Salina and held her hand. Salina melted.

"That's her happy expression," explained Marcus, "I think she's taken to you."

"Do you have fires here?" asked Jomo, looking around for any signs.

"We can't make it. I never learnt how to rub sticks properly. All I ever managed to do was get blisters on my hands," replied Marcus.

"Well, I can help you there. I've been making fire by rubbing sticks since I was about five-years-old, but I've learnt a new technique off the Caribs. They call it a bow drill. It's much gentler on your hands. I bought one with me and I can teach you how to use it."

"Brilliant," said Marcus, "that's a real godsend."

Jomo noticed a pile of dry sticks. "What are they for?"

"Traps. I've tried to build some to catch birds and animals but I haven't been very successful."

"How have you survived?" asked Jomo.

"On fruit mainly, a lot of coconuts and berries, and we catch the odd rat and bird... but we have to eat them raw. I shot a monkey once. When things are really bad, I sneak down at night and steal stuff."

"What about water?" Jomo enquired, ticking off a mental list of basic needs.

"Local spring. It's sweet," replied Marcus, "here, try some." He went to a dark part of the cave and brought back a half coconut shell full of water. Jomo sipped some, then handed it to Salina who nodded her approval after swallowing a mouthful.

"Delicious," agreed Jomo. "Has anybody come looking for you?"

"Yes," answered Marcus. "At least, I assume so, because not long after we escaped we heard some men with dogs in the area, but they never came to this exact spot. We've been careful covering our tracks and relieving ourselves some distance away."

"How many times have you heard them?" queried Jomo.

"Twice, but nothing for weeks now."

"Well, someone will come looking for us soon I imagine," said Jomo grimly. "We must make sure we don't leave any scent. What's the most pungent smelling plant you know of, Salina?"

Salina had relaxed. There was no threat here, only a young man with a vulnerable girl, trying their luck. *They are brave*, she thought putting her arm round Leila. "That would be the poon tree," she replied, "I saw one on the way in."

"That's great, here's the plan," said Jomo, feeling decisive, "we can have a fire and dry our stuff, there's plenty of cloud today to hide the smoke. Once that's lit, I'll go and collect some of this poon stuff to put by the entrance."

"While you organise that, I'll share out the food I bought," said Salina.

"I'm afraid you'll have to sleep on the ground for a while, my dear," Jomo said. "As soon as it's dry outside I'll build a room for us with a mattress of palm leaves, and cover it in moss. There's easily enough space for some privacy."

"Can't wait," Salina smiled.

“In fact,” said Jomo, taking in the full expanse of spaciousness in the cave for the first time, “it’s almost big enough to get lost in here.”

That night Salina and Jomo heard Marcus' epic tale. He was named after his father who, before Marcus was born, was sold from the Nevis plantation they were the property of, to a slave ship bound for Virginia. The boss’s tame slave had overheard a plot to murder the owner, became an informer and implicated Marcus’s father. Marcus's mother had died from puerperal fever when he was five, two weeks after giving birth to the speechless Leila. Nobody came forth to claim paternity but Leila’s light skin told its own story. Marcus didn't have the opportunity to ask his mother about Leila's father. Both children, the future cohort of plantation labourers, were adopted by his mother's childless best friend. Marcus was taught to look after his sister, which was easy for him because he loved her dearly. He became her voice in many ways. When she was about ten, Marcus noticed a white overseer taking an unnatural interest in her. That went too far one day when Marcus witnessed the man force Leila to fellate him. He had run and told his substitute mother but she didn't believe him, or didn’t want to, and told him not to talk in that manner again or they would all be in trouble. That was the way it was, she said and he was powerless to do anything about it. From that moment on, Marcus decided to protect Leila, and formed a plan to escape with her. He chose an occasion between the evening meal and bedtime, figuring out a route off the plantation by following the ravine of a deep ghaut, which led up the mountain. They had managed to get away. The tragic account upset Salina, who praised Marcus for his bravery and good deed.

"We'll help you protect and care for her," she told him, hugging them both.

Marcus was pleased to be able to share the responsibility he had taken on with Leila. There was a growing feeling of safety, of being far from everything, but they all knew they had to be on their guard.

The next day, Jomo was first up and out to micturate. He cautiously peered through the plant life at the entrance. The rain had lessened and the wind had dropped. A couple of ground doves nodded and picked at edibles amongst the damp leaves, and a squirrel nibbled a nut nearby, undisturbed. *This place is as perfect as it could be*, thought Jomo, stepping out, causing the squirrel to bolt. He walked a few yards before choosing one of the many trees to hide behind, and urinated. *I've got no view*, he thought, eyeing the dense foliage, *I'll go up to the top later*. Salina managed to squeeze herself out into the open, and squatted behind another tree. Jomo waited.

"How are you doing this fine day?" he asked when she returned.

"So far, so good," she replied.

"Are you happy to take this one day at a time?"

"As long as you are," she answered. They kissed. Jomo bent down on one knee, looking up at the woman he loved.

"I know we can't get married officially but... will you marry me?" he asked. "In my heart, I feel married to you already."

As Salina nodded, smiling, about to reply, they heard another voice; deep and male, and it wasn't Marcus'. Jomo stood up and quickly ushered Salina through the gap in the trees, then followed immediately after, glancing back. Nothing to report. Inside, adrenaline pumping and hearts pounding, they tried to control their breathing. They heard footsteps, feet crushing wet detritus, twigs snapping, then that voice again, "They must be here somewhere."

Jomo and Salina looked at each other, mirroring the same perplexed furrowed brow. They both thought they recognised the intonation. "Ibrahim?" mouthed Salina. Jomo nodded and slightly prized open some of the vegetation, enough for one eye. He saw the back of a black man facing a black woman. "Chloe!" he breathed. He opened the greenery further.

"Caught you!" growled Jomo. Startled at first, Ibrahim and Chloe looked scared but then laughed with glee. Salina followed Jomo outside, getting used to holding her breath and moulding her body through the gap. They all embraced. As they went to enter the cave, Jomo held Ibrahim back.

"It's best to let the women go first," he said. "You'll see why," as he invited Salina to lead the way, rubbing his hands in preparation, hoping to push her buttocks through the final hurdle, but disappointed when she showed her self-reliance. Like Salina's first time, Chloe became wedged at the entrance much to Ibrahim's delight. Inside, introductions were made. Leila was content; feeling included, safer and part of a growing family. Stories were shared; Ibrahim's being the most dramatic.

"When the hurricane was doing its worst, I saw you leave, Jomo," Ibrahim regaled. "I went and took a machete as well. As you know, it was pandemonium; people were hysterical, running around like headless hens. I decided that my time for revenge had come. I set out to find Opran and Slash-head. It was easy, nobody was guarding anything, everyone was just looking for shelter; the dogs had been locked up and, boy, did they yowl. I saw my targets hiding from the storm, talking at the rear of the sugar mill, just the two of them. I came up behind them and yelled. When they turned, I was the last person they saw. As soon as I knew they'd seen me, I swung the machete, and slit both their throats in one swipe. Very neat, I thought. Then I ran, found Chloe and we just made off. We guessed you'd done the same and seeing as we knew your plans, we hiked it up here."

"You took your time," said Jomo, grinning.

"We found a place to rest when darkness fell, a little further down. A tree had fallen and the branches had created a natural shelter, of sorts anyway. We were cold but it was drier to some extent, nothing compared to this though. We stayed till daybreak then carried on up. Thanks be to Allah for finding you."

The next night, the hurricane left the island completely to wreak havoc over on Puerto Rico. The death toll amounted to nineteen people, including Patrick, Opran and his foreman, eleven cattle, and four horses. Nobody counted the goats, pigs and chickens. Every wooden structure was flattened, fire had damaged half of Charlestown and only the stone-walls of the Big Houses and sugar mills remained standing on the plantations. A programme of rebuilding was quickly put into place and within a few months, things were pretty much back to normal. Huts were re-erected, wrecked crops replanted, materials and provisions replenished from unaffected islands and tensions continued between European powers. Replacement English naval ships arrived to safeguard and defend their interests on Nevis.

The day after the whirlwind, a pirate ship from Tortuga entered Charlestown harbour unchallenged. Fort Charles, which protected the entrance to Charlestown, had been abandoned. All the soldiers were away, following orders to help the white profiteers around the island, wrongly assuming that any visitation from the sea would be intending to help rather than attack. The captain of the brigantine and his band of colourful characters had been buccaneering in the region, tracking the storm from a relatively safe distance waiting for the landfall, knowing that there were easy pickings in a place devastated by the violent weather. Nudging floating wreckage aside, the vessel came to rest at a suitable anchorage. The pirates rowed to shore, armed with flintlock pistols and cutlasses which turned out to be unnecessary. They found just what they were looking for; a local population in a state of complete disarray, trying to come to terms with the natural disaster without the will to resist and, just as important, many undefended casks of rum. Having loaded their booty without a fight, they slipped away, with a smattering of extra shipmates.

A few days later, when Nevis Peak was devoid of cloud, Jomo and Ibrahim sat on the treeless summit watching ships coming and going, providing new supplies for the battered island.

"Now that our situation has completely changed, what happens about the slave revolt, the jihad?" queried Jomo.

"I'm finished with all that for the time being," replied Ibrahim. "I'll have to let B know that I can't be part of the Underground for the foreseeable future, and she can pass that on. I'll still fight though, if a plan gets properly put together."

"Do you think you have completed your jihad by killing Opran and that lunatic of an overseer?"

"No, that wasn't anything to do with religion; it was an expression of anger. Pure revenge for all the injustices they've meted out. A proper jihad would have to be bigger than that. It would mean taking on the institution of slavery. I know it probably wasn't the best way to go about it, but I'm pleased to have played a small part in showing my hatred of the system."

"I've been thinking a lot about religion, recently," confided Jomo. "As you can tell, I no longer do my prayers."

"Me too," admitted Ibrahim.

"The future now is all about staying alive, making sure we have enough basics to survive. Fasting during Ramadan would probably kill us. Anyway, how are we ever going to find out when Ramadan starts? God knows what my intentions are and I believe he will understand the decision I've made."

"What's that then?" asked Ibrahim.

"I'm going to stop feeling guilty about not being as pious as I was," Jomo replied. "We are living in extreme circumstances and I'm devoting my life to survival. But I still believe."

"I think that's permissible in this situation," said the ex-trainee marabout. "Islam makes allowances for difficult conditions and you can definitely describe our current existence as that. I've had similar thoughts. Let's allow ourselves freedom of expression. God can see that our motives are pure. Right now, I've got things on my mind that don't include piety."

"Are you thinking about Chloe?" asked Jomo.

"Mmm, I have a certain concupiscence," declared Ibrahim wistfully.

Two weeks after the storm, the group of hideaways were discussing ways of how to run their new home efficiently. Chloe was on watch when suddenly she heard dogs, growling and snarling, and then a man's shout. She swiftly slipped back through the gap and threw out some obnoxiously smelling poon-tree flowers and leaves onto where she had just been standing. Placing a wooden frame, covered in the same malodorous plant, against the inside of the entrance, she then ran to the others.

"I've heard dogs," she whispered. Leila whimpered and snuggled up to Salina. Everyone held their breath as their senses stretched, becoming fearfully expectant in the sudden suspense. Chloe tiptoed back to her position and strained her ears. People and dogs were directly outside; she heard a heavy sniffing and then a tinkling of water. *Dog's having a damn piss,* she realised, *cheeky mongrel*. But that was all. They weren't discovered.

Chapter 27 – Nevis Peak

Winter 1666 and onwards

After the downpour, B found herself with two pressing problems; the disposing of Patrick's body and the securing of her own accommodation, the hurricane having levelled Patrick's hut. Using her initiative, now that she didn't have to consider the wishes of a master, she decided to visit the rabbi. Her movement went undetected, everyone was dealing with their own traumas as opposed to policing wandering slaves. The rabbin quickly agreed to arrange the removal of Patrick's corpse and the digging of a grave next to Conor's remains. With help from some of Hilton's slaves, the second issue was settled by rebuilding Patrick's shack to a much better standard.

The escapees visited B occasionally, under the cover of darkness; separately to begin with, then sometimes together. On Salina's first social call, interesting news was exchanged. Nobody had asked about Salina by name. In the aftermath of the tempest, it was almost as if she hadn't existed and been forgotten, but not by the other person on the island w****ho mattered to her. Salina pretended to be shocked when B informed her that Opran and the overseer had been killed, possibly murdered. Opran's wife had suspected the culprits were her three missing slaves and oversaw a search party for them.

"We heard them," said Salina.

"Really?" declared B. "Word was that they never found a trace. There's been a lot of conjecture about how Opran and the overseer died. Both throats were cut, but their bodies were found under a heavy branch that had fallen. Some people say they were killed by the tree, but there are reservations. How were their throats cut? I've got my suspicions and I'm keeping them to myself."

"Who knows?" responded Salina. "They had it coming to them anyway." She didn't feel it was her place to tell the truth, but part of her felt guilty about not telling B what she knew. *B's better off not knowing for the moment*, she assured herself.

"There's been no talk of them searching again," said B. "I think the hue and cry is over now, especially after I started a rumour that some slaves had run off with the pirates."

"What pirates?" asked Salina.

"You haven't heard? A pirate ship looted the town after the storm, and I started telling people that I'd heard some slaves had left the island with them. Then I found out that some really had!" B laughed.

"So, you think Mrs Opran suspects we escaped with the pirates?" asked Salina.

"Looks like it," nodded B.

"And some slaves did go with them, you say?"

B nodded again.

"Good for them. Two chances of escape in as many days. You clever thing. Thank God for you and the pirates," said Salina admiringly.

Following an under-resourced investigation, a report was published nine months later, concluding that a sharp part of the fallen bough could have sliced the throats of the two men. In light of no further evidence, the coroner recorded an open verdict. He promptly filed and forgot about the matter, picking up his next case from the top of his overfull in-tray.

xxx

Hilton, Patrick's erstwhile employer and landlord, was an elderly and affluent man now. Suffering from arthritis and some memory loss, but still a highly-respected member of the plantation set, he spent half of his time supervising the finishing touches to the building of a stately home in the Dorsetshire countryside, paid for from the profits of sugar and slavery. Well, slavery mostly. Without the cheapest labour, profits may have only afforded him a townhouse. Hilton had been in England during the hurricane and when he returned he took B's position of slave without a master under his wing, before some enterprising entrepreneur realised her situation and sold her on. Outlining the facts, as he saw them, in The Court of Requests, that Patrick had worked for him, had no known family and hadn't made a will, Hilton argued that B's future should be his. The judge was persuaded and the slave known as Bridget O'Mahoney was legally and newly named Bridget Hilton. In her secret life, B knew she was losing her identity. She had become so used to thinking of herself as B and responding to Bridget that Bolanile was becoming a distant memory.

B had to let the family argument remain as Hilton declared. Although Jomo was related he would never be free to claim Patrick's possessions. Even if he had been, where was the evidence? She shook her head and smiled at the irony of being owned by Jomo. On leaving court, Hilton's face puckered as he turned to B, his new slave.

"Something's puzzling me, Bridget," he said. "I don't know if my memory is completely abandoning me but for some reason I seem to vaguely remember Patrick having another slave."

"You're correct Massa, he did. But she went missing after the rains. I've heard that some slaves took a chance and left with the pirates."

"Pirates? What pirates?"

B explained what had happened, realising she could embellish the story as much as she wanted.

"What with all the destruction and Patrick dying, and sorting myself out, I didn't even notice she was missing for a couple of days. I miss her terribly," added B, sounding all upset.

"Oh dear. Of course, naturally," Hilton responded sympathetically, nodding abstractedly. He went quiet for a moment, absent-mindedly, then tilted his head and lifted his eyebrows in relief. "Ah yes," he said with a sudden gust of energy, "that's what I was going to do. You, Bridget, are going to be a slave of mine for the shortest time. How long have you belonged to me?"

"About ten minutes, Massa."

"And that's as long as it will be," Hilton said decisively. "I noticed that you looked after Patrick admirably and even helped him with his drink problem. You were like a mother to him, so you deserve this. I am granting you your freedom and when I get home I will write up the appropriate papers."

"Thank you, Massa," said B, eagerly, hardly believing her ears, but determined that she would not allow him to forget his offer of emancipation.

"And you can stop calling me, or anyone else for that matter, Massa. From now on, I am Mr Hilton to you."

Hilton let B stay on his land. He was so impressed with the new hut and the way B worked and maintained the kitchen garden that he said she could keep her allotment and remain in the shed, rent free. He kept all the sugar-cane that Patrick had planted and pocketed the profits. B was more than content with the agreement. With Patrick gone, she had a double plot. She produced far and above what she needed and traded the excess, including home-made soursop jam, lime and mango chutneys, as well as hot chilli sauces.

xxx

Narrator's note:
There is an Ashanti saying: 'A slave who knows how to serve, succeeds to his [sic] master's property.'

xxx

Eventually, everything at the deceptively spacious grotto began to take shape. Living compartments were created, systems of food collection, waste removal, sanitation and keeping watch were expedited. Nobody bothered them and they annoyed no one, well, apart from the odd goat or chicken or yam. The following year, Nevis was spared from hurricanes. One day, Jomo and Ibrahim were taking advantage of a cloudless summit again, quietly admiring the scenery. Suddenly, Ibrahim broke the peace.

"Wait a minute... what the hell is going on?" he exclaimed. Ibrahim was looking north towards Saint Kitts. Jomo, facing south, turned around at the exclamation. Two bands of ships were heading towards each other in The Narrows, the meagre sea passage between the two islands. There was cannon fire and two ships on opposing sides blazed with flames and smoke. One group split up and manoeuvred, looking to surround the other, just as an enormous explosion shattered one of the ships. The sound echoed between the peaks of both islands. Jomo and Ibrahim saw men in the water, little dark drops in a sea of blue. Then one flotilla turned and scurried towards Saint Kitts whilst the other licked its wounds and floundered its way to Charlestown.

"What do you think that was all about?" asked Jomo.

"Who knows?" said Ibrahim. "White folk need to calm down."

xxx

Narrator's note:

They had just witnessed the Battle of Nevis between the English and French fleets.

xxx

B's yard became a safe haven. Sometimes, the Maroons went fishing in the dark, sneaking down to the sea. At day-break, they bagged their haul and holed up at B's place until night fell, when they continued to carry it back to their den, undetected. B benefitted from this deal. She was given a portion of the catch which she either ate fresh, or salted for the future.

Other runaways joined them; some stayed, some died, others moved on, but there were never too many, nor too few. Rumours circulated that Maroon settlements were better off on the larger islands. Those that left chanced their luck to flee all the way to Jamaica, a known popular hideout, with its greater expanse of wild, mountainous terrain. Out of these new absconders, some were Christians, mostly of the Anglican persuasion. Lengthy, in-depth religious debates occurred in a respectful way, with differences of opinion accepted as simply interesting. A couple had been teachers in their lives, pre-slavery. Books were occasionally presented to the group, eagerly read by the literate, who in turn taught others to read. Personal histories and skills were shared. People of all ages learnt wisdom, practical knowledge and new viewpoints as opposed to academia.

Salina and Jomo stayed and had a family. Jomo passed on his musical knowledge to his children and other youngsters who were interested. Broken or overstretched guitar strings had to be replaced with animal sinews or strong plant fibres; makeshift instruments were pieced together and new improvisations created. Ibrahim and Chloe also remained and had two children, one of which died at four-years-old from food poisoning, having ingested a rancid conch. The couple decided not to have any more offspring and devoted their doting attention to their remaining child who grew up confident but a little spoilt. B became a surrogate aunt to all of Salina and Jomo's three children. When they were old enough, Salina took them to meet her, carrying little handmade carvings and wicker trinkets as gifts.

"It's one way of repaying you for all you have done for us," said Salina, comforting an emotional B, overwhelmed by the warmth that the children brought to her childless life.

xxx

B outlived Hilton. The new estate owner was understanding enough to allow her to stay where she was as old age crept in. With a weakening body and failing capabilities, B's many friends from on and off the plantation took care of her. Salina visited as often as possible, sharing stories of her family and reminiscing about how important B had been in her life. When B peacefully and painlessly passed on, her chums buried her body near to the compost heap, identifying it with a crude wooden cross. The vegetable patch was replanted with sugar and the hut slowly deteriorated. The next hurricane that swamped Nevis swept away what was left of the Maroon's place of refuge and the area was carefully ploughed around the grave.

xxx

And so, the years went by as the community of Maroons survived further tropical storms and even earthquakes, through sheer determination, courage, inventiveness and resourcefulness. The strength of purpose, to remain free, flowed through each escaped slave. When Jomo and Salina's youngest child reached the age of twelve, Jomo held a family meeting.

"Now," he said, "I want you all to listen carefully to what I am going to say. You can decide for yourselves how important it is." Jomo informed them about his roots; that he was the son of a white, Irish man, who had been the grandson of a chief, and a mixed ancestry African/Arab princess, their paternal grandmother.

xxx

Narrator's note:

The powerful Europeans had introduced a series of belittling words for the offspring of miscegenation. In the language of the time, Jomo could have been called a caublasian, mulatto, half breed or leprecoon. Today shared-heritage would be the respectful term. Why do some people have a problem with political correctness when it is all about respect, and giving everyone a chance of dignity?

xxx

Jomo described the history of his slavery and escape, expounding on the fact that there were trustworthy and spiteful members of all cultures. He reinforced that they themselves had the blood of African, Arabian and European ancestors running through them.

"Variety is richness," he enthused. The children listened intently to their father's wise words. Jomo paused and looked at them. He wanted more for them than this rock shelter, but he was pleased with what he had achieved, given the circumstances.

"You are living outside of main society. I don't know if there'll come a time when you will be allowed to join in. I doubt it'll happen in my lifetime. Even if more opportunities are presented to us, you must remember that, we with dark skins, are considered to be inferior by those with white ones. Of course, this isn't true, but that's how the world is. So, although you have a white ancestry, you will always be seen as black and therefore treated as subhuman by those prejudiced people. Remember, if you don't know who you are, you won't understand how the world will perceive you. The bigots are ignorant, misguided in thinking that they're always right, judging you by your appearance, instead of what you truly are. You, however, have a duty to stamp down on that injustice. Just by surviving here we have fought back. Be confident, not subservient, you are as important as anyone else in the eyes of God. If you can develop a broad, balanced understanding on most things, you'll have done better than a wealthy man with a narrow mind. After all, wisdom is more important than wealth. In my experience, rarely do you find the two together in the same person. I believe the well-off don't take time to consider wisdom, they're too busy concentrating on how to increase and maintain their assets." Jomo took the opportunity to impart his ideas about religion at the same time.

"All religions have valid points and agree that people should be kind to each other. None of them should be regarded as superior to another. Ultimately, it's all down to your own relationship with God. You'll meet people who reject the concept of God and I can't prove or disprove his existence. All I'll say is it's better to believe, as faith will help you forgive those who trespass against you and protect you from losing your minds at the mistreatment and unfairness we have been subjected to. Failing that, learn patience." Jomo tried to share the knowledge that he had learnt about the big, wide world, to his offspring, even though their own was forcibly confined. Finally, he went on to show them and explain the significance of the seal. Whether any of them ever found their way to Ireland, or established that they actually owned land there, was in the hands of fate.

Jomo lived life as fully as possible, but the constant, physical nature of struggling for survival took a toll on his body. He came to terms with his past and started to pray again in his old age. He died naturally, worn-out but contented at the age of sixty-eight. He had never visited Ireland, nor used the name O'Driscoll. Shortly before his death, Jomo had confided in Salina.

"I feel my time is near. Thank you for sharing your life with me."

"We made it, Jomo, we made it," Salina responded, tears welling up in her eyes.

"We did indeed," he agreed, as they smiled at each other.

"Are you satisfied with your life?" she asked.

"Totally, but there is one thing that would give me complete peace of mind."

"What's that, my dearest?"

"Would you look after this?" said Jomo, placing the seal in her hand, "And pass it on to the next generation. I know you'll make a sensible decision as to who should hold it for the family."

Salina passed a year later, leaving three healthy, strong minded, self-reliant adults. In her final days, she handed the seal to the middle child; a steady, studious, serious woman, repeating once more the importance of its unwritten history.

xxx

Nothing is permanent, stories are altered slightly, and meanings are lost or become muddled; interpretations are reinterpreted, until, sometimes, the original is unrecognisable.

XXX

Generations of fugitives procreated and held out defying the odds, all born with the same desire: freedom. Free to be able to make one's own decisions, to have some choice, rather than no choice. Possessions were passed on, some mislaid, some forgotten. However, like survivors of slavery, some made it.

PART TWO

Chapter 28 – The Caribbean and Ireland

1710 – 2005

Millions of people were forced to endure the two or three-month journey, depending on the weather, from Africa to slavery in the Americas. It was unforgettable and unimaginable. Words rarely truly convey an actual experience, so, in honour to those who went through it, there will be no attempt to describe the depressing, despairing and fearful depths of emotion, or the debasing, degrading and humiliating treatment those poor souls had to suffer. Those that survived need constant praise. Descriptions of the human suffering have been brilliantly chronicled by previous authors, especially Lawrence Hill, and there is no intention in this narrative to try and replicate that. Please refer to the short further reading list at the end of this book.

Jomo's religion, Islam, lost its way in the Caribbean. There were too few Muslims, less marabouts, no equal rights, no mosques, no centres of learning and therefore, nobody to carry the cause forward. Some Islamic ideas slowly syncretised with a sack-load of Christianity and a pocketful of Animism. The Caribbean religion, Obeah, which is in itself a pooling of a variety of West African tribal spiritual customs and practises, amalgamated some Islamic and Christian concepts of good and evil.

African traditions, languages and music were frowned upon. They went underground and emerged in new forms, refusing to be wiped out. As a result, fusions of the past and present merged together to create the Creole tongues and lively dances in the genres of Soca and Calypso. Tribal, family and clan names were brushed aside with new identities being imposed; Christianised, Anglicised or Nationalised by the owners.

In the 1770s the white authorities added further insult to their African subjects by bastardising the words 'Negro' and 'Niger' into the derogatory word 'Nigger'. Another layer of humiliation and scorn. This emotive term has caused untold grief, physically and psychologically. Unbelievably, to this day, there are still some totally blinkered white people who misbelieve that it is an appropriate word to use in everyday language. It can never be averred that they have the moral entitlement to do that. More recently, black artists have commandeered the name. Arguably, they have the prerogative to claim the word, change the spelling and pronunciation, and positively alter its meaning to friend.

Slavery was popular. Sugar cane was king. But as the natural law of impermanence changes everything, so did attitudes to the former and the importance of the latter. Abolitionists prowled the headlines, growing more vocal day-by-day. The plantations began to suffer as cheaper sugar squeezed from beetroot was produced and manufactured by European machines on an industrial scale. Some plantation owners started to drift away from the Caribbean, leaving their property to nature. A few Maroons began to saunter onto abandoned land.

In 1807, Thomas Clarkson and William Wilberforce linked arms and minds with both black and white supporters, presented their humanitarian argument and won their case, causing the British Parliament to pass the Abolition of the Slave Trade Act. The poachers became gamekeepers. It was a start. The slave trade within the British Empire, not slavery itself, was abolished. It was a day of joy and celebration for some, but for the 97 men, women and children released from Fort James, having spent two weeks in impoverished confinement awaiting shipment, it was anything but. Their freedom took them to the edge of the island. Their eyes absorbed the swirling currents, crocodiles and the north and south banks: the way home. They required and enquired for a boat. Refusing the request, the soldiers laughed and gave them the choice to swim or starve on the island. Physically weak but mentally determined, the freed chanced the waters and all drowned.

Slave uprisings on a number of Caribbean islands occurred, testing the resolve of their masters. Fear became less one-sided. However, it took another twenty-six years for slavery within the British domain to come to a slow, shuddering halt. English plantation owners in the Caribbean received twenty million pounds in compensation, for their lost property. Most returned home to England, leaving everything behind, both animate and inanimate. The chattel leftovers, people who had only known fearfulness, degradation, and oppression, became free, but not with a pile of cash to help with their adjustment for their lost lives. Their reward for surviving was basically the chance to begin life again, or as the author Mousha Mehran describes, to start a 'different way of being'. They'd done it once before, they had to do it again.

During slavery times and long after, the Caribbean was owned by Spain, England, The Netherlands, France, Denmark and Sweden to varying degrees. Trading politics sparked wars between the Europeans which were fought throughout the region; islands were seized, lost, and gained. People died as a result.

For a long time, the Irish and the Africans worked in harmony, close to each other in similar conditions. Both parties had been suppressed at home and abroad. However, at some point in the early 1800s a stirring occurred within the damaged Irish psyche. Certain influential European individuals pronounced, based on their pseudoscience, that the false theory of white skin being superior to black skin, was true. Some Irish workers began to change their attitude and view themselves a status above the Africans in bondage, failing to support the abolition of slavery. The abused, abused; the abased, abased; the abashed, abashed. It seems that those Irish people were simply grateful not to be on the bottom rung of society's metaphorical ladder.

In 1845, Frederick Douglass, an African-American escaped slave-turned-statesman and abolitionist, visited Ireland to stand up for the rights of mankind and raise the profile of the demeaning treatment of slaves in the Americas. To his surprise, he found Ireland to be a home from home. The plight of the Irish peasant, ejected and rejected by the English colonial powers, reminded him of his original slave condition – poor, subjugated and othered. He befriended and joined forces with the Irishman, Daniel O'Connell, an emancipator of Catholics and another abolitionist who had never even visited The New World. Shamefully, their joint strong words and emotional pleas failed to convince all Irish men and women to undermine slavery.

In pursuit of anything better, rather than accepting their lot, many Irish citizens emigrated to just about everywhere, forced from their homeland by the British, and especially following the Great Famine of 1845. The potato blight ravaged Western Europe. Not many places relied on the crop as much as the Irish villein and for three seasons it failed. The land-owning usurpers denied food to the hungry, sending all other agricultural produce, grown or fattened on Irish soil, along the rivers to the ports where it was shipped to Britain and traded there, while over one million of the native Irish populace starved to death.

The Bajan community of British Isles exiles, the Redlegs, without a home either in their birthplace or on Barbados, stood up against injustice and discrimination. They began to integrate into society, slowly raising their lowly status.

Proceeding into the 1900s, the Irish continued to fight the English on a small but irritating scale, even in the First World War. The situation changed dramatically when the colonies started to become a financial burden to their governments. The case for independence raised its head. Pressure began to build, and something eventually had to give. For Ireland, in 1921, it was a compromise. Six counties of the province Ulster became Northern Ireland, continuing to be part of the United Kingdom. Troubles have flared and rumbled there, ever since. The provinces of Munster, Leinster and Connaught, together with the three remaining Ulster counties, became the Irish Free State, semi-independent but still subject to the British Crown and Commonwealth, the new name for the British Empire.

Before other deals could be achieved, another European war started. The proprietors of the Caribbean welcomed their black peoples, who volunteered for service in their armed forces. The men and women who made up the West Indian regiments believed that if Hitler won, they would be made into bars of dark soap. They still had survival at the heart of everything they did. It is worth remembering that during both world wars millions of non-white soldiers were recruited from all European colonies to join the campaigns of the Allied and Axis powers, hoping to gain some future leverage on independence. Those who enlisted included; Africans from all points on a compass; Indian troops, made up of different companies of Muslims, Hindus and Sikhs; Native Americans; Maoris from New Zealand and Australian Aborigines, all made their presence felt. Blood was spilt. People from many ethnicities and religions died for Europe on both sides, some of whom weren't even allowed full rights as citizens within their own country.

The Irish Free State remained neutral during World War II. Soon after the end of the conflict, legislation was passed by both Irish and British politicians which made the area of the Free State into a Republic, a sovereign nation. The Irish chose to name their country 'Eire': the Gaelic name for Ireland.

Migration can involve travelling 12,000 miles or a few streets away, and any distance in-between. The reasons for packing up are numerous. There are people who are forced to migrate, out of necessity due to war, violence, natural disasters, slavery or legal injustice. They don't choose or want to leave home, but departure is nonetheless imperative if continued existence is the goal. They are neither happy nor excited only hopeful that they will glean what they need, as opposed to what they want, and that one day they will be able to return.

Then there are those who move unnecessarily, perhaps due to a belief that they will have an even better lifestyle elsewhere. They dream of love, larger houses, more money and more land. Ultimately, they elect to travel and are happy and excited to do so and often, their fantasies are realised. They may miss home, but not so much that they need to return; luckily, many could if they wanted to. Every emigration requires immigration. Both forced and unforced migrants need to be welcomed. Before judging, we should find out their stories and ask ourselves, *What would I feel, think and do?* It could happen to you, your children or your children's children.

Another group of wanderers are those who neither choose nor are forced to up sticks. It's part of what they are, maybe call it instinct. Creatures like house martins have summer and winter homes, two emigrations and immigrations a year! And they are welcomed by the locals from both places. Is that because they are expected and accepted as part of the cycle of life?

A fourth group of migrants are those who are enticed to travel by being promised new opportunities. They spend their savings, and even borrow, to take the journey, only to find that the chances of success are miniscule. The sole positions available to them are deemed by the natives to be the lowest form of unskilled work, even though the immigrant may be highly qualified, skilled and experienced. They also find that, thanks to immense prejudice and discrimination, everything else that has been vowed, such as housing and education, is of poor, or even the poorest, quality, or that there are no jobs, accommodation or school places at all, especially if you can't hide the fact that you are from a Black or Minority Ethnic group. They have been lied to, or at best had their expectations raised by exaggerated propaganda. The recipients of this deceit find themselves in that space between the mortar and the pestle. Unable to return home due to lack of funds or just plain shame, they stick it out, persevere, and fight for their rights to survive and thrive. Again, through their own resilience and dedication, they overcame, succeeded and achieved.

Post-war, it became evident that the colonial powers needed their cast-offs more than the cast-offs needed them. "Please come to England, help us, we need you to keep the public transport running, and work in our factories and hospitals. We'll even pay you this time. Your Mother country is depending on you," the politicians pleaded. Nice word: mother. It conjures up ideas of nurture, care, warmth and understanding.

Those that answered Britain's desperate call came from the many colonies of the British Empire, especially the Caribbean, Ireland,

India, and Pakistan. The primary reason for the large influx of immigrants from these diverse areas, is because initially, the British went there, uninvited, and plundered, looted, captured and depleted their land, minerals, natural resources, economic structures and other prized possessions. Many stolen jewels, statues and other artefacts, even body parts, still remain in national museums and private collections. It's time to return them to their rightful owners, now, with no quibbling.

One consequence of this advertisement was that the British ship HMT Empire Windrush set sail from Kingston, Jamaica on 24th May 1948 with over five hundred hopeful Caribbean men, women and children. On 22nd June 1948, they disembarked at Tilbury Docks in Essex. They were expecting a promised welcome. But no. It felt like the general population had other ideas. "Go home, no Blacks, no Irish, no dogs," shouted back the racists, snobs and property landlords. But, as in most periods of the British Empire, there were some individuals who spread their arms wide open in a warm salutation; the anti-racists, the white people who were friends of the subjugated.

The body which followed the head of independence barged in, and further inroads on the political scene were paved. Self-determination and national status clamoured to cut the ties of subordination; eventually the imperialists severed most of their links with Antigua, Saint Lucia, Dominica, Jamaica, Barbados, Saint Kitts and Nevis. Unbeknownst to many, however, was the fact that the colonisers kept little strangleholds on their ex-possessions. For example, they still refused to allow the newly formed states to have complete legislative autonomy. Other governing arrangements were signed. Montserrat became a British Overseas Territory. The locals consider themselves to be Black-Irish and enjoy a public holiday to celebrate Saint Patrick's Day. Guadeloupe and Martinique remained French and are part of the European Union. The Irish had to be content with getting most of their country back, while the Africans, consisting of a multitude of tribes, customs, and languages from another continent, blended together and worked at making new countries.

PART THREE

Chapter 29 – Smethwick, West Midlands, UK

October 2005

Her friends called her 'Hawkeye' because she possessed the knack of walking into a room, scanning it, observing and memorising every important detail in seconds. This evening was no different. Elegantly dressed in a Wallis blouse and smart Debenham slacks, and sporting a recently coiffured French pleat hairstyle, Fiona Forrest entered the lecture theatre at Smethwick College and glanced round the room. There were two important things: a free seat, and a particularly good-looking man, sat three rows up, six seats in, hemmed in on all sides. She took the seat she had spied in row five, two seats in. As the class waited for the lecturer to arrive, she took a moment to look at the man again, noting his profile. He was white, middle-aged, scruffy round the edges, but handsome, and kind-eyed from what she could see, with a short full beard and a long chin. *Attractive*, she thought, *could do with getting rid of that pretend pony-tail though.*

A variety of heritages were represented in the auditorium, with a wide spectrum of skin colours on view, from extremely pale to very dark brown. Individuals from many walks of life had turned out for the lecture, with people of different ages, religions and ethnic backgrounds, dispersed throughout the audience. A range of accents could be heard; an array of fashion choices, and styles mingled respectfully, curiously and admiringly. Gathered in the middle of England, the group was an embodiment of what is great about Britain today, a rich diversity and an opportunity to find out more about themselves and each other. The sight epitomised the national mottos of Jamaica and South Africa, *Out of Many, One People* and *Diverse People Unite*, respectively. Multiculturalism works well if you want it to.

At 7.59pm, the lecturer came in, stood at the front and introduced herself. She was black, well-spoken, confident, smartly dressed and droll. She made her audience smile and feel at ease. They were in her hands now, attentive and keen. This evening was the first of ten weekly lectures on Black History.

"Tonight, we look at the career of Marcus Garvey... One of Black History's finest. He was a descendant of the Maroons of Jamaica. However, I won't assume anything here. Is anyone familiar with who the Maroons were?" There was a pause. Fiona watched as the white man raised his arm.

"Escaped slaves who set up their own communities," he said.

"Thank you. Yes, they were."

The class was enlightened about the rise and fall of the Black Star Line and the Pan-African Movement. Fiona checked her watch, surprised to see that it was nearly half-past-nine, and the end of the lecture already. The speaker hoped that she would see them all again next week, and people rose to leave. As the man with the short braid, Henry, turned to walk along the row, he saw Fiona for the first time. His jaw slackened involuntarily; all the lights flicked on in his head. *Oh man, she's gorgeous,* he thought, engrossed at how striking her bright, intense eyes looked against her beautiful, dark-brown skin. He tried not to stare, but failed; not even noticing that she had witnessed his reaction.

"Hmm," she hummed*, that's a positive sign*. She turned to walk to the end of her row, well-aware that he was watching her leave.

The second and third weeks went in a similar vein. Only the subjects differed. Henry and Fiona learnt about the exploits of Harriet Tubman, the innovative slave Underground Railroad, and the speeches of Frederick Douglass. On the fourth week, Fiona and Henry arrived at the college within seconds of each other, with him following her to the reception. Fiona opened the door, then glanced behind before letting the door shut. Henry reached for it as she kept it open for him.

"Thanks," he said.

"You're welcome," she responded. They ended up walking side by side, to the lecture room. *Say something neutral,* Henry thought.

"This week should be interesting," he said.

"I'm not so sure," replied Fiona.

"What do you mean?"

"Well, I'm interested in Black History but I didn't sign up for a lesson in Islam."

"You're not interested in religion then?" asked Henry.

"Oh yes, I am, just not necessarily Islam." *Okay...* he thought, picking up the message that Islam was off the conversation menu. Entering the auditorium, it seemed natural that they would sit together.

"Can I join you?" he asked, not wanting to impose.

"Sure," she replied.

"I'm Henry, by the way."

"Fiona," she revealed.

That evening, the presenter informed the group that a minority, but still a substantial number, of enslaved West Africans were Muslims. They had been responsible for slave uprisings and had refused to be Christianised. Islam itself had died out but resurfaced again in the Caribbean in the 1800s, with the arrival of indentured servants, this time imported from Bengal in India. It had only returned to Dominica in the 1900s after Arab and Pakistani students began studying there, spreading the word peacefully, eventually influencing some of the minds of black residents, as well as the small remaining Carib population who sanctioned their own mosque. Even a small building in Bath Village on

Nevis was reserved for praying Muslims.

"Amazing," said Henry, when the lecture ended. "What did you think of it all?"

"Well, I certainly learnt something that I didn't know," Fiona replied, neutrally.

"I've never really thought about it before this evening. I mean, you don't exactly associate Islam with the Caribbean. I've never considered the fact that some slaves were Muslims either."

"Well, that's what these lectures are supposed to do," said Fiona.

"What's that?" he asked.

"Broaden the mind," she replied.

Fiona stood up to leave and Henry followed suit. They said "Tara a bit" on the car park and Henry watched her walk to her new black Ford Escort with a personalised number plate: F1 ONA. *I've got to ask her out,* he thought, as he got into his old, battered, hearing-aid-coloured Nissan Micra. *The worst she could say is no... but if I don't, I'll regret it.*

When Henry walked in on the fifth week, his eyes wandered over the group, saw Fiona and noticed that there was a vacant seat next to her. Their eyes met and he smiled, pointing to the seat next to her as if to ask "can I sit there?" She nodded.

"How's it going?" he asked, as he sat down.

"Good, and you?"

"Yes, just fine." They had a couple of minutes before the lecture was due to begin.

"Have you had to come far?" he enquired.

"Only West Bromwich," Fiona answered.

"Oh, that's not bad, about twenty minutes, then."

"How slow do you drive!" she exclaimed, "about ten by my reckoning, if you know all the short cuts. How long does it take you?"

"Best part of half an hour," replied Henry.

"You must live in the sticks then."

"Tividale," he said.

"Tividale! I'd do that in less than ten," Fiona said emphatically.

Their conversation concluded when it was replaced by the passionate voice of the lecturer, who effused about the heroics of Mary Seacole.

"Now, that was amazing," said Fiona, at the end.

"True. You only ever hear about Florence Nightingale," agreed Henry. Walking out, Henry plucked up the courage to ask Fiona out on a date.

"... Fiona, do you fancy a drink after one of these lectures, sometime?"

"Yeah, okay, but I can't do the next two weeks," she answered, looking straight at him. His initial inflation rapidly deflated. *That's a long time*, he thought, *oh well...*

"How about tonight then?" he asked, hopefully.

"No time like the present, I guess," Fiona replied with a smile.

At Fiona's suggestion, they drove their cars down the road, rendezvousing at the Marriott Arms. Henry hadn't entered a Mitchell's and Butlers pub for years. His favourite beer was Batham's bitter. He managed a pint of Highgate Mild while Fiona sipped on a Malibu and lemonade. They sat and shared a few pleasantries, discussing matters such as their job, relationship statuses, families, which football team was supported and so on. Eventually, there was a pause.

Then Henry asked, "So, what's your ancestry? Jamaican?"

"That drives me mad," Fiona said, straightforwardly, shaking her head.

Henry's mind leapt, tensing up, unsure of what he'd said wrong.

"Everyone assumes that a black person round here is Jamaican," she continued.

"You're right, I'm sorry," he said. "I did assume and I keep trying not to. The only black people I've met have been of Jamaican descent.

"Fair enough," said Fiona, "there probably are more Jamaicans in this country than from other islands. But, that's because it's a big island. I'm from somewhere else. There are other places in the Caribbean, apart from Jamaica, you know."

"Of course… so, which island is your family from?"

"The small and beautiful island of Nevis," she replied proudly.

"The lecturer mentioned Nevis last week," recalled Henry. "Where is it? I can't picture it in my head. I know where Jamaica is, but not Nevis."

"Like I said, everyone knows of Jamaica," Fiona said resignedly. "It's in the eastern Caribbean. Anyway, what about you?"

"What about me?" asked Henry.

"What's your ancestry?"

"You're not going to assume that I'm Anglo-Saxon?"

"Why would I?" she responded. "By being a white man, you could be from any European stock."

"Well," conceded Henry, "I suppose I'm mostly a Celt. I was born and bred in England but I know that my father's ancestors came from Ireland and my mother's side was Anglo-Irish, from Dublin. So, I'm something of a mixture. I've never really looked into it, to tell the truth. All I know is that my paternal family clan came from a place called Baltimore, in South West Ireland." As the evening ended, they got up to leave. Henry was in a great mood.

"I'd like to do this again," he said, "would you?"

"Yes, that would be nice," Fiona answered agreeably.

They exchanged telephone numbers. Fiona rapidly tapped Henry's details into her up-to-date BlackBerry mobile phone, while he fumbled with his, trying to remember how to work the machinations of his out-of-date, Pay As You Go, Ericsson device.

"Would you like some help?" she asked, smiling. "You seem to be struggling."

"Yes please. I'm not very good with these things," he replied, underplaying his frustration with new-fangled gadgetry, whilst handing Fiona the handset. In seconds she had entered her number on his machine.

"There," she said, returning the phone. "That's old technology. Don't you know that we're in the twenty-first century?"

"I'm just a technophobe," he sighed resignedly. "Perhaps you can help me keep abreast of all the changes."

"You'd better be a quick learner then. I only say things once," she bantered, laughing. They parted company with a kiss on the cheek and returned to their cars.

The first arranged date, at a restaurant, went smoothly. Further meetings were agreed after that, all of which were successful. A game of badminton was played, Henry was whupped. Weeks six to eight of the course covered the incredible story of Olaudah Equiano, slave, freeman, traveller, writer and abolitionist pioneer; and the conquering feats of Toussant Louverture who helped to create Haiti, the first African run colony outside that huge, beautiful but serially abused continent. Details were given about John Edmonstone, slave, freeman and then qualified taxidermist, who, ironically, taught Charles Darwin. An account of a living example of a black man making history described the remarkable life of Nelson Mandela, who unflinchingly stood up against apartheid and injustice, eventually ending up victorious at a huge cost to himself and his family.

Week nine introduced other inspirational black men and women, including Martin Luther King who had a dream, Malcolm X who visited Smethwick, Rosa Parks who confronted racial segregation by sitting on a bus, and Sojourner Truth, one of the first black women to take a white man to court and win her case. To fill in five minutes at the end, the tutor chipped in with a couple of historical ironies. The song *Sweet Chariot*, usually sung with great gusto by the English rugby crowd, was written by a black man Wallace Willis, in the mid-1800s. The expression *the real McCoy*, readily used to describe anything worthy and genuine, refers to another black man, Elijah McCoy, who was an inventor in the late 19th Century, having invented a high-class train engine oil.

Fiona and Henry came in one car, his, for the final lecture. The programme concluded with a history of Black music; the discussion covered Gospel choirs, the Blues, Reggae, Dub, Soul, Hip-hop, Soca, and Calypso. Beethoven was identified as a biracial composer. References were made to the unique blend of chanting, West African drumming and North African strings of the Gnawa people of Morocco, who were the resulting fusion of many enslaved sub-Saharan tribes during the period of the Ottoman Empire, including the Fula, Wolof and Susu. New histories were being exposed. There was current ground-breaking research being undertaken, examining evidence of a possible link between the country blues from the southern states of America in the early 1900s and Islamic musical influences from Mali in the 1600s.

On the way out, Henry thought about how much he had enjoyed the course. Reflecting on the new information and perspectives made him think and open his mind. He felt tired.

"I don't really fancy a drink tonight," he said, as they got into his car. "Can I entice you back for a coffee at mine? I'll happily drive you home afterwards, or I can drop you there now instead, if you prefer?"

Fiona hadn't been to Henry's yet. That evening was the first time

Henry had picked her up from home. She didn't invite him in, being cautious with dating and firm in her decisions and actions. They had kissed, but paying heed to her perspicacious mother's advice, she was only interested in taking things further if she was confident about his good nature.

"Or I can get a taxi," she replied. "Have you got any dogs?"

"No..."

"Good, I hate dogs. Come on, Driving Miss Daisy."

Fiona entered Henry's house; it was a two up, three down Victorian terrace. Henry walked into the kitchen to put the kettle on, while she looked around the lounge. Minimalistic, with a dark green carpet, a light green settee, magnolia walls, purple blinds, pine coffee table, an open brick fire place, and a wood burner, full of soot and ash, with a slight but sweet smell of incense. An acoustic guitar rested in a corner of the room. Hanging on one wall was a delicate, pencil-drawn portrait of a Collie dog alongside a framed picture of what looked like a shield. Something about the design seemed familiar to her; she went up to have a closer look. There was a bird at the top, a ship in the middle and *Spes Mea in Deo* written underneath on a scroll. Further down, at the bottom were the words: *Armorial Bearings of the Family O'Driscoll.*

I know this picture, don't I? she pondered, *but where from? Henry's surname is Driscoll...*

Henry came back in. "Milk and sugar?" he asked.

"Milk and one sugar, please. And leave the spoon in," replied Fiona.

"Leave the spoon in?"

"Yes."

Henry paused. "So, stir it and leave the spoon in?"

"Yes. Is that too difficult?" she challenged.

"Er... No... Of course not," he mumbled as he went off back to the kitchen, shaking his head. He was starting to realise that it was better not to question her.

Fiona continued scrutinising the image. Then it came to her. *The seal! That's like the seal, I think anyway.* Henry re-entered the living room, hands full. He looked at her, sensing that something was bothering her.

"Anything wrong?" he asked. "You look as if you've seen a ghost."

Fiona was still staring at the print. She turned to him, "No... but... it's this picture. What is it?"

"It's a Coat of Arms," he replied. "My family crest. Why?"

"I think it looks similar to an old wooden seal that my brother's got. It's an ancient family heirloom." Henry put the mugs on the table, walked over and took the mounting off the wall.

"That's strange," he said. "I've often wondered when or why my side of the family lost the 'O' in O'Driscoll. I read a theory once that said it was dropped at the time of the potato famine in Ireland. Apparently, it made them less Irish or something, which pleased the British, who then gave the starving some soup to eat. Something to do with survival, I suppose. The Irish who did that became known as Soupers. I haven't looked at this properly for years."

With his hand, Henry brushed off the evidence of dust and spiders from the back before perusing the reverse of the frame. There was some exquisite calligraphy that explained the meaning behind the Armorial Bearings. It named a Sir Fineen O'Driscoll as the receiver of the heraldry. Henry showed Fiona.

"My hope in God," said Henry. "That's what the Latin means."

"Are you assuming I can't read Latin?" she said with an eyebrow raised. *Man, you're strong,* he thought, taken aback, *and beautiful as well.*

"Kind of," he said, sheepishly. "I'm working on it. Here, your coffee," and handed Fiona the cup with the spoon in. As she stirred, Henry considered that maybe she didn't trust people enough to blend the sugar properly.

She took a sip. "Mmm, not bad, not Nescafe though, is it?"

"Lidl's best," he replied, mentally noting what to buy next time.

"This is really puzzling me," she said, pointing at the artwork.

"Where does your brother live?" Henry asked, quietly assuming Nevis.

"Chris? He's lives in Worcester. I'm actually seeing him this Saturday. I'll phone him and see if he can get his hands on the seal. I've got to check this out." Fiona accepted the lift home.

That weekend, Chris gave Fiona the seal, which was now encased in a large see-through plastic coin collector's pouch. Other than some marks from water stains, it was slightly worn near the top, from the innumerable, unknown fingers that had rubbed the outline of the cormorant over the years, and had two chips in the edge. But the carving was still clear and true. Fiona examined it.

"I'm absolutely sure it's the same," she said to Chris.

"What the hell does that mean then? That we're related to this guy?" he quizzed.

"I don't know... I just don't know. I'll phone you when I've seen this and the picture together."

The next evening, the seal and the framed Coat of Arms were handled side by side. The outlines matched perfectly. Henry and Fiona sat in silence; they couldn't figure out what to think. The heavy atmosphere was finally broken by Henry.

"How long do you think that seal has been in your family?"

"I've no idea," replied Fiona. "All I know is it's very old. My grandmother gave it to my father, when they lived on Nevis. Dad handed it to Chris for safe keeping, because he's the eldest. I've always assumed it's supposed to be a lucky family charm. We've all known about it, but paid little attention to it. It's just one of those things that's always been about. Nobody's taken any real interest in it or understood what it actually meant. Not until now, that is." Fiona paused, looking bemused. "But what does it mean now?" she continued. "That there was an O'Driscoll in my family? There's a vague story about some white man, way back when in slavery times, but that was pretty commonplace, in those days."

"How would you feel about doing a DNA test?" Henry asked.

"It might be interesting," she acknowledged.

"I could do one too, just to see how Irish I really am." Their minds continued to churn.

"I know I shouldn't," Henry said, slowly breaking up his thinking, "but to move this forward, let's assume that the seal is from the O'Driscoll clan, and that it came from Baltimore in Ireland. How it ended up in your family is a complete mystery... but I have to say, I'm more than intrigued. If we can find out how old it is, then we can have a look at what was going on in Baltimore at that time. And I'll do some family research too."

"Sounds like a plan," agreed Fiona.

"Maybe the seal is the key to finding out that I own a castle or some land," he said, jokingly.

"Or, maybe I will," she shot back. "In fact, I reckon I've got more rights than you. You've only got the name and a picture of the Coat of Arms. I've got the actual seal. Imagine that, a black woman, Queen of an Irish castle! But... let's keep it real, eh?"

"Yes," smiled Henry, "but as they say in the metal detecting game, *you never know*!"

"Keep it real," she repeated, rationally.

Their interest in this joint familial relic grew rapidly, as their fondness of each other deepened at an equal rate. Fiona and Henry received the results of their DNA tests by email, on the same day. They agreed to meet at Henry's in order to compare notes. Henry's report showed that he was highly connected to Irish origins, but also had a combination of lesser portions of British, French, German, Scandinavian and Sardinian ancestry. There was even a zero point one percent link with Siberia.

"I never realised my heritage was that varied," said Henry after studying the details. "I always wondered why I liked vodka so much," he joked.

Fiona's DNA record demonstrated a majority West African lineage, which wasn't surprising. More of dual interest was that the test indicated she had a four percent Irish connection running through her veins. A slightly lesser percentage pinpointed an Arabian influence. "And look there at that, at the bottom," she said. "I've got zero point one percent Native American in me! I'd love to know how that got there."

Henry's internet genealogical search ground to a laborious conclusion, but not before he discovered that his great, great grandfather, John Driscoll was a member of the Church of Ireland, born in Skibbereen in 1809. The radiocarbon dating report took weeks to appear, causing both parties to start worrying about the seal, which had been posted by recorded delivery. It was a relief when it finally arrived back at Henry's. He tore open the package and put the seal safely in a draw. The enclosed letter indicated that it had been made from Irish Oak, cut down sometime in the 1500s. Now he had an identifiable period of time to investigate. After informing Fiona of developments, by text, he googled 'Baltimore, Ireland 1500s'. As he scrolled down the results page, trying to decide which website to open, he was drawn to a picture advertising a new book entitled *The Stolen Village*, by Des Ekin. It was the word 'Baltimore' printed on the front cover that had caught his eye. He opened the box and read the summary. It outlined the details of a Barbary pirate raid on Baltimore, Ireland in 1631. *I've never come across this information before,* he thought excitedly. Over one hundred English settlers and a few native Irish people had been seized, taken to Algiers and enslaved. Only two women were ever heard of again. Henry ordered a copy from Amazon, received it the following day, studied it and then decided to do further research on exactly who those captives were, the old-fashioned way.

With Fiona by his side, Henry travelled first to Baltimore, where he talked to people and researched remaining records. The seal which accompanied them, having travelled a journey of a strangely shaped figure of 8, returned home. Satisfied with their investigations, the couple moved on to undertake inquiries in Algiers and beyond. The oral tradition still held secrets that the internet could never hope to uncover. What they unearthed turned out to be truly extraordinary.

Epilogue

What are the chances? Are Henry and Fiona genetically linked to a single ancestor who lived 400 years ago, connected by slavery?

My thesis is that we all have common links that relate to the past, and one of the primary factors in that is slavery. Identify a place on Earth where the slave trade has not had some effect on the local population, and we'll have a debate. After all, there has been a known African presence in England since the 3rd century because of slavery, Roman slaves. A forced migration. In addition, Charlotte of Mecklenburg-Strelitz, a descendant of a union between a Portuguese monarch and an African slave mistress, migrated voluntarily in 1761, to become the second known mixed-race English Queen, when she married King George III. The first was Queen Philippa of Hainault, although not necessarily of slave lineage, who married Edward II in 1328. What about the unknown, or unrecorded?

Extending this argument, it follows that there is a mixture of many tribes, clans, ethnicities and other peoples in our genetic makeup, some more prevalent than others. The remnants of DNA cells of various ancestors, from who knows where, runs through our bodies. There is *no* such thing as purity. I suggest, therefore, that those of you who believe that your genomic ancestry is pure, for example, white supremacists, should take a good, long, hard look at yourselves and your predecessors. It's an absolute certainty that some of your ancestors were migrants, forced or unforced. It might make you change your mind, which you are, of course, allowed to do, and even embrace diversity with all its richness. In turn, this will improve your understanding of the world and help you lead a more fulfilled life. Why live a dull, boring, one-dimensional existence when you could be enjoying a more exhilarating experience? After all, there is delusion in extremist views. In addition, although you may not be able to identify the religions or beliefs of your forebears, imagine if some of them had been Muslims, Hindus, Jews or ... Are you aware that on April 23rd you are celebrating the patronage of a black Christian martyr, Saint George?

As we are a population that is so interconnected, here's a message from the majority, a hopeful assumption, of non-violent human beings to the minority, another hopeful assumption, of violent human beings, *Stop killing, hating, oppressing, enslaving, raping, warring, scheming and stealing*. There, I think that covers it.

Furthermore, you should talk to each other. We're all family. We could unknowingly be related to someone who lives around the corner, or even next door! The least you can do is cease perpetuating the attitudes of superiority, arrogance and pomposity that privilege encourages.

xxx

A rant:

Some white people continue to believe in the racist attitudes that justified enslaving Africans. New forms of verbal and physical abuse have evolved including certain graffiti; malicious, vitriolic words; the throwing of bananas at football matches, and the childish anti-social posting of dog mess through letter boxes. All serve to inform the migrants and their offspring that they aren't welcome or that they are, at best, second rate. Every hour of every day, people from ethnic minorities are at risk of racism, from the subtle to the blunt. To those offensive white people, please just stop what you're doing, put yourselves in other people's shoes, and imagine and extend your minds to understand how it feels. Then, after much soul searching, conclude that the hatred is unnecessary and must end. Take personal responsibility for one's self, to learn and realise that our white ancestors made it all up to satisfy their self-centred greed – that a dark skin is inferior to a pale one. Fundamentally we are all human beings, one race. Look beyond the superficial. By examining themselves, individuals can establish what influenced them to think the way they do. It's usually parents, friends or the media. All negative thoughts are just that. Intangible thoughts. They are all inside the head. There are always other ways to think.

Historically, the United Kingdom has been regarded as a Christian country. Questionably, it still is. Have we really forgotten how to do unto others as we would have them do unto us? These are the same sentiments as Islam. We have more in common than not.

It is reported that Britain is a tolerant society. Is that it? Is that the best we can do? To tolerate is to accept begrudgingly, to say "I don't like it but I'll put up with it." That's not good enough. Isn't it better to work towards what was originally suggested – "we welcome you", and mean it?

Certain things have changed, of course, for the better. When opportunities have been afforded some black people have achieved, much to the frustrated surprise of some of their white counterparts who hate to be outshone. Statutes have been enacted to provide safety and security for people of colour and other minorities. Over time, laws that are enforced can alter people's opinions. However, it is nigh on impossible to overcome ingrained attitudes, they have to be unpicked. If the cap fits, pick at your beliefs, increase your knowledge and don't rely on just one newspaper, one television channel, one radio station or one point of view. Having said that, as with all negative mind-sets and destructive behaviours, one must want to change. Create a window in your schedule, ensure enough time, space and energy is available, and concentrate. You will be rewarded for your efforts. The benefits outweigh the costs. Hatred and fear, both depressing and emotionally expensive, can be replaced with respect and understanding, both uplifting and emotionally freeing.

There are individuals who wish that those that are, or who look like migrants, would return to the place from where they originated, or have ancestral roots. If, by some quirk, that became a legal obligation, then those desiring that, and wanting to be fair-minded, must agree that the law should extend worldwide. So, as Europe expels her African, Caribbean and Asian minorities, true Australians, New Zealanders and North and South Americans hope that their many generations of immigrant majorities, sometimes erroneously and anomalously called ex-pats, would return to Europe. European minorities would also have to come back from Africa and Asia. Then complain about lack of jobs, housing, hospital beds, school places... But that would be ridiculous. Repatriation is not going to happen. Let's share what we have and stop behaving selfishly and spoilt.

As an aside, if there is something on a black person's shoulder, it is not a chip. It's an enormous burden of never having been taken seriously, persistently denied opportunities, continuously pushed lower and lower and invariably dismissed. Also, nobody takes a position of employment, everybody has to apply and be accepted. Jobs are given not taken.

XXX

Sadly, slavery was, and still is, prevalent. It's a fact of life. Just because it's traditional doesn't make it acceptable. Traditions don't and shouldn't last forever. Slavery involves theft; the stealing of lives, freedom, choice and identity. Consequently, everything gained from slavery is tainted, rotten, and as some might say, cursed. Now that we know which guilty parties benefitted from these crimes, shouldn't those responsible be humble enough to pay compensation?

It has been estimated that twenty million pounds in the 1800s would have the buying power of over one billion pounds today, less than the value of Buckingham Palace. Could the Crown Estates Commissioners consider selling this pile of stone, and allow the monarchy to compensate former colonies? There would still be some change left over. The Queen has other roofs over her head atop the properties of Sandringham House and Balmoral Castle. Or perhaps those wealthy families, who can trace their gains to slavery, could contribute as well. Their names are known. They may feel pleased with themselves to offload a few million quid which is superfluous and just gathering interest and dust. What an enormous amount of respect they would gain in their place.

This would be a positive step towards drawing a line through the still ongoing grievances from the past. Even discussing the principle of making amends would be a start, instead of ignoring the national guilt. Karmic accounts have to be balanced before order is restored. That includes personal and national karma. Being just, fair and reasonable always helps.

XXX

Now, time to move on. History catches up with the present.

If you think Fiona and Henry are related, have you worked out who the common male ancestor would have to be?

THE END

Glossary

ADHAN – (Arabic) Islamic call to worship recited by the muezzin.

AGNUS DEI – (Latin) Invocation to Jesus in Catholic religion.

AQIQAH – (Arabic) Islamic naming ceremony.

ARQUEBUS – (German) Long firearm.

AZALAI – (Tuareg) Camel caravan.

BAKRA – (Creole) Literally 'back row', referring to your place in church. There is a second meaning – white person.

BARQUE – (French) Three masted sailing vessel.

BATISTE – (French) Fine, plain-woven cotton especially for dresses.

BEDISTAN – (Turkish) Slave market.

BODACH – (Irish) Low life, pig.

BOWAAB – (Arabic) Sentry.

BRAT – (Irish) A mantle or cloak.

BREAKING WHEEL – Torture device.

BRIGANTINE – (Italian) A two masted sailing ship popular with pirates.

BURKA – (Arabic) A one piece veil that covers the face and body, leaving a mesh to see through.

CAC – (Irish) Shit.

CARIK – (Turkish) Curled up shoes.

CAROLUS – (Latin) Gold coin minted in Charles 1st era, value £1.

CASBAH – (Arabic) Fortress.

CAUBLASIAN – Mixed parentage of Caucasian, Black and Asian.

CLAIRSEACH – (Irish) Triangular harp.

COFFLE – (Arabic) A line of slaves fastened together.

COIRM – (Irish) Beer.

COLCANNON – (Irish) – A meal of mashed potatoes, cabbage, milk and other bits and pieces.

COLLEEN – (Irish) An unmarried woman.

CRAIC – (Irish spelling of English 'crack') An enjoyable conversation.

CURRACH – (Irish) A boat constructed with a wooden frame covered in an animal skin, usually ox-hide.

DHOTI – (Hindi) Long loincloth.

DIMIJE – (Turkish) Baggy trousers.

DOUBLE CROWN – a 10-shilling silver coin.

DUDEEN – (Irish) Clay tobacco pipe.

EIRI AMACH – (Irish) Irish Rebellion.

FEAR GORMA – (Irish) Black men (literally 'blue' men, from the colour of clothing worn by North African tribes.)

FEINNE – (Irish) Legendary Irish warrior, folk hero.

FLAMBEAU – (French) Flaming torch.

FOGGARA – (Tuareg) Underground irrigation system.

FUNGI – (Creole) Cornmeal.

GAEILGE – (Irish) Gaelic.

GERBA – (Tuareg) Goatskin water bottle.

GHAUT – (from Hindi) A small cleft in a hill through which a rivulet runs down to the sea.

GOZDE – (Turkish) Favourite.

GRIS-GRIS – (French) African charm or amulet.

HADITH – (Arabic) A report describing the words/actions/habits of the Prophet Mohammed.

HALAL – (Arabic) Permissible especially in relation to food and drink.

HAJJ – (Arabic) Annual Islamic pilgrimage to Mecca.

HIJAB – (Arabic) Literally a partition or curtain but often refers to material covering the hair worn by Muslim women as a sign of modesty.

HIPI – (Wolof) Open your eyes.

HMT – Hired Military Transport – A ship prefix. The Empire Windrush was originally a German ship, acquired by the British as a prize of war.

JAUNTING CAR – Two wheeled cart for a single horse.

JERKY – (Quechan) Dried lean meat.

JIHAD – (Arabic) Literally means spiritually struggling with a praiseworthy aim but also refers to an Islamic armed struggle against unbelievers.

JINN – (Arabic) Supernatural spirits or demons.

JUMU'AH – (Arabic) Congregational prayer that Muslims hold every Friday, just after noon, instead of Zuhr prayer.

KABYLE – Berber jewellery from Algeria.

KAFIR – (Arabic) Unbeliever.

KERNE – (Irish) Foot soldier.

KUFI – (Yoruba) Brimless short rounded cap.

LEINE – (Irish) Shirt.

LOBLOLLY – (Old English) A broth made from boiled maize to a thickness of porridge.

MARABOUT – (Arabic) Muslim religious leader and teacher.

MAROON – (From Spanish 'cimarron' meaning wild, savage) Fugitive black slave.

MEGRIM – (From French) Migraine, headache.

MNA GORMA – (Irish) Black women.

MOBBIE – (Carib) A distilled spirit made from water, sugar and fermented sweet potatoes.

MUEZZIN – (Arabic) A man who calls Muslims to prayer.

MULATTO – (Spanish/Portuguese) A person with black and white parents.

NEGUS – A drink named after its inventor, Colonel Francis Negus, an English military officer.

NEGRO – (Spanish/Portuguese) Name given to people of African descent from Spanish meaning black.

NIBIMA – (Twi/Ashanti) West African plant used to treat Malaria.

NIGER – (Latin) Black.

NI MOR RIACHTANAIS – (Irish) Needs must.

NIQAB – (Arabic) A veil covering the face and hair, leaving the area around the eyes clear.

NYIRI – (Fula) Mixture of grease and flour eaten with soup.

OAKUM – (Old English) Tarred hemp/jute fibres to seal gaps on ships. White oakum is the material before adding tar.

ODALISQUE – (Turkish) literally chambermaid, but also refers to concubines.

OONT – (Hindi) Camel.

OUD – (Arabic) Short necked lute.

PANYARING – (Portuguese) Kidnapping.

PASHA – (Turkish) High ranking official in the Ottoman Empire.

POTEEN – (Irish) Distilled liquor from cereals and potatoes.

QIBLA – (Arabic) Direction of Mecca.

RAMADAN – (Arabic) The ninth month of the Islamic calendar set aside for fasting.

REVERT – In Islam, a person who becomes a Muslim, after believing another religion, is called a 'revert' because it is said that all babies are born Muslim, and the person has reverted.

SEBSI – (Arabic) Moroccan cannabis pipe.

SHAHADA – (Arabic) A Muslims declaration of belief in one God and Mohammed his final messenger.

SJAMBOK – (Afrikaans) Leather whip.

SOUK – (Arabic) Marketplace.

TASBIH – (Arabic) Prayer beads.

THALER – (Czech) Silver minted coin in 1520s, anglicised to dollar.

TORIES – (From Irish ‘toraidhe’) Irish outlaw.

VILLEIN – (Latin) Tenant farmer.

WALLAHI – (Arabic) I swear unto Allah.

YATAGAN – (Turkish) Ottoman curved single-edged sabre.

ZUHR – (Arabic) Noon prayer.

Further Reading

'African Music, a peoples art' – Francis Bebey – Hill and Co. 1975

'Servants of Allah – African Muslims enslaved in the Americas' – Sylviane A. Diouf – New York University Press 1998

'The Stolen Village' – Des Ekin – O'Brien Press 2006

'The Book of Negroes' – Lawrence Hill – Black Swan 2007

'Swords, Ships and Sugar: A History of Nevis' – Vincent K. Hubbard – Premiere Editions International 1992

'Small Island' – Andrea Levy – Headline Review 2004

'Rosewater and Soda Bread' – Marsha Mehran – Random House 2008

'To Hell or Barbados' – Sean O'Callaghan – Brandon 2000

'Sacred Hunger' – Barry Unsworth – Penguin 1992

'Exotic England' – Yasmin Alibhai-Brown – Portobello 2015

Analecta Hibernica No. 4 October 1932, documents relating to the Irish in the West Indies – Rev. Aubrey Gwynn

Acknowledgements

During the writing of this book certain people have made important different contributions, all of which have helped to create the end result. I am grateful to all the following parties.

For painstakingly proofreading and providing feedback and a black perspective – Mr Tony Kelly (UK).

For reading, feedback and an Islamic perspective – Mr Asif Ali (UK).

For reading and feedback – Mrs Jayne Rumble, Mr Bernard Hill, Mr Bob Cashell, Mr Keith Heyes (all UK).

For a variety of information, friendship and encouragement – Mr Steadroy Benjamin (Antigua), Ms Judy Bailey (Barbados), Mr Abdul Mehter (Barbados), Mr Oliver Driscoll-Hill (UK), Mr Adama Taal (Gambia), Mr Cherif Keita (Mali), Ms Anne O'Regan (Ireland), Mr Alfusainsey Jallow (Gambia), Mr Christopher 'Markey' Boswell (Saint Kitts), Mr Mckenzie Liburd (Nevis), Mr Orville Payne (Montserrat), Ms Sheena Jolley (Ireland), Mr Dominic Thompson (UK).

For IT assistance – Mr Mike Rumble, Mr John Howells (both UK).

The public librarians of Dudley Borough, Barbados, Nevis, Saint Kitts and Montserrat.

Lastly, but not leastly, the staff at North Staffordshire Press, especially Ms Megan Turney and Ms Emily Moore. Megan's editorial thoroughness and expertise has improved the original script considerably, while Emily's artistic skills have brought the book's cover to life.